CON

Rob Donnelly

Create the Day Publications, Hobart

Rob Donnelly/Create the Day
Hobart, Tasmania, Australia

Publisher's Note: Certain names, places, and events in this novel are drawn from historical sources. Others are entirely imagined. This book should be read as a work of fiction.

Book Layout © 2016 BookDesignTemplates.com

Cover design by Pascale Hutton

Book CON/ Rob Donnelly. -- 1st ed.
ISBN 978-0-6485822-3-6

I acknowledge, with deep respect, the traditional owners of lutruwita (Tasmania), the palawa and pakana people, and the traditional owners of the other lands in which this novel is set.

Sovereignty has never been ceded.

It always was and always will be Aboriginal land.

FOREWORD

This book is a work of historical fiction grafted to many verifiable details about my ancestor, Cornelius Donnelly, his brother James, and the conditions of life in Belfast and in Van Diemen's Land in the mid-nineteenth century.

My ancestor's life was more than records found in the hardbound books of the social engineers and colonisers of that era. The fullness of his life, and the many experiences he and other exiles went through, have been overshadowed for too long by the limiting title "convict." Cornelius was a man who reinvented himself, pursued opportunities, loved, sought justice, and sometimes unravelled when times were hard and the bottle was too close at hand. I look at the verifiable details of his life and find that he is not a stranger to me.

The past is never too far from our present. We carry secrets, in our dreams and predilections, that reach back further than our years. Barely known histories electrify our instincts. Deeply buried traumas murmur through our souls. Sometimes the work of recovery needs to lean into spirited imagination to trace those threads that weave our complication.

In memory of my father, Don, who began the work forty years ago. And in memory of all my ancestors who were forced into exile from their native lands because of the violences of colonisation, transportation, poverty, and the brutality of that genocide that has long been misnamed a famine.

Rob Donnelly
Cushla, Lachlan Tasmania
September 2025

Our freedom must be had at all hazards. If the men of property will not help us they must fall; we will free ourselves by the aid of that large and respectable community – the men of no property.
Theobald Wolfe Tone

Nothing appears more surprising to those who consider human affairs with a philosophical eye, than the easiness with which the many are governed by the few.
David Hume

To the living we owe respect; to the dead we owe only the truth.
Voltaire

PART ONE

CHAPTER 1

I am bound in a tangle of snoring brothers, and I can't sleep for the bruises. The world is creeping from the shadows. I look for the ravenous creature that lurks in the paint flakes and smoke stains above me.

I hear her voice come back to me.

The majesty in the muck of it all. Would you look at it.

Her fingers wove with mine, our arms stretched out above, tracing circles in the air. That soft, thin hour like no other.

Who do you think he'll eat first? Better not be me or who will feed the lot of you?

Memory brushes sweet to bitter through me. I'll take what it gives me regardless. Better to taste the bitter than have good memories fade. I won't have a part in forgetting. The others go weeks with no thought of her. Seems there is nothing in their world but what's planted in front of them.

I don't hate them for it. They can't help the way they are. Maybe that's why they sleep so soundly. How free they look with their soft shut eyes, their thick heads planted, and their mouths wide in that drooling chorus.

I hear the day begin with the stir of Da across the room. His steady stream's right into the pot. You can hear the relief of the man: one gush and all will be well. Save for the grief. There's a stoop to him that wasn't there before, and the shadows hang deep round his eyes. His cruel curve spells the truth. Death gives love a great weight.

There's a fierce knock on the window. Curse the devil, the old knocker-up, walking the streets with his bamboo pole. The lot of us dance to that devil's jig, tap-tapping the township

1

awake.

Best you be up now. Sure Ma. Don't risk the lockout. I won't, Ma. Mind the young ones. I will, Ma. And that Jimmy. God help us, Ma.

She'd give me the look, like there was some deal made between us and she expected me to keep my end of it. I nestle into the memory as I watch the others stretch and scratch their way to stumbling wakefulness.

We scrape together what we can to eat. Da has made us tea. It's hot and bitter. I press the cup to my cheek for warmth, then swallow down to the gritty dregs. It's just enough to get my belly murmuring.

Jimmy gives us all the nod, like he's the man in charge. Mary tuts and gets her sharp grin on. Jimmy and his notions. We pile out the door, before Mary gets a word in, and join the same old staggering herd. There's nothing about but thick heads and murmured words, and we're soon swallowed in fog.

Young Tommy, from across the way, has his eyes on my sister's rump. She's got the matter-of-fact stride about her, a formidable thrill to the boy, and he's itchy as a dog at a gatepost.

"Best watch yourself," says Jimmy to Tommy, "she's the heftiest shin-kicker in all Antrim."

At that, Mary spins round to spy us.

She's got the dagger in her eyes, and the flex in her cheek, and a general snort of contempt blowing out her nostrils.

"What's your business, Tommy?" she says.

And there it is: my sister's clipped tone – the one that could sink an armada. She's steely as a sabre at the ready, and the boy's all ablaze in the cheeks. He's a rosy glow in the too-early dawn. You can see the fear take hold of him right down to his nervous extremities.

He mumbles something about all of us Donnellys:

2

troublesome mob that we are, and some of us with a record to prove it. We eye each other, at the boy's sour tone, and let out a laugh at the truth of it.

Mary's got tears from laughing. She turns back and saunters on. There's a mockery in her gait now – bait on the dangling hook – but poor old Tommy has opted to trudge with his eyes cast down. He's a pitiful conquered thing, and I feel sorry for the boy.

Everyone knows his father's forever three sheets in the breeze, and his mother has a brittle nun's piety. They're at it, day and night, with belligerent cursing from his drunken side and vengeful praying from hers. And now here's Tommy, the poor worn spawn of their troubles, reduced to a shambles by Mary.

I don't say a word to Tommy. It would only make matters worse for him.

Jimmy has gathered an unlikely pace. He's striding forth, ahead of the pack, with his chest thrust out in the territorial manner. He has a black eye from last night's roadside banter: a little back-and-forth with the never-surrender boys. He takes pleasure poking those sore bears to have them dance for their supper. And there's no sorer bears than the Proddies right now. No drums and no marching, by order of their own Saxon Parliament. A quiet July. Imagine it. No tooting. No banging. No orange flags fluttering. No fat toy soldiers processing. Nothing for them but their aggravated spleens and phlegmatic bluster and the taunt of their unstruck goatskins.

Oh, it's the sweetest pleasure: Britishers betrayed by none other than their own. Oh, the treachery of it! Oh, the forsakenness of it! Union-jacked, the lot of them, and with the tide of repeal rolling up to their necks and beyond.

We continue up the street as more of our mob join us. We've nothing ahead but the mill and the flax, the dust in the air, the stoop and the drag, the murderous machines, and the grind of the day. The only thing worse is the hunger of lockout and that gormless grin of the gatemen. The pitiful lordship of pitiless men; I spit at the thought of those creatures.

I look at my brother. He's now hunkered down with the wage-slave scowl set firm: thunder in the brows and a hard knot at the jaws and a solid block of ice in his eyes. I should know better than to speak to him. It'll be nothing but his older-brother scorn. I know better, but the words come out anyway, all soft and full of that hope that's made for being dashed.

"Do you think they know how we hate them?"

He gives me his deadeye look and shakes his head at me.

"We're nothing to them. Only a fool would think otherwise."

Enough said to put me in my place. The broody bastard slouches off to grumble through his day. I'm left on my own to be what the mill would have me be.

This place rankles me. It always does. As soon as I'm here, I'm restless to be anywhere else. The old workers say this is the way the world is. They say the only peace is knowing your place and settling into it. They say don't torture yourself getting tied in knots about the why of it. I can't stomach the rheumy defeat in those old men. I meet their eyes and feel their cloying melancholy. I won't have it. I'd rather die young and free than sink in the abyss of their misery.

I take my place at the flax mound. It's all retted and brittle as straw and ready for the crimper and scutcher. My back stoops low to it. My hands dig into the brittle and lift. First load with twelve hours ahead. I haul it across to the crimper. The rolling drums crack the outer husks. The machine has no end to its appetite. It's a mindless, careless thing: a rolling menace to crush all contenders. I've one finger lost and another one broke, but everyone's body is marked in some way. We work 'til we're broke beyond useful.

They know there's always fresh bodies for labour. Every day knows the shudder of birth in this town. Children are thick on the tenement ground and hanging from mothers like fruit off gnarled trees. By the time they turn eight, they're slaves like the rest of us. And then there's that sorry remnant who come drifting in from the country. Their eyes are ploughed wide with desperate need. One step inside the mill and they know they've met their defeat.

I haul the cracked flax stems across to the scutcher. I set my feet firm to its fast-spinning blades. They pummel the bundles as I hold them in place. My body is filled with its fury. Large pieces of husk fall to the floor. Fine dust fills the air. It covers my face. It gets in my eyes and into my mouth. I breathe and it's there in my lungs. I stand in the dust 'til the flax is stripped bare and there's nothing but supple strands.

Off they go to the world of spinners and doffers and weavers. Back I go to the next flax bundle. Back to the crimper. Back to the scutcher. Back to the blades and the dust and the coughing. The stooping and rising. The back ache and headache. The hunger and thirst. Mind blurred to nothing. Senses subdued. A body in motion. Hour by hour. Six until six. Meshed with machines. Nothing but work 'til the gloaming.

It's the starlings that herald the night.

How her eyes came alive at the sky-bound wonder of them. Everything in her turned quiet, and there was that gaze of hers that could soften the world and make it a home.

We are barely out of the mill when hundreds of them take off above the Lagan. They merge and become a dark, twisting cloud that sweeps above our town. The bird cloud moves in a perfect circle, then breaks into two like a wave torn apart by a rock. The two clouds make their own paths, one clockwise and the other anticlockwise, rapid and graceful, every starling surrendered to the singular motion. They weave back together, and briefly seem solid as iron, then turn into strands allowing the light to shine through.

"There's Connie at the birds again," says one of the old men as he passes me.

"You'll break that neck of yours, looking up like that boy," says his crotchety mate.

I don't care that those old dogs laugh at me. They were born with downcast eyes and not an ounce of wonder in them. But I am my mother's son and she told me to never stop looking up. The promise is up, never down, child. She'd have me follow the flight of birds as though she was training my eyes to it. Up, never down, and never mind those who say otherwise.

Even now I could whisper to her. The words tease, eager at my tongue. We had our ways, didn't we? How I feel it still, just a hint beyond, that once-upon-warmth now faded to a dream. There's no home for the soft twixt us now. If I spoke what I felt out loud, it would only add fuel to those old fools' fire. They'd name me Mad Con, or a soft-headed boy who murmurs to ghosts, and there'd be no end to it.

How I hate the endless dig of dimwits.

I look up again. There's a pulse to the aerial spectacle: this dance of mingling and separating. Eternity is traced in our town's dying light. For a moment, there's majesty to behold: it's no one and everyone's possession. It lasts a moment, then breaks into threads as the birds descend to roost and the gates of the mill are locked for the night, and dark despair creeps back up our streets.

Stand by the Lagan long enough and you'll see the bruised fruit drop. There's plenty I know who are not quite alive and not quite dead. They linger at the choice that's ahead of them 'til they lean right into the dark, add rocks to their pockets, then jump. The foul water takes care of the rest while the dark prowls the streets looking for more. It's a thing more noxious than the Blackstaff Nuisance. Its dank stench lingers everywhere.

Some in this town redouble their prayers when they hear its malicious whisper. They murmur their way through the beads. Pray to Saint Jude. Confess. Take communion. They bless themselves when they feel the deep grave beckoning. And something of the older ways ripples through their souls: the way a feeling is read; the hint of unseen presences; the lingering stain that makes a place cursed; the soft water that promises miracles; the signs – and those things to be done – to ward off the bad and beckon the good. It's the old druid thread, woven through Catholic cloth, and never mind over-schooled thinking about it.

Others look to escape the despair with drink. They look for the craic and the comradeship of the bottle. There's desperate joy in the moment: a rollicking song belted out on the edge; noisy blather, a laugh and another, the edge ever closer, the laugh all the louder. A staggering shift from joy to effrontery. A mutter, then, *what did you say?* Some old grievance brought back to life with a slurred incantation. There's the curl of a sneer, a blood-charged leer, the long glance to measure things up. Then a shove and a threat, a staggering dance, the spin of a world that's all fists and smashed glass and tomorrow's mysterious pain.

I'm roused from my thoughts by a grubby wean. He's tugging at my sleeve. I pull my arm away and give him a look as though I'm ready to clout him. He juts his chin defiantly and gives a snort as he backs away: a wee raging bull in the making.

"Your brother says to come."

"Tell him I'll come when I'm ready."

I know I'll cop a knock for that one later, but I don't care. I like this time when the mill is behind me, and the whole night is ahead of me, when there's nothing but a stir across the waters. I

7

can feel something better in the air, stronger than that boney reach of despair. It's hid in the quiet, in the dark folds of the street, like a treasure that's still untarnished.

I know all this thinking is madness to everyone but me. No one wants to hear it. It's not a thing expected of a boy. Not in this town. I know what the old men would say. Have a drink and have a bash. Time is made to snuff out dreaming 'til there's nothing but a man left. I know I will need to slip my skin again and join the rest and be the thing expected. That's why Jimmy is after me. He feels a brotherly duty to try and iron the peculiar out of me. There he is, down the end of the street right now, and marching in my direction: the determined man out to catch the stray.

"'Mon little brother, let's be at it!"

I can hear the joy in him. He's such a different creature in the night. He's friendly when there's a chance for hard business and that raw togetherness that's spiked by drink and fused into knuckles and blood.

"What's up with you?" he asks as he comes closer.

He doesn't want to know the answer, and I know better than to tell him.

"I'm ready as any man in Belfast, so I am."

He laughs at that.

"'Man' is it?"

He throws his arm around my neck, locks my head, then rubs my hair until it stands on end. I feel the fire burn away the dreaming in me then, as he has my face pushed into his stinking armpit.

"Get off me, you horse's arse."

He rubs all the harder, at that, and laughs. He's happy getting the fire up in my blood. He stands back and looks me over like I'm a soldier out to be inspected.

"Not quite a rooster, but at least you've got the comb."

His eyes are dancing about and he's near jigging in anticipation of all the bloody glory that's to come. God knows I might hate this town, but Jimmy loves it.

CHAPTER 2

Barrack Street and Sandy Row are two ends of a fuse. They run into either end of powder keg Durham Street. Barrack Street is the finest in The Pound. It's lined with shops and is the natural place for a boisterous gathering. We find our way to the usual crowd, standing around a fire. Jimmy takes a swig from a welcome bottle.

"Sláinte."

He hands it to me and I drink. A quick shot burns a trail down my throat and into my belly. I'm oven-warm on the inside as the bustle swirls around me. Street balladeers are singing the latest deeds of the Liberator and charging the growing crowd with a patriotic fervour. The great spread of history – made alive through the singing – curls around me and starts to take a grip. I welcome the mad, hot spin of it. A few more swigs and I'll be fully in, my empty made a fierce voice in the streets.

"Deliverance!"

I toast the crowd, who look at me perplexed.

"What's yer man about?" someone asks Jimmy.

"God knows," Jimmy says and winces.

He shakes his head and shoots me a crooked look like I'm spoiling his moment. I drink some more, despite the moody cur, then bluster and play the big man with the best of them. Desperate for the weight I'm yet to gain, I slap the back of a friend. We raise our fists as though we're contenders. We try on our fiercest looks until we crack apart with laughter. I hand him a bottle that someone handed me. He knocks back a shot and winces.

We're well on the way with drinking, but the headiest brew is now the air we breathe. It's charged with anticipation. I wink at a girl I fancy. I feel my heart beat all the harder, then I hear a wave of laughter from some dark corner.

Everyone's pockets bulge with stones – the poor man's ammunition. Women hold more in their aprons. A group of them are itching for battle. Eyes sharp and tongues all the sharper. My own sister is there in the formidable thick of them.

I listen as the grog sparks life into others, even the quiet ones. Heat is rising. Everyone's a little louder. Soon a litany of savage recollections is recited: all holy relics of our precious outrage. Those from the country tell stories of atrocities carried out by the Orangemen and the Armagh Peep-O-Days. The fact it's all been heard a thousand times before doesn't matter. The telling is important. It makes those distant outrages personal until there's no telling where one wound ends and the next begins, and we are all made raw the same way.

The talk moves to the daring tales of the mighty Ribbonmen, who set the scales right, and exact Irish justice on the invaders and their miserable spawn. I'm full drawn into the brotherhood then, through the listening. It gives a sharpened point to all the peculiar want inside me. I'm thick in the mob and charged with our ancient business. It thunders in us so we're ready for action, as though the destiny of our one true nation relies entirely on the outcome of whatever street fight is approaching. It's Ireland for the Irish, one street at a time, one cracked jawbone after another.

I see some men have sticks or brickbats. Some have spiked bludgeons. There's rumour of a gun. Better we have it than the others, though they're sure to have more on their side. It's always been that way.

Now word gets around that the others are near, moving up Durham and gathered at Christ Church. They are near enough that we can hear their shouting. There's more in the field behind Mullholland's Mill. The cry goes up and we all move together. Our shouts blast down the streets. Our ammunition is at the ready.

When we face them, they yell like they're the ones that's invaded.

"You'll not be visiting Sandy Row tonight, you papist scum!"

"Seems you're the ones inclined to come calling, you pox-ridden Proddies!" yells Jimmy.

This whole business is a dance of violence, worked out at county fairs, then brought to Belfast streets. Our dense-packed town is a crucible. Everything boils to a concentrate here: a dark shot of heartbreak and hate; nectar of the old vengeful gods who came tumbling off the longboats.

First there's the words.

It's the women given over to razor-sharp taunting. A furious verbal torrent to cajole, provoke, emasculate the po-faced Proddies on the other side.

There's a violent artistry to a well-honed taunt and delight in seeing it strike. Seeing the receiver squirm in his boots. Knowing in that moment he's been bettered. Mary's aflush with the vigour of it. She's struck more than one mark already, and the night has barely begun. It's no small thing to have the sharpest tongue in town, and our own sister's vying to own it. She has the humour as well as the barb. That's what makes a good taunt remembered.

Soon that po-faced squirming, on the other side, hardens to revenge. A pair of dark eyes is there, marking each vocal offender for a future bruising.

"You watch it, you bastard!" I yell at a boy, on the other side, who's eyeing Mary like he's ready to pummel her.

He's shouting back at me. I'm straining at my skin to be at it.

"You going to fix him for me, little brother?" Mary says.

The girls beside her laugh. Young Maeve Ryan is giving me the soft eyes with a well-lit fire in her cheeks. I grin and nod to Maeve with a saucy cock to my eyebrow.

"I'll see what I can do for the lot of you," I say.

They laugh at that.

"We'll do plenty enough for ourselves, thanks, boy," one of the older girls says.

Most lads are verbal blunderers compared to the girls. We are full of bluster and itching for the release that will only come through a well-swung fist meeting a jaw, the taste of blood on lips, and the solid jolt of a knee deftly driven right into a pair of sorry Proddy balls.

I add my voice to lads who are striking up a chant for repeal, a chant for King Dan, and Irish sovereignty. It's soon met with the other mob's reply.

"To hell with the Pope."

"To hell with King William. Long live King Dan."

"No Repeal!"

"It's coming. At long last it's on the way."

"Not where we live."

"Time to sweep out the rubbish then!"

"You'll be hearing it."

"You'll be copping it."

It's the weans who first get worked up enough, in the back-and-forth, to start hurling stones. They set them flying, then watch to see if they hit a mark and draw blood.

It's a bloody game played by darting children who spend their daylight hours doing the dangerous clean-up crawl under mill and factory machines. It's the same on both sides – rattling breathing, maimed hands, bleak lives ahead – with more in common than sets them apart. But all that is nothing to the mad heady buzz of battle and that feeling of thunder in the veins. Each child is a warrior-king, come to reign in the Belfast streets and smash the lot to smithereens.

Their shouts echo down lanes as they scatter when a rain of rocks comes down in their direction. All of broken Belfast is flying through the air. Rocks and brickbats and paving stones are coming out of nowhere, exploding on the ground, striking flesh, drawing blood, breaking bones, smashing windows. We are all in it now and, before long, we're scrambling to gather more ammunition. Fingers pry up cobblestones and grab loose timber for clubs. I feel the tide take hold of me with its iron-hard resolve to stand our ground and drive them back as far as we can make them go.

"Ireland forever!" someone cries, and we all roar our reply.

In the finer houses, eyebrows are raised. The poor are at it again. As long as they keep to their wretched streets, it's no concern, but God help any who cause damage to the mills. The idea stirs a flurry of consternation in the thick of the pipe smoke and sherry. The wretched refuse is one thing, but the protection of one's investment is another. There's a dry chuckle, proving a genteel calm, and then a bell's rung. A servant is instructed to go and get word to the constabulary.

It doesn't take much for a mob, on the streets, to make an effigy: some straw in hessian bags tied into a head, a body, arms and legs; an enemy-coloured sash; a long stick shoved up the baggy arse; a firebrand at the ready. On the Protestant side, they raise a green-sashed Dan O'Connell; a half-stuffed puppet they jig about with disdain.

"Here's your Liberator! Hanging by the rope he deserves!"

No sooner is fire racing up O'Connell's straw man legs than we raise up none other than an orange-sashed King William III.

"Look who we've dragged from his cursed grave. Your orange saviour, ready for a roasting just like he's getting in hell! No hope for you lot now. No orange man to come and rescue you."

Up goes William of Orange in flames, and up goes a torrent of abuse and rocks. We surge forward through drifting embers. A thick boy charges me like a bull. He takes a swing. I crack him in the guts. I let him know my knee as he doubles up. The night's

14

alive and I can taste the blood. I cop a blackthorn cudgel to my ribs. I gasp for breath. The street's a spinning storm. Grown men are pummelling children. Bludgeons swing, collecting jaws. Blood sprays. Bodies fall. Some are pinned down, kidney punched, and gouged. Fists grip rocks to give them extra clout. Women claw and bite. Nothing but the dark ecstasy of the Belfast night. A wild-eyed exuberance is all around. Everything's unbound as the blood of both sides mingle into one.

Then Tom Verner, the justice of the peace, arrives.

"Go back to your houses and I'll be answerable to your protection," he says to one side and then rides across to tell the other too.

No one budges. Verner can see it. He frowns. He threatens to read the riot act and call out the troops. Weans answer him with rocks. Each hopes to be the one to cause the horse to rear up and send his lordship flying. The moment is precarious. Verner has only twenty-five police, with bayonets fixed, standing between two forces that are hundreds strong. Twenty-five police to serve the whole of Belfast and one's already down, thanks to a well-aimed rock to his head.

Verner sends word to the barracks. The only hope of restoring order is the troops. He reads the riot act, then starts with the arrests. He's careful to show an even hand. The leaders of both sides are cuffed. Stewart Lafferty on the Catholic side. William Quinn on the Protestant side.

People start dispersing when word of the approaching troops spreads. Verner draws a breath but knows the trouble is now likely to spread. There will be flare-ups right across the west of Belfast. The large mobs split into small groups. Some go home to rest. Some spy on the movement of the other lot to check they're not doubling back. Some squat in shadows and plot.

"Those living where they don't belong need be driven out."

15

"Cullingtree Road then?"

"Sure enough!"

I watch a mob rush past me.

"'Mon Connie!" they call.

I wander in their wake, but the fight's gone out of me. There's pain in my ribs from being hit, and blood is pounding in my skull. I feel apart from everything around me. Ahead, I see boys lobbing rocks through the window of a house. They barge through the door, then there's a great smashing racket, then screaming.

"Get out of my house, Papist."

"Get out of our territory, Prod."

Fists and boots hammer at a man to break him. His children cower in a corner. A woman wails at the injustice. The home is smashed beyond repair. Chairs are broken, a table upended, crockery turned to shards. There's nothing noble about the mob now. They laugh at the fear they've struck in the children, mock the groans of the man they've ruined, then sift the debris hoping for a drink before they pay a visit to the next house.

The family stumble onto the street to find their way to safety.

"You'll get yours," the woman spits at me in passing.

All the savagery and sorrow of the broken world is there, and I have no reply to it. I know any remorse I feel tonight will be lost in the heat when I'm back in the streets tomorrow. There is no room for sympathy in this town. It's better to look away and not let feelings in, give a cheer, and laugh when your own mob expect it. There is no other way of belonging in a world like this than keeping loyal to your own and hard-hearted for those opposite.

A Protestant mob is also at work on Cullingtree. They will ruin eighteen houses before the night is through. They have busted into the house of Cosgrave, the shoemaker.

"Leave him! He's dying of consumption!" cries his wife.

"Damn the papist – he is going to hell and we'll only send him the faster!" they reply as they drag the old man out of his sick bed, then pummel his frail body with their boots.

The woman tries to stop them, but she can't. There's no reasoning with the devil. Once the mob have gone, she holds her man. There's nothing but bewilderment in his eyes. She brushes his face and rocks him back and forth and curses the day they set foot in this town.

Outside, there's a brief peace just before the dawn. The bruised and wounded limp back to their homes, and grab a moment's sleep, just as the knocker-up starts his work. His feet are familiar, weaving across a world of broken glass and bricks and blood. He gives it little thought as he starts his bamboo tapping on the windows. The mills and factories pause for no one. Night is done. Another day begins. I wake listening for the sound of her, but there's no time left to find her.

CHAPTER 3

There's no grip fiercer than a Belfast burial when there's matters to consider. The priest is up there, beside the hole, attending to redemption. The crowd of mourners, pressed inside the gates, is attending to retribution. Poor old Cosgrave, dead on Friday, and now he's down below with all the rest of Plaguey Hill's boney congregation.

There's such memory in these clods you can smell the grievous weight from the cholera to the penal laws. Everything that's about us, and muddy beneath us, is made to spark the fuse inside us. There's no away from it. It presses all about. And there's old Cosgrave's wife, the state of the woman, so pale you'd think she was a ghost herself. But is it any wonder with what the woman endured? Seeing the old man dragged from his sick bed and pummelled and there was nothing she could do about it. Nothing at all. And those scurrilous sons of whores, with their sneering faces, had their boots pound into the man 'til he was nothing but breathless, bruised and near dead for the effort.

Poor old Cosgrave indeed.

Sure, the man could make a pair of boots though.

My brother's got the hard look. I dare say I have too. We're all primed after processing past the Sandy Row mob on the road to Friar's Bush. There was no avoiding them. They could have stayed at home, but they didn't. It wasn't enough they killed the old man. They sniffed his funeral as chance for further provocation. The bastards were near salivating at the chance for it. You could see it in the spray of their words and the wobbling desperation of their jowls: a pack of mongrel dogs who best know they are due a beating.

It was only our repeal wardens that kept us on the road through the shower of taunts and rocks. All about us was the

18

Prods' Pope-cursing, fast followed by our repealers' murmuring.

"Don't give the bastards what they're after, and let's give the old man the peaceful burial he deserves, and bide your time, lads, and steady as she goes now, boys, and our day will come," and all the rest of the palaver.

We all know, once the old man is buried, it will be back to business on the double.

Sure, the repeal men are still desperate to keep the peace. They say don't give the English any excuse for holding back from doing what is right. They even say, for now, we'll talk up being loyal to the crown if that helps us get a government of our own. Some repealers would sacrifice their mothers to advance the cause peacefully in accordance with the directions of O'Connell.

That's all well and good. They can vote for fine sentiments in their weekly meetings, down in Chapel Lane, but I'll tell you one thing straight, on our Belfast streets we'll bide no sacrificing justice in the name of a peaceful process.

"Did you hear what that spotty cur, beside the Malone turnpike, said?" Jimmy mumbles to me, though I'm sure he knows the answer already.

I turn to him.

"The spotty one, with the face gone wrong, is that the one you mean?"

Jimmy nods.

"He said, best get used to it, papists! Dig a few more holes while you're down there."

Jimmy gets his savage grin when he hears me say it. He leans across to me.

"That weedy little bastard's own mother won't recognise him by time I'm done with him."

I nod at Jimmy's sentiment, feel its contagious heat, then keep my head bowed for the priest's blessing. God give us strength to do what needs be done and do it thoroughly so it's

19

remembered. We cross ourselves and that's religion done. We walk back from the graveyard, hundreds strong. Some say it's more in the order of thousands, given those come down from the country.

I'm with Jimmy and the other men. We've taken the lead, knowing trouble is ahead. It's nothing but passing niggles, from a few stray Prods, for a while. A "to hell with the Pope" here and there. It's the kind of half-baked effort easily ignored. But once we're close to the station, it's a different matter. There's a mob of them ahead of us and, while the wardens call out for us to keep the peace, we've no mind for restraint. The old man is buried, we did our peaceable bit, and now it's back to work, and so the cry goes up from one of the old men in the lead.

"Let's be at them boys. Anois. Anois."

We run at them like stampeding bulls. Horns levelled to the target. Everything inside us made all the stronger on account of our keeping it corked-up before. Stones are flying. Curses flashing out. Dead set determination is hard pressed in our eyes. I see a boy in front of me throwing punches wildly, so I grab his grubby shirt and smash his forehead with my own. We stare at each other, bloody-eyed and bewildered for a moment. It's a dazed look that could be between friends as much as enemies. We both shake it off, and then we're fists and knees at each other. There's whistles blowing loud in my ears. Verner and his peelers are pushing into the thick, but it's well beyond an easy settled thing. Verner cops a hail of rocks. He is looking about wildly for his assailants. His constables are just another bunch of bodies in the furious mix where it's fight back or be beaten to a pulp. Verner's yelling orders, like a drowning man, and now looks set on just collaring us Catholics. The clear injustice adds a further fury to our fighting. Then word goes round the 53rd are on their way. The Prods start pulling back down their alleys. Jimmy grabs me by the arm and hauls me along.

CHAPTER 4

It's Wednesday and I'm on the road with Jimmy. We've been locked out one too many times from the mill. Now we are out of work, overdue the rent, and walking hungry. There wasn't even a sip of tea for breakfast. My belly's some fierce creature gnawing me. My head's the worse for it: dizzy and aching. Jimmy is moody as all hell and buried in his head. Just as well. If he came at me with his needling, I'd clout the boy without a hesitation.

I'm looking out for food as we walk. A handful of blackberries would be enough; purple-stained fingers and sweet popping in my mouth. The sheer glory of a thing like that. Even a tart old crab apple would do the trick. Anything to feed this desperate beast.

It's times like this, imagining turns devil itself. All manner of thoughts are pitch-forking in my skull. Potatoes cooked with bacon fat. Sweet Jaysus, the thought of it. I can almost smell it. The smell would be enough. My stomach quivers at the thought. My heart starts pounding through my head. Nothing but the ravenous beast in me. A man can do all manner of things to see it gone.

It's hunger keeps the magistrates in a job. Stealing bread. Stealing a miserable oat cake. Stealing a hunk of pork. Down comes the unjust gavel on it all. Three months' hard labour. Six months' hard labour. A trip on the high seas. That's the old assizes in a nutshell: well-fed magistrates, full of gas and porcine bluster, judging the poor for grabbing an answer to their deadly circumstances.

There's nothing new in any of that drama when it comes to me or my brother.

And now I'm all awash with the dark. The good old, age-old family legacy: a memory seared by all that's wrong; a heavy frown and narrowed eyes to fit. When there's no food, teeth can bite and rip that bitter flesh: injustice. We once were kings or something close enough. I look at Jimmy. He's in that same place. Ruminating just like our old Da: the family curse of moody cogitation.

Surely life is something more than this. Something more. Such a troublesome thought, that something more, when all around what you see is something less. And all the less boils down to this. Everything that was our ancient best was stolen by the bloody English.

It's a short walk over the bridge and past the Marquis of Donegal's estate. They say he's the world's unluckiest gambler, yet there he is, splendid in his poverty. I wouldn't mind a share of that kind of misery with the fine house and the beech trees and the view across the Lagan to the town. I think I could do quite nicely in such deplorable circumstances.

"Jimmy, how about we knock on Chichester's door for a drink?"

My brother is not in the mood. He doesn't even bother to look my way. He just keeps on with his dogged stride: head down and on a mission.

Ballynafeigh is a world away from the crowded tenements and back alleys we call home. It's country cottages, vegetable patches, elm trees and green fields, backyards with chickens, and a house cow on larger properties for the milk and butter. It's a place where a clerk might make his home. Enough wealth to employ a servant: if not every day, then a few days every week. Enough wealth to take on day labourers for fence mending and the like. Enough wealth to have something worth stealing but not so much that it's safely tucked inside the thick walls of a manor-house.

More than one local gives us the up and down. We're the kind who don't belong. They can see the desperation in the hollow of our cheeks and sniff the native Catholic in our sweat. They've been edgy out this way since May when a house was stripped of all its linen and clothing, by a daring band of midnight robbers. The family slept right through it. A house full of plump chickens that woke up plucked.

"Keep your eyes open," Jimmy says.

I give him the grunt he deserves.

We come to a house and there's a pile of fine clothes in a basket beside the door. Seems there's no one around. I look at Jimmy, and he looks at me. His crooked grin signs off on the plan. I reach out and feel the material in my grip: fine linen from the underpaid slavery of a mill; a thick coat to ward off the worst of the approaching winter; the fluted contours of a brocade pattern on a jacket for the kind of occasions I have never known. I feel that handful of fine woven wealth, and I could let it go, but I don't. There's a fierce possession in my grip. If the world won't set things right for the likes of me and my family, then I will. My will is there in the grab and take. This is how I claim the life I want. My heart thunders with a fearful spark of liberation as me and Jimmy bolt down the road – clothes in hand – without a hesitation.

And now it's noise and voices, cries of distress and outrage. There's a steady rising sound of boots on gravel, like a dark wave rising up behind us, and the air is torn through with their ferocity.

"Thieves. Thieves."

We are running, me and Jimmy, running for our lives. We are running till the air is burning in our lungs, and our hearts are close to breaking with the urgency. And all we need is to get back across the Lagan and lose ourselves in the thick of our own. All we need is the safe fold of our home and our Da's cranky wisdom and our Mary's cutting judgement, and our little brothers with their eyes full of wonder looking up at us as though we ruled the world. All we need is a chance in a world that's desperate poor in giving chances to our kind. And we are almost at the bridge, even as our legs are straining with the speed, even as the clothes are dropping from our hands, but the voices are closer and I can feel the heat of them behind me and I can feel the grip of hands about me and then I'm twisting and falling and all the world is falling down on me and I am gone as ever I have been as all the life is knocked right out of me and I am an empty, fallen boy hard pressed to the gravel.

CHAPTER 5

It takes millennia to shape a land: to glaciate, roll out the long scouring slide of gravity, mound sediment into tear-shaped drumlin hills, melt, recede, leave a legacy of plains to be seeded into green, a trace of something ancient in the stew of marshlands. All around is the thick writing of the land: the long true story told by it. And everything else is the blink of an eye: a stoney fortress is built on a mound; a former slave turns missionary; an ancient faith is part supplanted by a new one; a high king leads a native alliance into defeat; invaders graft themselves to the land with stone forts made for future ruination; strangers turn native; generations decay back into earth; oppressive laws come then recede; old ways retreat to a rocky western fringe then creep back through the power of the culture; leaders make their hopeful noise, stir up the crowds, then fall into silence; people starve; people leave; people thrive; all of it in the blink of an eye.

If there's any place to feel the whole pulsing truth of it, then it may well be Dun Padraig.

It doesn't matter that old Holy Patrick and the others are mouldering in their nearby graves. We are men wholly in the dark. That's the way the punishment begins. You steal a few meagre possessions, things of little consequence to the wealthy, and they in turn steal the world from your eyes. They steal the sun. They steal the hills and the grass and the laneways. They steal the stars and moon. They steal the daylight warmth on your skin and the stir of a breeze across your face. They grab and shove at your body, as though you are nothing but a beast, a thing to be transported in a covered carriage, then controlled and corralled in the airless thick of a stone-cold cell. And all of this is long before any gavel falls.

"Are you alright, brother?" Jimmy asks.

"I'm alright," I answer. "It's not the first time after all."

Jimmy doesn't reply straight away.

"That might be our problem."

I can hear the sunken weight in him. What am I to do with that? Am I the one now meant to stir hope for both of us? I haven't an ounce of it, and I don't have it in me to pretend. Jimmy wouldn't have it anyway.

"Better that we stole some food and had a decent feed before we were caught."

Jimmy doesn't reply. Maybe he's asleep.

"Are you asleep, Jimmy?"

"I might be if you shut up about it."

He's gone from reassuring to sullen now: the cranky man's back to brooding in his cave. I lie down and stare above, but it's so dark I can't see a thing. I'm all dry blood and bruises, and it hurts to breathe, but that's not the half of it. It's the voices are the real torment. I can still hear the spat-out contempt of those jowly bastards as they pushed me and Jimmy along. I can hear their threats and feel where they gripped me with their sweaty claws.

Brave men in a crowd, sure. How I crave just one of them should appear before me now. I can feel the volley I'd deal out: busting lips and teeth. Hundred-fold payback in my knuckles. My heart jolts imagining it. My whole body's roiled, in this dark, and I'm close to throwing punches through the air.

And there's old Jimmy sleeping like a baby. God help us, how can a man be like that? Why amn't I like that? I swear he could sleep right through the punishments of hell with no hint of disturbance. It's me born with the torment of a brain, I suppose. Oh, that I might have been born with a duller one. Imagine it. Walking through the world barely touched on account of the blessing of dimwits.

Oh, I know you're there, Mamai. Of course you are.

Disappointed, are you? Best you burn Saint Jude's ear and be done with it. God knows there's no more powerful tyranny than a mother's broken heart: that look of disappointment that could cause the world to wither with the shame.

Second conviction's not a good thing. Jimmy's right about that. He has a nose for the worst to come, just like Da. Make the most of today boy, it's likely worse tomorrow. There's the old man's voice fired up at all the unjust defeats that life dishes out. God help us, the misery of the man. He can look up at the clearest sky and talk of nothing but the likelihood of storm clouds.

What is to become of us? Maybe double what we got last time: twelve months hard labour. Six was bad enough. A year of breaking stones and all the hemmed-in trouble of the lock-up. But maybe it will be transportation. It's possible. Van Diemen's Land has an evil sound to it. Just the name: demon's land. What kind of name is that for a place? Who thought that one up? Some Dutch bastard, I suppose. Enough. Let me have a minute's sleep at least. Just a drop of my brother's dull-headed forgetfulness. Let me lose myself and fall until I wake tomorrow.

***

We shuffle down a tunnel from the prison to the courthouse: a pair of clanking Antrim boys bound for a Down judgement. There is the Downpatrick courtroom: officials at their well-polished tables; papers piled high; guards ready to pounce on any trouble; the petit jury, to the side, primed to pass judgement. Barristers are centre-stage, soothing the magistrate with their well-practised bows and reverential words; all learned friends of the bar playing their part in a largely mundane drama; strutting peacocks delighting in their occasional games of one-upmanship.

The air is thick with their language: arguments and rebuttals; points of order; flourishes of precedence; whispered agreements; eyes to the magistrate; eyes to the jury; a quick glance at the accused; further whispering; a word to the bench; a gruff magisterial response, then a prod to get on with it. Ordinary people shuffle into this other world to act as a witness or to be judged. Their manners are made foreign by the airs and graces of this room. They stumble through their words, get flustered by the magistrate, and know they are an amusement to this judicial class with their wigs and gowns and ungodly worshipful ways. And, through it all, justice is little more than the artistry of winning an argument; throwing out a well-baited hook – made to appeal to prejudice as much as to reason – to snare and reel in the jury.

The Crown Trials of the Downpatrick Quarter Sessions has commenced. Bridget McCarty and Alice McGee are guilty of stealing the potatoes of James Wallace. They have already been in prison seven weeks. A further week is added. Samual McDowell guilty of stealing the iron horse tree of James Murdock at Killyleagh. Six months' hard labour. James Kelly not guilty of stealing a top coat on account of his mental incapacity. Recommended to be sent to the workhouse. Arthur M'Arthur guilty of stealing parts of mill machinery from Beersbridge Mills. Twelve months' hard labour. James Campell for stealing several articles of clothing from Henry Smith. Four months' hard labour. Ann Magee for stealing three yards of muslin. Three months' hard labour. Ann Carlisle for stealing a cotton frock. One month hard labour.

"Cornelius Donnelly and James Donnelly."

We are brought forward to watch our trial run its course. We are charged with a crime that is similar to those of others. Stealing several articles of wearing apparel, the property of John Macmullan at Ballynafeigh, on the 13 September 1843.

The charges are laid out. Witnesses are examined. Concluding arguments are made. The magistrate gives his instructions. We wait until the jury comes back with its verdict. The paper is handed to the judge. He peers at the finding, then looks to the jury.

"How do you find them?"

The foreman looks across at us.

"Guilty, your honour."

I'm not surprised. I brace myself for what comes. I hear Jimmy draw in his breath. The magistrate's eyes are down as though we are nothing but rough notes jotted on a page. He lays out his consideration of our past crime and the likelihood of future offences. He stares up at us. I see more indifference than contempt in his eyes. I swear the man looks bored. We are nothing but another pair of brother criminals; boys who are not likely to be set right with a further six months' hard labour. There's only one answer for recidivists like us: seven years' transportation. Down comes the gavel to seal our fate. I stand here, staring ahead, not knowing what to feel. It's like staring at a door that's just slammed shut in my face. Jimmy's saying something but I can't take it in. I'm startled as the guard grabs my arm. I let myself be led without causing any bother.

DUBLIN
1843

The bellowing symphony of cattle-economy Ireland filters into the Smithfield Convict Depot. There's the groan of cattle, the trample of shit-splattered hooves, the bleating of sheep, and the almost human cries of pigs as they are prodded and jostled into pens.

Farmers smoke their pipes as they look on, one foot on the rail, muttering asides. They sometimes find good cause of amusement: a boy landing arse in the mud as he tries to trap an absconding pig. Get after 'im boy. The squeal of the creature, the curse of the lad, all good for a laugh.

An ill-tempered horse rears up in the horse market. Every town dweller is an expert, from their safe distance. The farmers' laughter rolls through breath mist and coughing. There's the long tail of a joke as it's repeated. A hip flask is offered to take the edge off. All the while, eyes gather in the quality of the livestock, the chance of rain, and the likelihood of competition in the bidding.

There is still that outside world: a muted place my senses barely reach; the lingering song of Ireland beyond the walls. It's the sound of life getting on without me. Maybe that's the hardest punishment: not gone but already forgotten in this miserly prison at the arse-end of Dublin.

Old Crooner, in the corner, has started again. Every day it's the same baleful dirge. All those songs about treacherous women and men's ruined hearts – there's something ominous when there's too much of that sort of thing. You can hear the moody thinking, just below the surface. He's a well-stropped blade waiting for the moment.

"I'll tell you something," I say to Jimmy, "As long as that old bastard's serenading the world with his aggrievances, you know where he is, but once it stops, God help us all. I'll be putting as many bodies as I can between old cut-throat, the balladeer, and me."

Jimmy frowns.

"Never mind that, you owe me baccy."

Some say having family locked up with you must surely be a consolation. More fool are they for believing it. Old Jimmy has refined his cantankerous to a state of endless pettiness. Nothing but a war of clawing demands, with his face hard set, and eyes stabbing at me. It's just damned baccy, I say to him, but he won't have it. You'd think his life depended on it. Transport me and let him stay back here. I wouldn't mind one bit of it. I'll gladly face the wilds on my own, whatever savagery and consternation comes, at least I'd have some peace from the boy.

"Oh come on, you can't be that desperate, sure," I shoot back at him. "I'm done with the coir picking."

"You're done when you've paid me back, boy. What else did you have planned for your day anyway, a promenade along the Liffey with some mad girl who doesn't know any better? Who do you think you are, a man of leisure? Get yourself a coconut and get at it."

We give each other a half-hearted shove, then settle into the peculiar work.

"Nuts like these would cause a horse to blush."

I don't even get a snort of appreciation. Jimmy's the determined, serious man: all eyes on the work and not to be interrupted.

"So here we are then," I add despite him, "exports cracking imports."

I hammer the nut repeatedly until the husk breaks open. The

31

dense-packed coir fibres wrap around a smaller nut inside. The smaller nuts, that hold the white meat and the milk, are for the market. The layer of fibres around it are for weaving mats and stuffing mattresses.

"They won't be making fine linen out of this," I say as I tug at the insides.

Jimmy offers a grunt. It could mean anything, but I'll take it as evidence there's life in the old boy yet. I know there's no use chasing him for a conversation, though. He's not one for talking when he's got the scowl on like that. There's nothing for it but to settle in the quiet and keep on cracking nuts and stripping out the fibres. It's not hard labour. It's nothing like twelve hours at the mill. It's just a thing to do for the snuff gratuity.

There's no real task work here. The special-skilled boys, the mechanics, get a chance of payment for making shoes and socks and nets and furniture. Meanwhile, the chatterers are happy talking through the day: the lot of them mull about, all with something to say, and none of them inclined to listen. The younger boys get taken off for an hour's schooling. Those inclined learn numbers and at least enough to write their names. The rest of us are left to stare at the walls or pick coir.

There's madness in doing nothing. You can tell those given into it. They murmur and mutter, rock and hiss like devils, and lurk about in the shadows sniffing for the freedom of a frenzy. I know enough of it to feel it in me – the fiery charge of Belfast in my veins – but it would be the end of me if I gave into that side here. Once gone, there's no coming back, and the likely end is dying.

Charlie, with the broken nose, interrupts my thinking.

"Old Crooner's at it again."

"Like a dog that's lost a bone," I reply.

"Don't want to catch that shifty look of his," Charlie says. "I'm eyes down getting past the man."

Charlie picks up a coconut, then goes on.

"I don't know what he did to get in here, but you can be sure it wasn't picking pockets."

"He wouldn't know how to keep his mouth shut long enough," I say.

We both start laughing at the thought of the man, trying to dip his shaky hand in a well-loaded pocket, and keeping up a tune at the same time.

"My money, he's a slasher," says Charlie. "He's got the homicidal brood about him."

"Exactly what I thought," I reply. "He's bound to turn, just wait."

"Blood on the walls and cries for mercy."

"God, it's desperate."

Charlie crackles about in a nervous, friendly way. There are pock marks on his face and a scar across his right cheek. I like him well enough, but I can't shake the feeling he's always after something. I reckon that friendly way of his could turn to treachery if he saw an advantage. Jimmy agrees with me on that. But still, Charlie's good for a laugh and that's a thing in here, and he's better at knowing the gossip than anyone else.

"You know this place was a regular prison before it was a shipping-off place for the likes of us," Charlie continues as he bounces the coconut in his hands.

"That's no surprise," says Jimmy with his bleak gaze grazing the grim room.

"They thought they were closing the prison for good a year or so back, and didn't the temperance crowd make a song and dance about it. 'Here's the fruit of sobriety,' they said. 'A sober Ireland, at last, and there'll be no more need for prisons!' They had quite the celebration with their victory signs and the bands playing."

"A sober Ireland!" Jimmy laughs.

"A little early to the punch," I add.

Charlie chuckles and starts stripping the fibres.

"What do you boys know about the colonies?"

I sigh. It's the question Jimmy loves. I'm sick to death of hearing him trot out his tired stab at humour. I give the nut a good crack in anticipation.

"I hear the natives eat scrawny samples like yourself for breakfast, Charlie," my brother says in that same old manner of his. "Roasted on the fire until the meat's fair hanging off the bone."

"Well, they've an appetite for the best then, Jimmy. I'd be the finest meat they ever had."

"And if the natives don't get you," Jimmy perseveres, "I have it on good authority there's snakes there that can kill you just by looking at you."

"Good authority, is it? And what if you've a mirror?"

"Do you have a mirror, Charlie?" asks Jimmy.

"No, but I'm sure I could get my hands on one if there's a call for it."

"What do you think a snake would do if it saw itself in a mirror?" I ask.

Jimmy draws a breath.

"Don't be bothering us with your philosophising, Connie. Just get on with the coconuts and paying off your debt, and leave the snakes to look after themselves."

"I'll tell you something though," says Charlie. "There's only one sure thing in this world."

"What's that?" I ask.

"Aran agus bainne."

Aran agus bainne. Bread and milk. Is it any wonder I was salivating at the thought of Charlie roasted on a native's fire? The famished intent of that cannibal convict would have nothing on me. I'm always hungry in this place. The food is much the same from one day to the next. It's a breakfast of one-quart stirabout seven days a week; then it's nothing but bread and milk, for all other meals, apart from Sunday dinner when it's boiled beef with rice and vegetables. They say boiled beef, but what we get is a gristly remnant of something that might have once been passably good.

"The hardest labour in this place is taking a shit," says Charlie.

Jimmy starts laughing then. Typical.

"Have you ever heard McCafferty going at it in the morning?" Charlie continues, "Squat down and bellowing like there's no tomorrow. The other morning, I called out to him, 'Are you alright McCafferty?' 'Christ on a donkey I'm not!' he roars back at me. The noise he was making, you'd have sworn it was the donkey itself coming out his bum hole with hooves kicking up a fierce resistance."

We're all laughing now as we sit in the middle of the cracked coconuts and coir fibres. We laugh even more when McCafferty trudges through the room.

"Thar she blows!" calls out Charlie, and there's tears streaming down all our faces as McCafferty scowls at us with bewilderment.

Jimmy's up for a piss, and Charlie leans in my direction like a conspirator out to hatch a plan.

"You're the brains of the operation, I reckon."

His mouth has gone crooked with the utterance like he's thrown in a hook and set it dancing for a fish. I'll be no fish for Charlie or anyone else for that matter.

"For all the good it's done me," I reply.

He leans back like he's had a second thought.

"Do the two of you have much family you're leaving?"

"Ma's dead. Da's still around. There's our sister, she's a one, and a couple of younger brothers."

35

He nods his head as though he's almost interested.

"What about you?" I ask.

"There's no one that will miss me here."

He says it, but there's no melancholy in him.

"What do you think it'll be like?" I ask.

"Like nothing we've ever seen." His eyes have got a shine now. "I listen to the smart ones. You know, the old pipe and slippers brigade planted in the corner of the big room."

"Yeah. And what do they say?"

"It's seven years slavery but then countless opportunity. That's what some say. A blessing wrapped in a curse. Good country for sheep, no more bother with bailiffs, a chance of owning land, and a decent enough distance from England."

He pauses, then goes on.

"You know, there's some of them set themselves up to get nabbed just so they'd get transported?"

"I heard it."

"Anything for a better life, Connie. Here's hoping they know what they're talking about."

The conversations ebb and flow around me. My head is a stew of noted facts and unbound wonder. I try to conjure grand thoughts of heroic daring. Once the seven years are up, anything is possible. A new land, however it might be, and a new identity. Cornelius Donnelly: fortune seeker, explorer, landowner, witness of wondrous visions, noteworthy man, up-and-comer, a sun-baked colonialist, lord of all he sees. Even half of what I dream would do me well.

The politically serious – the secret society men – sharpen their theories in the shadowy corners of this place. There's no blessing in the curse for those boys. They apply their grinding philosophising to the political intent of transportation. They say all of this is just another chapter in the savagery of the British invasion. They talk with a murmuring passion about true Irish

36

sovereignty and justice. The empire could exile them anywhere, but it can never take them away from the grist of the Irish fight.

"The Saxons will have this island cleared of all the Irish, just wait and see."

"No hope at all save for King Dan and the tide of the monster rallies. I was at that early one at Trim. You should have seen the man. Passion and intellect combined. The crowd was tens of thousands, and every one of them on fire with it. You could taste the independence in the air. I've seen it and I'll tell you there's no stopping it."

"Sure the meetings are a spectacle, I know that myself, but O'Connell plays it too safe for my liking. Too much the diplomat. Not enough the rebel."

"Plays it too safe, you say? Is it Dan O'Connell you're talking about? Sure, he plays it as safe as is needed in the moment. In the moment. The thing about the man is, he knows the English. He knows they need no excuse to storm in here, looking to plant their heels down on Irish skulls, and then it's '98 all over again, isn't it? And where would the movement be then? It would be massacres and burning men alive and all the rest of their brutal civilising."

"It's all about the timing, see."

"Sure it is. He plays them smart. Plays the loyal card for now. Goes about the business with brains before brawn. What would you be having, another half-baked pike rebellion? God save us and preserve us. It's Dan O'Connell, and his way, that'll win us independence, or we won't be having it."

"But we won't be here to see it."

"No, more's the pity, but still our home forever."

Once the political vigour subsides into the sad fact of exile, one of them breaks out an old Jacobite number. It threads the air with a sad ache and sounds out all the injustice we've ever suffered. Those who know the language hear it all. Some join in singing the chorus. Their eyes are set on a place that's out beyond, sweeping the bogs and marshes and green fields and the rocky headlands and the vigorous sea. The whole of it is conjured through the song. It's there enough to give a decent jab. I don't know the meaning of most words, but I know it through the heart-tight grip that takes me. And everything that matters – more than I can put in words – is there in singing the old language into life. And something true in me is in it too, but maybe, even far away, this will still be true. Maybe there's room for both things: the future blessing on the other side of the curse and the old belonging that can't be conquered by the distance.

Night is a different beast. Smithfield depot has no lighting. It's pitch black when we are locked up in our cells when the sun goes down. It's three to a cell for the adults. Five to a cell for the young ones. The bedding is filthy and riddled with lice. The acrid stink of the common waste bucket poisons the air as the night goes on. The animals in the market are kept better than this.

Despair creeps along the corridors. It's supple enough to slip under any cell door. It's heavy enough to drag the biggest man down and drown him in his worst thoughts. It looks for any crack to crack some more, any doubt to stretch into a crevasse, any grief to shape into a darkened pit. It needs little time before it strikes a flow of tears: a boy pining for his mother; a man aching for his wife and family. Then we are all folded into the grievous black and made fodder for that bruising beast that grinds us with the quietest and the bleakest thoughts.

I feel it whisper its way into me. It puts me back in the dock: the boy whose trial is never allowed to end. Everything I say in the day is bluster. How can I deny it? All that chatter and humour and talk of the good to come is a lie. I don't really believe it. No one else is fooled by it. This treacherous dark isn't fooled by it. I am on the precipice, just like everyone else. We are all set to be erased from this world, like bodies tossed into an unmarked pit.

I will not have these tears. I will not be the weak boy. I cannot afford to be that one. Not here. But the folding dark now starts its cruellest ways upon my soul. It sets aside its ruthless prosecution and lays a soft, consoling hand on me. It conjures thoughts of home, memories of Ma, anything to prize the cracks in me until they're stretched to a fierce aching. How can the dark be so gently cruel? I tell myself I will not break. I cannot. But the night wields all I love to bring me down, and there's nothing I can do to stop my falling.

DUBLIN
JUNE 1844

Charlie's at it again. He's always bright when a rumour's taken hold of him: the smiling man bustling through the prison and eager for any pair of ears inclined to listen. Most of us were like that in the early months. We itched with the threat and promise of our deliverance from this dingy world. The cry would go up – the boats are in, the boats are in, did you hear the boats are in – and we'd be close to lining at the door to get this wretched place behind us.

Just seeing a decent patch of sky, and breathing air that's free from the stench of men and piss and market shit was cause enough to stir excitement.

I was moved by the rumours as much as any man until the constant disappointment smothered the spark in me. I sank into the daily proven fact that we are stuck in this abyss. Even the squealing pigs, next door, are moved on faster than us.

"It's different this time," Charlie says, taking note of my look, "mark my words."

He comes to me, before most others, these days. Charlie isn't one for reading between the lines of other men. It's not that he's stupid. It's more he's a dog with a bone when an idea settles in his head. He babbles on until men walk away or give him a good belting. I can't count the times I've found him bruised and bewildered on account of his fevered chatter. He's no idea how annoying he's become to everyone, including Jimmy.

But I have a soft spot for the mad boy, despite myself, and he knows it. God knows I pay the price for my fondness.

"I've told you, time and again, Charlie. I'll believe it when we're marching out the door."

He sighs at that and shakes his head, as though I'm the fool for not believing him.

"Mark my words, that's all I'm saying," he says with a note of sadness.

"Yeah, sure," I say.

It says something that Charlie still has it in him to get excited by a rumour. The constant disappointment has barely made a dent in him. What makes a man like that? He doesn't feel the weight and grind of time and disappointment like the rest of us.

I wouldn't mind an ounce of what he has. I'd never look to spray it around the place, though. Men in their misery tend to hate a cheerful man. There's plenty who have settled to hating Charlie. Complaints about him range from jokes to murderous plots. If I had his dim-witted joy I'd keep it quiet to myself. It would be my secret fire where I could warm my tired bones with barely a smile to give away the secret.

I watch him move down the hall. He's hunting for anyone who will listen, and there's McCafferty barking at him to get back in his hole, and there's Charlie giving McCafferty advice. I wait for the fight, but neither seems to have the inclination.

"What did he want?" Jimmy mumbles when he comes into the cell.

"The usual."

Jimmy snorts.

"You know we've been here longer than the whole time we were sentenced for the watches."

"I know it."

Jimmy stares at me for a moment, then drops his eyes.

"They're looking to drive us to the madhouse, brother. Are you telling me that pack of bastards who built an empire that spans across the whole world, can't organise the timely arrival of a few ships for a pack of prisoners? You know what it's about, don't you?"

He's not after my opinion. He never is. He's been sniffing around the world of the politicals the past few months, and now he's one for having a view. Jimmy and his notions. I barely nod my head before he's off again.

"Leaving us to stew here is their twisting the knife to bring us lower. That's what it's about."

"Who are they, Jimmy?"

He snorts and levels his eyes at me.

"Don't play the fool, boy! The English. You mark my words, once they think the spirit is worn out of us, the boats will arrive. Then off we'll shuffle with no fight left inside us. That's how they want us, beaten down and compliant, slaves to their system."

"Do you really think we're so important to them, Jimmy, that they give us that much thought?"

He flares at that.

"You've no understanding the way this world works," he fires back. "We are the colonised and they are the colonisers."

"Ah, Jimmy, you're just dishing out the scraps you caught from the smart crowd's table."

He shoves me out of his way as he storms out of the cell, desperate-clinging to his new-baked certainties.

I shouldn't have said it, I know it, but I'm not the younger brother I used to be, tagging along behind him and staying in his shadow. I measure my words with the hard men in here, of course, but not so much with Jimmy anymore. Enough provoking, and I give him the full charge of what I'm thinking. Quick as a flash and set to burn. Anyway, I can't abide him acting like he knows better. All he knows is what he hears from others, and half the time he even gets that wrong.

I've only one certainty in my head. This place is driving the lot of us mad. And am I any different? I spent months dreaming of escaping. I had it mapped out in my mind: make a rope of sheets, jump out the window, hope for the best, and climb the outer wall.

Charlie told me there were plenty of locals who would see it as their patriotic duty to hide away a Smithfield escapee. I could see it in my mind's eye: the buxom young widow who would gather me into her home, her heart racing with a patriotic fervour. It would be you poor thing and you darling boy and you gallant lad and we'd be at it, with her soft, eager thighs about me, charging towards a splendid liberation with a hearty yell to go and wake the neighbours.

I couldn't get the smile off my face when I was thick in that dream. I should have just enjoyed it on the quiet, but I made the mistake of telling old brother of mine. Didn't I cop it then: the look on his face, sour enough to curdle milk.

"You're an idiot," he barked. "You want to escape? Where would you go that you wouldn't be found? Under a pile of rocks in Connemara, or stuck in France with all their foreign babbling?"

Of course, I had neither a real plan nor intention. It was no more than a happy dream. But the way he carried on left me thinking I ought put a plan together despite him.

"The trouble with you is you've lost your courage," I said to him.

That was all it took, and then it was fists flying, and word soon got around that the Donnellys were at it again. We'd become so regular at it, we barely drew a crowd. I know one thing. He was a sorrier sight than me by the end of it.

The months have dragged on since, with Jimmy trying to be political and Charlie with his constant gossip, and Old Crooner still throwing out his tunes and every other mad bastard barking at the moon and looking to brawl for little reason.

"Connie, did you hear?" Pete Doherty says to me.

"Hear what Pete?"

"We're going."

"God help us, man, has Charlie been at you too?"

"No, not Charlie. I heard it from Old Bung Eye."

Now this is something of a different order. Old Bung Eye isn't a turnkey inclined to start rumours or say much of anything to the likes of us. He shuffles about as though this is his purgatory and we are his much-despised tormentors. Cards close to his chest, that one, and cudgel even closer. On a bad day he's a bastard, and on a good day he's cold indifferent.

"What did he say then?"

"We're to be – what's the word he used? – disposed of – that's how he put it. We're to be disposed of in a matter of days."

"And what the hell's that mean?"

"Shipped out, Connie. We're going. We're finally going. And doesn't it make sense? Didn't you notice the priest going on about exile the other day, like he was preparing us for it?"

"Can't say I was listening."

"Well, it's definitely on this time. No shadow of a doubt about it."

Pete's near bursting with excitement. He goes off down the hall, checking if others have heard. I follow along. Everywhere I go, there's chatter. It's more than the usual tired rumours. We're off. We're going. It's happening. Knock the cobwebs off the irons, we're going for a ride. A ship is due at Kingstown. It might be there already. Even Old Crooner has started up a sea shanty, and Charlie's jigging about to it with his clumsy feet. No one is denying the likelihood of the news, and my heart has started to sound a stronger beat. Even Jimmy has an itchy look about him.

"Do you think it's true?" I ask him.

"I think it might be, brother."

He gives me a grin. There's a turn-up for the books.

"Don't let your political mates see you smiling. Aren't you meant to be aggrieved at the injustice of our exile?"

"Don't bother me with your nonsense," he says, then wanders off.

I can feel a lightning charge right through me, but dread is nipping at its heels. That dread is not a thing to show. I see some are given over to it, getting shaky in their boots, pale as ghosts, as though willing themselves to die right here and now. The shady men linger around them, with sharp threats or soothing promises, like crows to a carcass. I keep the crows away from me and bolster up my bluster. I'll have them know I'm a wild colonial boy in the making. It makes no difference that I'm far from convinced by anything I say. We are going – that seems to be the only certainty.

One more breakfast and then I join the line-up for the heavy irons. The fourteen pounds are clamped around my ankles. I am hobbled like an animal. My wrists are bound. My final steps on Irish soil are nothing but this clumsy shuffle. What once was, never to be again: that fleet-of-foot boy, brawling bold in his all-familiar world, lost down a Belfast alley and gone for good. He is gone. He is gone. I am this man now, pushing through this heavy rain of thoughts.

Better to not think at all. Better to just move.

Someone's started with the doleful sniffing. I steady myself. I won't have that sound hook and drag me down. There's a mutter of annoyance from another man. I ball my shaking hands into fists and set my face as hard as I can.

Jimmy is close, but he's planted himself deep in his own head now. His eyebrows are knotted, and his jaw is set tight. He is the contained man. He'll be giving nothing away to them. He will give nothing away to anyone. Each to his own, just like old Da says. I dig to find the man I need be as one of the officers starts barking his commands so loud it makes my head sore.

"Keep your mouths shut. Be quick about it. Cause no trouble or we'll send you to sea black and blue and with broken bones for good measure."

We are prodded to start the shuffle through the dark hall towards the entrance. The sound of the market is loud, now the door stands open, but so is the sound of the drop and drag of the chains. I am walking against an undertow. The last lingering claim of our land is beneath my feet. More than a hundred generations are in this dust. My footsteps are soon lost in the shuffle of those behind me. In seconds, there's no trace left of where I've been; soon, no trace that I have been at all.

I look up to take in every drop. Old Viking Dublin: that raggedy, glorious thing. I glimpse the nearby buildings and take a last full breath of the shitty market air. I am struck by a shard of light from the glistening Liffey down the street. Not far from us, there's people getting on with their lives as though this is just another day.

What is this state we are in now? Are we made ghosts before we are even dead? We are here but not here really: passed beyond the notice of the crowd.

There's a line of carriages outside. The peelers have circled around. Some face towards us as we emerge. Some face out to keep an eye on all the alleys. Each has a cudgel at the ready. They tap a beat in their cradling hands. There's a hint of nerves about them: a restless shifting about on their feet and a fierce kind of muttering. They are reading threats in every shadow, and they want this business done before there's trouble.

Word came through to us about the riot at Kilmainham back in April. One hundred and sixteen men had to be moved. A great storm mainly brewed because there was a famous ribbon-man among them. Nothing stirs the pot like the presence of a patriot. Get close to a patriot, and stir up in his defence, and there you

46

are—a patriot yourself.

A turnkey let it out that the papers told of a riotous, disorderly mob and that the governor of the gaol wasn't so much afraid of escape but that the mob would slip whiskey to the convicts. Imagine that.

The news stirred the imagination of us Smithfield boys. We cheered at the idea of a rowdy drink at our departure. Some hoped that boisterous sympathy that shook Kilmainham might still be astir in Dublin at our leaving. But now I look around, and there's nothing much to see. I wish there was some drama. Surely being hauled from home and all we love calls for some drama, even if it's a few drunk locals looking for no more than a raucous opportunity? Just a bit of noise would be good. Just a few voices sounding out the wrong would bolster the spirits and say what's being done to us matters.

What I'd give to hear Mary's vehement voice. Those down-from-the-country constables wouldn't have heard such a murderous roar. They'd be shitting their pants and packing their bags and running for the hills at just the sound of her. My sister's more warrior than the rest of us combined. But I know there'd be a tremble at the edge of her voice, and that would be too much for me. Maybe this quiet is better for all concerned. Our leaving is just the business to be done today, and tomorrow it will be another fifty to the ship, and then they'll have the sails up and we will be lost to the horizon.

I need to stop this thinking. It's cutting me too deep. There's plenty enough men in our ranks now keening like old black-wrapped women at a wake. To hell with them and to hell with this. I shuffle along, then step into a blacked-out car and squeeze into a sandwich of bodies and chains.

There's discomfort and the common stink of men and a strange brew of neighbouring emotions. Every man is pressed together, and we're all wondering what's to come next. There's a lurch, then a jerk and pull as the horses move. Their hooves start up a rhythm straight away. The sound of the convoy echoes through the alleys. It's nothing but the empty sound of leaving.

I presume we will be in the car for the ten miles south to Kingstown. Those who know Dublin mutter at the blacked-out windows and try to work out the direction. One man is crankily contending with another about the likely path. There's relief in the normal sound of stupid arguing. The more vehement the two men get, the more the rest of us are amused. We poke at their aggravation to spur them on.

"I think your man has a point," says one spectator who's put on a quizzical look.

"No, the other one's the truer Dubliner," pokes another.

We are no sooner settled in for a long bout of curmudgeonly entertainment than we come to a sudden halt. Everyone is puzzled at that, even the argumentative Dubliners.

The door of the car opens and we are ordered out. I step down and see we are still in the thick of Dublin, but now beside the river.

Someone mutters, "North Wall."

Another points at a steamboat and jokes, "Looks like we're on the slow boat to the colonies."

A third boy chimes in, "Tell the authorities they'll be needing a bigger boat."

And for a moment, we are lads having a laugh as though there's no care in this peculiar world. Our sudden free spirits put the guards on edge. They start pushing and shoving us towards that unlikely steamboat.

"Get moving, get on there," they bark.

We shuffle on and take our seats. Once the boat is full, it sets off down the Liffey and across the bay.

I see, across the water, the ships at anchor at old Dunleary.

Great groaning beasts of timber; all masts and sails and made for crossing oceans. Each one a sorry drop ready to move through the veins of the noxious British Empire.

Now it's heavy in my soul. I am leaving in the belly of one of those things and I'll never be coming home. I swear I can't breathe. I think of you, Mamai, and your grave that I will never see again. I think of you, Da, and your grief-heavy eyes and the mumble of your voice in the morning. I think of you Mary, fierce with all your friends, and whoever the sorry man will be to marry you. I think of you, Johnny and young George, Belfast brothers, out there on the streets and left to battle on. All of you, save for Jimmy, is soon to be lost across the sea with no trace left but lines in a few brief letters and the unsteady grip of memory.

Tears press at my eyes. I curse the restless push of them. Once they start, who would know the end, and, in this world of regular brutalities, tears are a weakness that I can't afford. I don't dare to look across at Jimmy. The sight of him, troubled in the same way, would sure set me off and, if he didn't seem troubled, it would probably set me off the worse. I press my face tight and will myself strong as the boat pulls into the dock. My eyes drift over the square-rigged masts of a barque. Strange it has a simple girl's name, as though it might be something warm. This thing in front of me is nothing warm. Emily by name but not by nature.

We shuffle, single file, up the gangway. No one dares look down. That water adds weight to the irons. One clumsy bastard could be the end of all of us. The twitching town and country peelers want the business finished. They want to get home. They bark like dogs to keep us moving. The soldier-guards, on the ship, feel the need to make a first impression. They yell the louder when we break silence, as our feet find the safety of the deck and we let loose with sighs and a general mumble of relief.

"They don't see men. They see a herd of animals," the boy beside me mutters.

An officer notices straight away.

"You are not to speak to each other. You are not to speak to ship's crew or the guards unless you are spoken to; you are not to speak at all until you're below decks."

The officer has collared the boy and is eyeballing him.

"Have you got that clear in that thick head of yours, Paddy?"

The boy takes a moment. I know that calculation. I can see it in his eyes. He looks straight at the officer, cold as ice, just long enough to make his point. The air is charged with whatever might come next. The boy shows the slightest flicker of a sneer before he nods his head to show he understands. It's enough to keep the peace without selling his soul outright. The officer stares him down a little more, but he can see his words have caused a bitter stir among us. He yells, "Move on," and so we do until we're brought to a halt to be addressed.

"I am ship's surgeon, John Munro," a man announces from a height, "I have one concern: that every person on board this ship gets to the end of this journey in a healthy state in body and soul. It is my singular concern, and it should be yours as well. Be clear, your good health will rely on every one of you adhering to the rules and regulations of this ship. They are there to maintain good order through whatever the ocean might deal us in the weeks to come."

He draws breath, then tries on the face of a grave father.

"I will not abide foolishness. I will not abide sloth nor ill-manner nor plotting nor general bad behaviour. I will not abide disrespect in any manner. You will learn the rules. You will obey the rules. You will respect the authority of those who are commissioned to govern you onboard this ship. If you prove unruly, I can assure you it will be on your record and there will be repercussions both onboard and when we land. Do you understand?"

No one answers, and another officer gets red in the face and starts barking at us.

"Answer the surgeon when he asks you a question, or there will be no end of trouble for you."

We manage a murmured yes, and the surgeon continues.

"You will be kept busy in the daily routines. The cells will be cleaned every day. The bedding will be aired every day. There will be time for exercise, and there will be education for the younger boys. You will not be given time for your Irish brooding."

There's a murmur in the ranks at that. I've heard it said some English see us as a savage breed, as less than human, with little hope of civilising. In their minds, we are unconquerably backward, distemperate, lazy, lost in mindless superstitions and papistry. We are a waste of good land, impoverished vermin to be cleared, an endlessly needy people, one famine shy of extinction.

Is that the way this surgeon and the other glowering officer see us? Do they see a savage when they see the likes of me? I see the curl of their lips and hear the disdainful tone. They think they're better than us. The surgeon's playing the condescending lord, and the other one's his yard dog. I feel anger press against the irons, and I hear a stir of muttering around me. Now the guards bark us into a line-up to be recorded. An official scratches my details in a ledger. I'm given the once-over by the surgeon, then prodded to go below.

I descend into a dark world that rocks and creaks to the rhythms of the sea. It smells of timber, tar, and salt. I stoop to pass through a gated doorway and find myself in a long cell. There are tables and seating. There's hammocks and bedding packed away to the side. It's the place to eat and sleep and stare at walls: the belly of the beast; our timber and iron cradle to the other side of the world.

"Here we are then," says Jimmy.

"I thought our ticket gave us better lodging," I reply.

He smiles at that. What's got into him? I swear he's in good spirits – peculiar boy.

We find ourselves a seat, over by the corner, and watch the shuffling procession continue. It's mainly faces we know from Smithfield. Michael Kelly, the lifer, shuffles into our cell. He's the one sentenced for stabbing a constable in the jaw with a knife.

"There's one who can give that surgeon a hand," Jimmy murmurs to me.

Little Robbie McKeaver, the book thief, and young Jimmy Fitzpatrick are directed to a cell just across from us.

"Temptation's to be kept at a distance then," says some dark character, sitting to our side, as he stares at the boys like a devil on a leash.

"Best you calm that grubby tongue," Jimmy snarls at him.

The other man turns quiet but continues staring.

Those boys, in the opposite cell, have little to no concern for the devil sitting beside us. They are all darting eyes, and general excitability, despite the chains. Strange children and with tongues so sharp they could cut a hole through this ship's timber. They are fierce-honed by the streets. I'd guess they have little family to grieve their leaving. They'd carve the lecherous bastard beside us up for breakfast if they met him as a gang, but any one of them, trapped alone with him, would be dealing with another matter.

The cells are slowly filling with a shuffling tide of men: violent murderers and bacon thieves; rapists and young pickpockets; wheat thieves and highway robbers; soldiers gone wrong and desperate hungry farmers.

Some are putting on the hard face as though none of this is any bother. Some don't have to put on the hard face. I suspect they came out of their mothers looking fit to murder. And there are the sad others, sniffing in the shadows, and given over to grief. They are mostly left alone, though the noisier ones are cursed for the disturbance.

"Is this boat not punishment enough, you weeping bastards? How about you find yourselves some balls so we can have some peace?"

I don't curse the grievers. I can understand their tears, but I can't afford to dwell on their common feeling. It's too deep a hole, and I fear there'd be no getting out of it. They might mourn and curse themselves to an early grave. I choose to look ahead and live.

EMILY II – DEPARTING IRELAND
14 JULY 1844

Old Crooner is in our cell. It seems the songs have left him. I've felt his eyes on me but haven't dared to look back. This boat's too small a place for entertaining curses. It is strange his quiet doesn't trouble me the way it would have in Smithfield. Maybe it's because the irons are still on us.

I'd never heard him speak, in a plain way, until last night. Suddenly, he had plenty to say.

"Come here to me," he said with his eyes looking around at us. "The English, with all the far reaching of their empire, don't know the truth of the sea now. Not for all the maps they've made and all the books they've written about it. No map can hold the truth of the sea."

He let that one hang in the air until we were all ready for what's to come.

"Ancient Bran and his crew, in their currach, they were the ones who knew the truth of it. But they only came to know it by passing through the fiercest waves and all the tribulations that the deep could throw at them. They knew through the plight of enduring it, you see? That's where the truth is found. But, tell me, do any of you know of Bran and his journey?"

"Are you talking about Saint Brendan?" asked Jimmy.

"No. His pious self is another matter," Old Crooner said with a hint of disdain in his voice, "Our man Bran, he was from far older times and not so inclined to sanctity as old Brendan and his monks. With those old holy boys, it was as though they never really left the monastery. Even when they were miles from any shore, they kept at their prayers and ceremonies.

But Bran and his crew, now they were men like us, you see,

54

when they decided to go out on the ocean. Further than the fishermen they went. Further than anyone had imagined before. They went so far it's hard to reckon how deep the depths were beneath them. Fierce deep, be sure of that, and who could say what strange creatures lurked there: all manner of coiled and restless briny monsters and all astir in that chaos we are all born from."

The old man looked around at all of us. He took a sip of water, then nodded.

"So there was Bran and his fellow men, the lot of them, brave as a band of men could ever be." He raised his hand at that, as though pointing out their presence in our midst. "They went so far, didn't they meet the warrior-king, Manannan himself, in all his fiercest and finest glory? And it was himself told them that they were on their way to the otherworld."

He paused again to let the name of the destination settle in our minds.

"The otherworld no less: a world beyond all reckoning and further than any imagining can reach. Then Old King Manannan made the risk clear to Bran and his crew. Death was more likely than life if they continued. But Bran and the crew, well, they had set their minds on making the journey, so they kept going in hope they'd find a mighty good on the other side. Not knowing but going anyway. That's the mad courage that is hope. And do you know what they found once their strength was close to spent?"

We murmured no and waited for it.

"An island full of the most beautiful women that could be imagined."

We let out a laugh as he arched his eyebrows and looked around at us.

"Indeed, it was. Beauties beyond anything you itchy boys could conjure in your minds. And, tell me, can't you just see the delight of old Bran and his men near jumping out of their skin at the sight of all those women whose beauty would cause a man's heart to burst in excitement at the sight of them. And wasn't there great feasts and song and dance and the like and the women with no end of hospitable ways about them."

There was a murmur through the cells then, and someone said that transportation was sounding all the better by the minute.

"Now you might think, well, there's the end of it then, and it would be understandable to come to that conclusion. What more could any man want than what Bran and his crew had on that island?"

There was rowdy agreement on that point.

"Well the pious might be more inclined to old Saint Brendan's godly ways with the island of saints and the glorious light and the like. But between you and me, even at the age I am, my preference is for Bran's otherworld, thank you."

We laughed at that as he took another sip of water.

"But here's the thing," he continued. "The story can't be left there because that's not where it ends. No, it isn't. There's always more to a thing like this, just like the sea itself."

He paused again.

"So what happened next, you ask? Well, even there, in a place as close to the fullest joy and satisfaction as any of us could imagine, there was a longing for home, you see, among the men. It was even felt by Bran himself. It was there, in them, like an itch that got fiercer by the day."

The old man looked at us to see any signs of sympathy on that point.

"We must depart from here," Bran finally said when that itch was close to driving him mad, and all the best of that beauteous world seemed like nothing worth considering.

And so they set off. Back on the currach they got and out to the sea and back to making that rough crossing with the monsters of the deep lurking below, and all the waves crashing about them. And, here's the truth, the pull of home was so formidably great inside their souls, they continued through all the tribulations without a moment's hesitation. And so, in time, they found themselves just off the shore of their home, that is our own good country."

He stared into the distance on that point, then nodded again.

"So there they were. And what do you think should happen, but people on the shoreline saw them out there in their currach. But what happened then? Was there a great joy of welcome and celebration that the heroes, who had gone, were now returned?"

"Sure, there must have been," said a boy who was caught in the spell of the story.

"Well, you would think as much now, wouldn't you?" replied the old man, "and I wouldn't hold it against you if you did. But what happened wasn't that at all. Oh no. It was as though those country people, out in the fields, were looking out and seeing nothing but strangers in a tiny boat. Strangers! Just imagine it. All that time, and the fierce claim of the ocean, had made Bran and his men strangers to their own people. Too much time has passed, and they had become nothing but a half-remembered story to their own kith and kin. But one of Bran's men, well, he wouldn't have it, no, not at all, so out he blunders from the currach, full of determination to be home and done with it, and what do you think happened?"

We all sat quiet not knowing what to say.

"No sooner did he plant his foot back on the land of his birth than he turned to ashes then and there. It was as though God himself had sent a lightning bolt down to end the man."

Old Crooner settled back on that point as though there was

no more to be said. Some of the older men seemed inclined to sit and quietly wrestle with the point of it, but a young boy spoke up with the question the rest of us were wondering.

"But what was the truth of the ocean then?"

There was a further pause, and Old Crooner stared out to nothing in particular.

"There's no going back to the place you once knew."

We were quiet for a while, and then an old country man started singing. *Mo ghrá den chéadfhéachaint thú, Eileanóir na rún.* It wove the strange, sad feelings tight about us. *You're my love at first sight, Eleanor my secret.*

Grief was so tight about my soul, I couldn't sleep afterwards. No going back. I spent the night staring into the dark with the sound of the sea beating its rhythm. No going back. No going back. No way to stop this thing from happening.

I hear the sound of leaving. It's muffled by this coffin timber that creaks and groans about us. Some faces are washed pale with grief. It's not just those who have wept all the way. The most bedraggled souls are mostly wrung dry and lost in silence. They've hid themselves in the shadows with their dead eyes staring at nothing at all. Now it's hard men who are breaking into tears as though they've just woken to the loss. Home is a place already lost to our eyes. They've stolen it from us, now forever. The boom of the captain's commands drifts down from above. The deck drums with the sound of scurrying feet. Movement is across the deck. Movement is through the rolling sea. Somewhere above, sailors are scaling the rigging. A great cascade of canvas falls, and the sails rustle into life and smooth into blustering tension. I feel the ship surge forward. It becomes an awkward, lurching thing: sliding sideways, one moment, then down to a briny crash before rising, suspended for a moment, then crashing down again. I am gone, and home is lost to me. Níl cara ag cumha ach cuimhne. Memory has no friend but sorrow.

CHAPTER 9

We are tossed between a cruel god and the devil. Even Jim Owgan, who killed a man with a shovel, now has the look of a shivering, scared child. The murderous Gilligan brothers, those formidable stickmen, are pale and moaning like ghosts in the corner.

No one is a hard man now. No man is above the rest. The old country men are groaning in the native tongue. Dia ár sábháil! Dia ár sábháil!

Everything rises, then falls with the heave and splatter of vomit. The stench burns my throat. I can feel it curdling inside me. Across the way, the desperate pious are going at their sorrowful mysteries like grandmothers in a frenzy. Jimmy has taken to chiming in with a blasphemous response that's sure to make matters worse.

"For Christ's sake, Jimmy, will you stop stirring the pot!" I yell at him.

He looks at me, all grey jowls with a tinge of green, then he vomits about my boots.

"You can thank me later," he mumbles as he wipes his mouth, then brings his blaspheming back up to the rhythm of the Hail Marys.

And now the convulsions are at me. Every miserable burning morsel is surging through me and into the common stew that's sliding about the floor. This is it then. This is how it ends. Sick-splattered and wrung until I'm heaving nothing but stale air. And up we rise and down we crash again. Dia ár sábháil! I'm sure the old native speakers want nothing but to die. Their eyes are full of horror. Their hands are clawing at their faces.

We're all struck mad and desperate, iron-locked in the belly of this splintery beast as death rides the waves with vengeance, slamming the sides of the ship like a Friday night brawler, then tossing us up to jar us with a savage kidney punch.

Mother of God. Jimmy has quietened down to an empty shell beside me. His mouth's agape, and he's staring at the ceiling. Don't be dead, Jimmy. Don't leave me to this on my own you selfish bastard. I elbow his ribs, just in case. There's his reassuring sneer levelled at me but I can see despair eating at his edges. He looks like he's lost something and it's not coming back. A jolt of panic races through me at the sight of it so I elbow him again.

"Pray for us sinners now, and at the hour of our death."

The desperation and the praying all blur together. Some praying types have gone quiet and some soulless types are now pounding heaven's door with a panic to make their souls right before it is too late. Hope in the hopeless storm. At the hour of our death. Amen. Amen.

And then, like some answer from above, we hear boots clambering down the stairs.

Munro, the surgeon, seems taken aback at our miserable state. He staggers across the cell, lurching one way and then the other, and half-skidding on the vomit that's all about. There's a blood smear on his apron from bleeding the soldier boy who turned sick before we left Kingstown. Now, I suspect, that boy's the lucky one, lost in a drift of wine and opium.

The surgeon goes from one man to the next. He checks each of us and, for some at least, he offers a tender tone. He seems most concerned about the old native speakers. He asks for help to find out what they are saying.

"Well then, sir," says one of them who has some English, "they claim they feel close to death, but maybe baccy might ease their final suffering."

"Tell them I will consider it," murmurs Munro.

Every other man in the cell sniffs the opportunity, despite Munro's attempt to keep it quiet. They strike up their own claim for the need for consoling baccy in the storm. Munro has a limit to his sympathy and a nose for exaggeration. His kind tone breaks into brittle British commonsense.

"You men are young and in a fair enough state to my mind."

"But surgeon, can't the heavy irons at least come off us?" pleads someone at the back.

"They stay on until the weather is calm, and they will only come off if good behaviour warrants it."

"They guarantee our death if the ship goes down," snarls one of the former soldiers now turned convict. "You know that well enough, though, don't you?"

The surgeon eyes the man and marks him down as trouble.

"The weather is rough, but this ship is sound and well-captained," replies the surgeon, "I advise you calm your minds, attend to your prayers, and don't go rousing yourselves with unwarranted consternation. It does you no good. We've a long journey ahead of us, and this will not be the last storm we face, so best you get accustomed to it."

Munro leaves our cell to inspect the others, and we are alone in our misery again.

"They'd sooner we drown than survive a shipwreck that might give us our freedom," chimes in the former soldier. "These irons are a death sentence once the sea cracks in. Better that they hung us all back home and be honest about it."

"Enough with your cheery chatter, you horse's arse," pipes in someone else.

The former soldier bristles at the insult. He sprays threats through the dark. It leads to nothing but a chorus telling him to shut his trap. For a moment, some forget that we are about to die. There's some would fight the cursing soldier now if they weren't in the irons. There's relief in the sniff of a fight and the familiar surge to action. They're almost happy as they strain against the cold weight, and curse him and his mother, just as we rise to a monstrous height, then fall.

I close my eyes and give in to the brutal back-and-forth. There's no end to it. I've never known a violence I couldn't contend against, or escape, but anything I can muster is nothing to this monstrous ocean. I swear the timber wails, as though in mortal pain. I keep my eyes closed and fall into the empty. Nothing but dark, inside and out. Nothing but cold sweat fingering my skin. Nothing but the push, off the cliff, and crash that jars the marrow from my bones.

And then it comes to me: a blue so pure I forget to breathe, the sight of wings, their ever-upward flight, the sound of bodies weaving to a flock, skin and feather and all that gentle, and her whisper in my ear. Up, never down, Connie. The earth disappears, the air lifts me to flight, and something more surges through me 'til I am close enough to reach it. Maybe heaven for me after all. Maybe all the wretched life is left behind. I am so close I can almost taste the sweet of hope. Then comes a savage lurch of gravity, and all the good is lost to me again.

The sea has paused its fight. It's so calm, it is almost troubling. Maybe the ocean's taking breath before a final onslaught. It's devilish to allow us a lick of hope when it intends to kill us. I see men, about me, who are bright and smiling as though there will be no more trouble. The fools have the memory of fish. I hope the sharks take them first when they start to circle.

"Look at them," I say to Jimmy. "You'd think they were heading home for supper."

"You know who you sound like?" he says with the sly-dog grin I like the least.

"Don't say it," I reply.

"And you reckon I'm the one most like Da," he says, clinching the deal, then signing it off with a laugh.

God knows I hate it when he gets up himself that way. He's

all strutting peacock and thinking he's the clever one. I give him a shove just as Munro's coming down the stairs.

The surgeon's walking through the ship, drawing up his plan. He's spelling out his dictates to a pair following in his wake, the boatswain of the prisoners and the boatswain's mate. They are little men in the little ordered world of this unconvincing bucket. They give the servant's nod and note the surgeon's every word as though it's gospel: the holy gospel of the illustrious surgeon as noted by his gormless disciples.

"All floors are to be dry scrubbed with sand and stones. Make sure of that. There will be no buckets of water brought down. Damp invites contagion. A thorough dry scrub over every inch of deck; is that clear? The sand will soak up the worst of this and make it ready to be gathered and tossed overboard. Get the men busy about it and make it clear the work will be thoroughly inspected and any half-baked efforts will be noted and with consequence."

The servile pair are about to get to business when the surgeon calls them back.

"And have you found me a more satisfactory cook?" he asks.

"One of the older men, James McDonnell, says he can do it," says the boatswain.

"As long as he's not a poisoner," he pauses. "Do we have any of them on board?"

"Just the simple variety of murderers sir, knuckles and sticks men, and McDonnell isn't one of them anyway. I hear he gave a woman a kicking on account of her stealing from him."

"He will do," says the surgeon, "And what of a teacher for the boys?"

"William Reilly was a clerk before," says the boatswain's mate, "he seems smart enough."

"Age?"

"He's twenty."

"And his religion?"

"Protestant."

"Well, it's writing and basic arithmetic he'll be attending to, so it shouldn't cause aggravation. God knows the papists can get prickly about that kind of thing. I'll tell you now, I won't abide sectarian nonsense on this ship. I haven't the patience for it. Whoever gets the job done is good enough."

He looks about for a moment.

"Right. I think that's all for now. Get the men busy. I want this filth removed, and bedding aired, before the evening. We will have good order on this ship and a healthy arrival at the colony."

I am set to work beside another man. He's a boy, maybe my age. He has the northern sound about him, like me. We are quiet about our business, for a while, tossing sand across the greasy floor and sweeping up the soaked-in debris. He throws a grimace in my direction and I fire back a comradely nod and, so, there's an ease between us.

"The sweet joy of ocean travel," he says as he pushes a clotted mess of sand and spew towards the cell door.

"Sure, just breathe that fresh air."

We stop for a break, and he asks me where I'm from. I tell him Belfast.

"Were you around to see that aeronaut with his balloon?"

I feel a charge of delight at the question. It brings a grand day back to me like a treat.

"Charles Green, you mean? Yeah sure, I didn't have money to get up close, but I saw him go up from a distance. All the town was out for it. It was as fine a spectacle as I've ever seen."

"Sure it was."

"So are you from Belfast yourself?"

He squints at me before he answers.

"From further north, but I spent my share of time in the

64

town when I was younger. You know that Green reckons he will fly to America in that basket of his one day. Think of that. Getting from one side of an ocean to the other without setting foot on water."

I laugh and look around at the floor.

"Steering clear of water sounds good to me. Maybe that's how they'll be transporting our kind in the future," I say. "They'll have us piled in a basket. Just imagine it. 'You are sentenced to float away in the clouds for seven years!' The colonists would be looking up for rain and see an Irish cloud, fit to burst, instead! Just imagine, they'd be scurrying like rats at the sight of us bearing down on them from above."

The boy laughs at that one.

"You know what I remember most from that day with the balloon going up?" I ask him.

"What's that?"

"It's how the old ones couldn't cope with the sight of it. 'It's not natural. It's the work of the devil himself.' God, the consternation in them. Their arms were flapping about, crossing themselves like there was no tomorrow, and the holy water! God help us all, the whole town was near drowning in it. The priests would have made a fortune if they were selling it by the gallon."

He smiles at this, but doesn't take up the story as I'd expect, so I know for sure he's one of them. We settle into silence and work on. Whatever is likely to come next has turned to a hard knot inside me, and I don't know how it's undone. I know this boy is a Protestant, but there's something in this moment that warms me to him despite it. I don't want to say anything to sour the air between us.

What strange world is this? All of us gradually turning upside down and made more together than apart. Maybe that is the spell of an otherworld just like Old Crooner told it. Maybe all the old ways will be getting unbound, despite how hard they're knotted, and something new is going to be made. The thought is as wild as the ocean out there. I look at the boy and I like him. It really makes no difference to me what he is.

"You know what I'll miss the most?"

"What's that?" I answer with relief that he's still friendly.

"Looking up at Cave Hill in the evening."

I'm struck hard at the thought of it.

"Oh, you're not wrong. My Mamai, she loved that hill. She called it the old sleeping giant. Were you one to go up there for Easter?"

"Sure, some years when we were in town when I was little."

"And the Danish gold?"

He laughs at mention of it.

"We looked about but clearly had no luck."

"I swear me and Jimmy and my sister and other brothers looked over every cranny of that hill from one Easter to the next. We were sure we were going to find it. Our Da always coaxed us. "Off you go, make us rich." He'd say it every year, without fail, and we believed him. I used to have such visions of digging up the buried chest and digging my hands into all those riches like holding pieces of the sun itself."

I stop, caught in the thick of the memory, then feel it ripped away.

"But like you say, here we are, and we won't have a chance at it again."

He starts on a song, at a murmur, just to give some pulse to the work. I know the tune but not the words, apart from the "will you go, lassie, go" line. I'm partial to a work song. It makes things easier, and, on this ship, there seems to be no trouble dished out for singing or talking. We've been told the only thing that matters is getting the work done to satisfaction and without grumbling or back-talk.

"Where do you think we might be in the world?" I ask him a while later.

"I reckon we've gone past Portugal by now," he replies like he knows it. "I've got fair memory of a map I once saw. It was such a fine thing. The prettiest writing and drawing I've ever seen. Just between you and me, I would have swiped it if I had half the chance. More's the pity I didn't. But I still have the picture of it lodged up here." He taps his head. "I reckon we'll be going between Africa and America for a long way down, but I'm guessing they'll keep us too far from anywhere to see."

"It's a strange thing, isn't it?" I say.

He looks around at the boat, down at the sand, then smiles back at me.

"It surely is, brother."

CHAPTER 10

I'm glad to have the heavy irons off me. Once they were undone and put aside, after the sea turned calm, I swear I could have flown away like that aeronaut. The surgeon laid out his rules about how releasing us from the irons was an indulgence, easily rescinded if there was even a hint of trouble. He's training us the way you would a dog: a friendly pat on a well-lowered head, but always the hovering stick demanding full obedience.

His threats are nothing compared to what the rolling deep can dish out. There's no shaking the thought I might die on this crossing. Maybe I'm so far from home it doesn't really matter. And if nothing matters, then those bastards have no power. There's a grim satisfaction in that thought. How strange final freedom might be found cradled in the dark of likely death.

I don't tell anyone what I think, not even Jimmy. He'd have words to say about it. There would be no end to his head shaking and blustering at me, as though he knows a thing. I have no need for that. I tuck the good scraps of what I think inside myself so the best of me is hidden from everyone. I keep my head down and avoid the attention of the surgeon or his yard dog, McLerie.

That McLerie itches to play the pompous military man. You can see it in the way he struts about, all hollow regalia and bombast, desperate for a military campaign. He disdains that he and his Redcoat lackeys are reduced to nothing but prison guards on account of us. His nostrils flare at the sight of any prisoner. There's no greater mockery, for a man like that, than an enemy he's not allowed to kill.

Jimmy said he'd heard the man was made an officer on account of saving the life of England's prissy little queen. And they call us the criminals! The man can't have a drop of Gael in his blood, committing such a sin of omission. I'd put money on him being a mason to boot. That's the way those kind go. They offer their secret worship in that dark world of devilish temples and do all manner of evil things for their advancement.

I look about this world of timber and rope and all that great canvas bustling above. The whole thing works to an order, just like a mill or factory. It starts with our names listed into three divisions and hung below decks. Those who read make sure to read to those who can't. The doors open every morning and one division after another is let out to shuffle up the steps and onto the open deck for the morning muster. Prayers are said, then the list is at hand, each name called, a quick reply or there will be trouble, then we're inspected.

Some have a go pleading ill-health to the surgeon. He brings heavy brows and squinting eyes to bear on the subject. It's a scalpel-sharp reply when he knows a man is putting on the bluff. There's plenty who give it a try. What's a man to lose when he's already lost the world he knows? But Munro can spot a lie a mile off. I heard him say he's done this voyage before and will probably again, and there's nothing that he hasn't heard a thousand times before. He does have a kindness for those genuinely sick – I'll give that to the man. He keeps a particular eye on the old men in our cell.

I've heard the soldier-guards are more prone to illness than our boys. It makes you wonder how they will fare in the colonies. They're all brass buttons and bluster and no balls. The natives will eat them for breakfast, though I doubt those ones would make a satisfying meal.

Once we are inspected, buckets on ropes are dropped into the ocean, then hauled back up. One after another of us steps forward and cops his early morning dousing. The cold ocean is a shock. Men half-asleep on their feet are immediately awake. Some boys seize the opportunity to put on a performance. They shake and stomp as though some grave injustice has visited them. Those who get too carried away dance right up to the edge of trouble.

There's pleasure watching what might happen then. There's some boy, dripping wet, puffing out his chest to play the comic rebel. There's just enough murmured encouragement, in the mob, to stir the boy further just for the laugh. And there's a Redcoat guard, happy to throw off his boredom, and throw his weight around. The young soldiers, who feel the need to prove themselves, bark like dogs straining on the leash. The old ones don't bother saying much. They just wander over and make their point with one hefty belt across the comic rebel's ears. More often than not, things settle after that, and that's the end of our excitement for the morning.

It's the former soldier boys, the ones transported for attacking their superiors, who seem most prone to march headlong into trouble. There's plenty of them on this ship: the ones who didn't take well to orders and the others who didn't take well to staying where they were meant to be.

They're restless men with a distaste for the uniform they once wore. They are men not made for the army but who joined it anyway, thinking they might see the world. No sooner did the uniform go on than they were landed back in Ireland to be used against their own. More fool are they for it. What did they expect, selling their souls to the British?

The Tipperary man, John Flannery, agitates from dawn to dusk. He's always on the sniff for other men's unhappiness. He sees one desperate crack in another's soul and he's hard at it, prizing it open all the more. On occasion he dares to whisper, into gullible ears, his thoughts about mutiny. Most tell him to shut his hole, but some of the young ones get excited by it. Flannery knows how to play to their feelings. He offers them something to counter their restless boredom. So they soak in his every word, bristle at knowing something others don't, then whisper contagiously among themselves as though they were the rebels of '98.

Jimmy gave me the eye when he saw Flannery talking to me when I was with the man, on deck, airing out the bedding.

"Steer clear of that one, boy," he said to me.

"But Jimmy," I countered to put him in his place, "your man promised I'd be captain of the ship all the way from here to Siam."

Jimmy didn't laugh. He was all for teaching me a lesson.

"All it takes is one poor spoke word, joke or not, and they'll be tearing strips off you," he says with his earnest tone. "You mark my words. That Tipp arsehole is going to do nothing but bring trouble down on himself and those he gathers to him, so you make sure you're not one of them 'cause there'll be nothing I can do about it. You hear me?"

I know he is right. It's not as though I didn't know it already. I swear, sometimes my brother presumes that I'm a fool.

The one unforgivable sin, among the high and mighty on this bucket, is any talk of mutiny. Any hint of it sounds a rarely spoken truth that would unravel the lot of them: there's more than two hundred of us onboard and so very few of them.

They rely on our meek accepting of our fate. That's what keeps things calm. The bars in the cells and regulations would be nothing if we rose as one against them. I look around at every prisoner, and look inside myself, and hate that we are as they want and need us to be.

That's where Flannery is different from the rest. He doesn't accept his fate. It goads him, and the fact that the rest of us aren't interested in anything beyond going along with the ordained arrangement goads him all the more.

"Where's the rebel in the lot of you?" he mutters. "Are you content bowing your heads and accepting the fate of slaves? All your grumbling and bellyaching, and what are you doing about it? Nothing! Where's your balls? Where's your manhood?"

He spits his diatribe at us and it sure stirs up an anger, but not the kind he wants. It isn't about the business of being transported. Most have settled into just getting on with it. It's anger at the agitator himself for pushing the idea there could be another choice and, if we were real men with even a modicum of bravery and effort, we'd make that choice and claim a free life that's hanging right there ready for the picking.

"Shut your mouth, Flannery," says one who's primed to cut him down, "you're bound for a noose and to hell with you taking any of the rest of us with you."

Flannery's taunts dig into me. There's a vengeful twist in the idea I'm not acting like a real man or a real patriot. All the old anger has flared right up in me, like a fever, and I hate that Tipp bastard for stirring my embers.

I know Jimmy is brewing dark like me. We don't speak of it on account of the shame, thinking that bastard might be right and his judgement of us might be true. It's like he's sewn a treacherous malady in us and it can't be shaken. Without a word said, among the men below, there's a common feeling that something has to be done about the bastard.

It's only above deck that I feel a calm come back to me. Something of a better, bigger world steals right into me there. Just enough of it: the smell of salt that clings to my body long after it's dried; the sores and abrasions, where the irons rubbed my ankles raw, that sting for a while but heal the faster for it. I feel that oldest god, the ocean, licking good right through me. I look at all its glistening expanse until the wonder of it comes in me like a tide and dances with my dread. They spin together like they've always belonged, an endless flashing spin of light and dark, hope and despair, each cradling its opposite, flying and falling and rising from heights of heaven to depths of hell. My heart is stretched by it as though making room for the whole of it, as though this strangely changing world is mine to claim and I'm a man who's made to ache for it. It's a sweet trouble that brews in me, this claim of something more that no one has the power to deny me.

We have a time, most afternoons, when the sea is calm, when the morning's work is done, inspected, corrected, and finished to the surgeon's nit-picking requirements. The food is dished out and eaten with ravenous speed. On best days it's pratties with a good lick of fat. There's grunts of satisfaction all through the cells then. All that ocean makes a formidable appetite. The pots and utensils are gathered afterwards, hauled above, and cleaned. And then the space is cleared and we have our small serve of afternoon liberation.

I thought I was struck with an equatorial fever, and my imagination was getting the better of me when I first heard the surgeon, Munro, speak of it at morning muster early in the voyage. He was taking forever to get to his point, much as he always does. We've become accustomed to that now. What is it in a man that makes him feel the need to say so much? It seems worse among those with the higher social standing. Too much education or titles and a man, like the surgeon, will flap his gums from dawn to dusk and say nothing for all the words that come spilling out his mouth.

I half listened as he went on about the need to keep melancholia at bay and establish acceptable means for expelling nervous energies rather than having them ferment into trouble. There was a murmur of hope in the crowd that the man might be working himself towards announcing an increase to the quarter pint serve of the watered-down rotgut they label wine, that we get every second or third day. No sooner was that hope voiced than it was promptly dashed.

"Where there is consistent good behaviour," the surgeon finally said, "I will allow a time, in the afternoon, for dancing for the purpose of bolstering health and general good spirits. I have decided, on occasion, to allow some of you to receive instruction and some possible competition in the commendable and manly art of single sticks."

This caused a murmur among the men.

"Bear in mind, all of this is an indulgence and easily rescinded if there are any problems. Best you keep in mind there is not a minute of the day when you are not under scrutiny."

"What did your man say?" an old one mumbled in my ear.

"He'll have us dance."

"Dance, did you say?" the old man asked with his eyebrows raised and his mouth crooked with bemusement.

"That's what he said."

"What devilish business is he about then?" the old one said with a hint of annoyance. "Is the cur adding mockery to our imprisonment? Will he have us perform like trained monkeys for the amusement of the soldiers and their wretched families?"

"It's to stop us feeling miserable," I said.

The old man let out a raw laugh at that one.

"Well, here's a better thought, if that's your man's concern. How about he turns the boat around and has us home?"

I liked the old man's aggravation. It made me think of Da, in all his dark vim and vigour, spraying spit and curses at the damnable, unfair world.

"Why don't you put your suggestion to his lordship? I imagine he'll be all ears," I said.

"I'll give the cur all ears alright."

"So you're not one for dancing then?" I asked.

"I'll have you know, boy, I'm Sean-nós to the marrow of my bones. You're not likely to cross paths with a nimbler pair of feet than these ones. I have the tradition thick in my veins, I do, and best you not be fool enough to doubt it."

I looked down at his rough-stitched leather boots and saw no sign of nimble about them, but I decided not to provoke the old man anymore. There's plenty enough cruel men on this bucket. I have no interest adding to their numbers.

"Then I'll be looking to learn a thing or two," I said.

"If you're lucky and you've the mind for it, but I doubt you have either."

One man interjected from the crowd with a question for Munro when the surgeon had finally managed to stop speaking.

"But surgeon, sir, how are we to have the music?"

"One of the crew is a fiddler," replied Munro.

At this, everyone laughed and someone yelled, "Tell us something we don't know," and then a guard started bellowing to get us back in order. Munro went on to say, again, that the whole arrangement was conditional on good behaviour and the coarse manners we had just displayed would not serve our standing well.

God save us from the humourless tyranny of the prissy queen's prudish men.

There was some puzzling, among the ranks, over the mention of single sticks.

"Bataireacht," suggested one of the ruined soldiers in our ranks.

"What's that then?"

"Stick fighting."

This caused a stir.

"And will they give sticks to the Gilligan boys, over there? Those ones don't need instruction when it comes to dishing out a deadly wallop with a stick. Sure, half the boys on this ship are here because of what they can do with a decent stick, an honest drink, and a head full of hate. The surgeon might as well just hand the ship over to us now and be done with it."

And so, we dance in the afternoon. It's far from a graceful

business, but it's something I look forward to anyway. Jimmy stays to the side and finds amusement, caustically observing the unruly sight of us. He calls our sound a cacophony of clodhoppers.

"You're as graceful as cows jostling in a market pen," he says.

I don't care. He can mock all he likes. Dig me in the ribs. Call me a clumsy oaf and talk about the embarrassing sight of my boisterous gambolling. To hell with Jimmy and his mockery. Give me a jig, any day or night, and I'll hammer my feet around as good as any man and be glad to make as much noise as I can. I'll let the whole span of the ocean, and the strange lands we pass between, know the fact that here I am alive. Alive despite everything. Alive in every hammer of my heel. Alive in the boards, beneath, now made a bodhrán to our stamping feet. Alive in the bounce of my body in the crowd's restless heat. Alive in the tempo climbing, and the joyous sound of the whole, building to a blast that won't be muted. Alive in the small moving world of this prison ship, even as the miles from here to home unfurl behind us and we're swallowed into the unknown that's ahead.

CHAPTER 11

I overhear we are nearing the bottom of Africa, and then there will be nothing but the great stretch of a southern ocean. The wild has already set us rolling about, as bad as the first days, and the blustering cold has caused the surgeon to order the return of our woollen winter dress. This emptiness hones the marrow-stabbing blade. I have on all the extra layers, but the icy gales still cut right through me. It's worse than winter days back home.

The ocean has uncovered all that's raw and desolate in everybody. There's no face that is reassuring to me. Jimmy is away somewhere in his mind, thinking or not thinking. His cold gaze is mostly fixed on nothing. Who can tell what the man's thinking? I elbow his ribs sometimes just to hear him curse me. Sometimes the curse is enough to give me back my balance and push aside the worst of the loneliness. I make the most of any crumb I can get.

I'm tired of it all: the stench of close bodies despite the washing, the bored, cruel appraisal in the eyes of the guards, the bickering of men about things that don't matter, the unsteady stagger to fetch a cup of water. I am tired of the groaning harmonies of ship timber and maudlin souls and those fierce nights when the violent water finds a crack and rushes in to drown me as I'm dreaming. I'm tired of the constant struggle to hold in check the boy I am but must not be: the boy who panics and would have fear written on his face. No good comes to a desperate boy like that. Not on a boat like this. A boy like that is carrion. I will not be that boy. I will stay the steady course, show the solid man, and to hell with all the rest.

Flannery's agitation grows day and night. It's like the battering wild outside has gotten right into the man and turned him madder and more daring than before. One of his boy followers has managed to steal a clasp knife from a sailor. The way the sorry plotters carry on, you would think they had already managed to pull off their mutiny by virtue of an act of petty theft. They talk about their plan more openly now. They don't even bother to cover their contempt. They mutter and curse at muster. They sneer when they're given an order. They even showed indifference, the other morning, when the surgeon spoke of recent mutineers, on other ships, who ended their days in the hangman's noose in Cape Town.

"Don't listen to those who profit by your fear," Flannery says with the tone of a high commander in the making. "Taking a ship has been successfully done more often than it's failed. The likes of Munro won't talk of that though, will they? Of course they won't."

"If you lot knew anything of geography, anything of the world, then you'd know what hope is and you would see that any risk is worth it. You would know that there are islands between the colonies and America where a man can live his days warm in the sun and with his pick of exotic beauties to have his way with. Listen. It takes a little courage to gain a glorious life, but with no courage, you'll be slaves to other men until the day you die."

He can sniff his chance among those agitated by the rolling sea. It's fuelled his daring. It's made him all the louder.

"And what of you, young Donnelly?" he mumbles in my ear. "Haven't you still got some northern rebel in your blood?"

I smile at him and give him a nod, but agree to nothing.

There are rumours that Flannery is already a man undone. The boatswain is well on to him. The surgeon has singled him out and warned him about causing trouble. Some men in the cells have made general complaints about him. Most see him as a raging arse boil fit to burst.

We wait for those above to do whatever it is they are going

to do. They are going to do something. We are sure of that. We make our bets, with baccy and rations, over the likely outcome. A few say it will end with a hanging. Most doubt there's been enough trouble to warrant that. A good number bet on a flogging or the box. Some bet it will be a double dose of both.

The betting has turned the tables on Flannery. He's become the carrion that the hungry crows are eyeing with delight. Some, who can't stand sight of him, now greet him in friendly terms like men who give a lucky pat to a horse they've put their money on. Their good fortune will be his dancing corpse or torn flesh or savage containment. Flannery sees that change in other men's regard, but he doesn't understand it. His head is too full with his own bombastic dreaming. He presumes the friendliness is a sign that he has won men over to the cause. He bristles with feelings of likely success. I almost feel sorry for the bastard.

Then comes the guards, as we all knew they would, and off goes Flannery, who is back in heavy irons. There's a ripple of dark glee in the cells. The speculation and betting is now at a fevered pitch. Tomorrow's muster will give the likely result. It makes for a restless night charged with an unusual air of eager anticipation.

We are brought up. I see Flannery is already bound to the triangle on deck. Ropes are digging into his wrists and thighs and calves. His back is bare and splayed. His body made a thing. One of the hard men murmurs, "Meat ready for the tenderising," but there's something desperate about the scene, and the hard man's words are nothing but foolish to our ears. The pious cross themselves at the sight and lower their eyes to pray. I don't feel that inclination. I do feel a dreadful weight of remorse. As bad as Flannery is, no man should be brought to this. God help us that we joked about it, that we laid down bets about it. God help us that we've come to be so hardened.

I don't dare look at anyone else to see if they feel this, too.

The feeling is too much, and I can barely hold it in. The guards are lined up opposite to share in the witnessing. Munro is to the side with a grave look on his face. McLerie is beside him, in his full regalia, frowning up a storm to see the dread work done with vigour. Greaves, the captain of the ship, is there beside the others. Everyone, save for the soldiers' families, is present.

"I had not wanted there to be a morning like this," the surgeon says. "Good behaviour all around, and there would be no need. But here we are. Most of you know why. Some of you have colluded with Flannery, and I can assure you that we know who you are and any hint of further trouble, you can be sure you will be next."

"Flannery is guilty of plotting mutiny. He orchestrated the theft of a knife as a first step. He has caused dissension and threatened the safety of this ship and all on board. These are serious matters warranting serious punishment. He will be flogged this morning. He will be in the isolation box for a number of days, to be determined, and he will remain in heavy irons once he returns to the general cells."

"Let this be a warning to you all," chimes in McLerie, "Any plotting, any troublemaking, even a whisper of dissension, and it will be you strapped to the triangle. Best get that clear in your thick heads. And I will tell you now, I will not have any man turn their eyes from this business this morning. If I see it, and I will, you will suffer for it. Do I make myself clear?"

We bark "Yes, sir" back at him. We turn our eyes to Flannery. For a moment, there's nothing but the waiting and the warmth of sunlight on his back. The sea is calm. There's a beauty in the streams of light that break through clouds and make the ocean glimmer. Just another morning. No. Likely not so bad. No. The flagellator approaches and pulls at Flannery's limbs to ensure the man is well secured against the frame. He is tight bound to it. I see the dread cat in the flagellator's right hand. The knotted nine tails dance about like some child's entertainment: a thing whose jiggle would captivate a pair of innocent eyes.

The flagellator takes position and sets his feet so he can swing and land the heaviest blow. He leans back with his arm stretched out behind then thrusts forward and lands the nine fierce tails on the flesh. Flannery stiffens at the strike but makes no sound. First trace of blood on his back, and back the flagellator leans then thrusts again. Whistle and thud. The number called. Whistle and thud. The animal-shudder and muted groan. The number called. The whipping arm is a machine moving back and forth to the task. Whistle and thud. The number called. Justice now a thoughtless blur of bloodied thongs and shredded flesh. Whistle and thud. The number called. A body judged. A body owned. Whistle and thud. The number called. The repetition building to a scream, muted, the whipped man locks despair in his silent, bloodied frame. Whistle and thud. The number called. The tear-streaked face of hard men witnessing. Whistle and thud. The number called. The surgeon's eyes assessing. Whistle and thud. The number called. Again and again until the body is slumped. The broken victim is untied and dragged away. A trail of blood is left in his wake.

We stand as witnesses of this violent lesson meant to educate us for our betterment; this cursed vision that we may, in time, treat as forgotten for the sake of those not tainted by such things. All of us, at muster, will forever be veterans, locking up the evil of the world within our silence. And maybe tomorrow's good will exorcise the devil in our memory. And maybe the soft music of the breeze and the strange expanse of all the new to come will drive the worst away. But maybe only death will truly still the bone-deep tremor in our limbs and grant us peace again. Some days are so much hell I feel too tired to live.

CHAPTER 12

Flannery's heart has been cut out of him. He shuffles about, in his heavy irons, like a bedraggled ghost. His mind is bent, beyond repair, from the days and nights they had him crammed inside the box. The spiteful men, in the cells below, now take pleasure goading him. You can see them stir to the task as he approaches. They peruse his cowered form with crooked grins and dark asides. One man elbows another in the ribs. "Here's a chance," he mutters as he nods in Flannery's direction.

They ask the faded rebel the progress of his mutiny and the likely day for the uprising. They rub their hands with glee as though savouring the imminent prospect of it. They ask him for bawdy details about the island, with the native women, that he had promised as the final destination. They call him Scribbles on account of the torturous map that is now, forever, writ across his back.

He never replies. He stumbles along his way. I suspect a man could give him a thorough beating and he wouldn't raise a fist.

I shouldn't care. I had no belief in the man's mutiny. His boisterous posturing caused me as much aggravation as anyone on this bucket. But it bothers me to see the way he is. Something in him has fallen into an abyss. I doubt it will ever come back. The pious say the man has lost his soul. They cross themselves and don't dare look at him, in case it is contagious. I'm not afraid to look at him. I meet his eyes and see there's nothing there. It feels like standing on a crumbling edge, and I wonder if the pious have a point.

The surgeon and the guards can do what they like with us on this boat. Sure, they talk about reason and the legal nature of their actions. They clip their words to make them sound of common sense and Christian virtue. That's just the way those well-coiffed bastards fool themselves. Flannery deserved something. No one would dispute it. He was a nuisance to all of us, but they flogged the soul right out of the man. It's better to hang than to have such a fate.

The truth is they used him to grind us all under heel, and there's not a man, on this boat, who hasn't succumbed to the slavish choice. I do the same. I know it. There's no great thought about it. It's like the wind blowing at the sails and the sun moving from rise to fall. We get up every morning and do what we are told. We don't look for trouble, and we steer clear of those inclined to it. We tailor ourselves to be unnoticed, men who are there but barely there at all. We check ourselves when there's a surge of temper, remind ourselves it wouldn't be worth the trouble. Sure, we murmur and mutter when it's safe, and tell ourselves our mute rebelliousness is who we truly are. But it is mute, and we are as we are told to be. They barely need raise their voices for us to do their bidding.

Is it better to blaze with a glorious defiance, the way Flannery briefly managed, knowing it risks a likely smothering, or is it best to temper the defiance and keep the deep coals glowing so it lasts?

Jimmy accuses me of thinking about these things too much. He gives me the old up and down with that look of sullen judgement, pushes his finger to my chest, and says all my thinking will be the end of me, and he's damned if he'll be dragged down with it.

"Where's your thinking ever led but trouble?" he says. "You know, as well as me, that you think too hard, and the hate starts up and the hate will be flicking your reins to get you going where it wants. And, before you know it, you're the one squeezed inside to stew in that little box of theirs, for days and nights on end, just like old Scribbles over there. Just take a look at him, brother, and learn the lesson. I know you think you're the smart one. Maybe you reckon you can think your way towards better terms. But I'll tell you, it's thinking is your enemy."

EMILY II – SOUTHERN OCEAN
NOVEMBER 1844

CHAPTER 13

I am on deck washing dishes and spoons. The work isn't any bother to me. It gets me out of the cells for longer. Sometimes there's scraps left that I have no hesitation eating. There's never a time when I'm not hungry. I'd barely know myself without that gut ache now. It's such a part of me. Even when I'm in the middle of eating a meal I'm already hungry in anticipation.

There's an ease in the cold, the ocean is calm, and there's a light breeze flicking about. I've heard we are moving towards a southern summer. It will bring heat in December. One of the simple boys asked why we haven't fallen off yet, since we're upside down on the world. We all laughed at him despite not having the answer. It's peculiar to think about such things. It doesn't feel any different than at home. The sky remains above and the ocean is rolling below.

My eyes are down, working on a crusty dish, when someone above yells "Land ho!" and there's great excitement on the deck. All the guards are gathering to one side, talking and gesticulating, as they peer across the waters. I take a look myself when no one is looking at me.

There's a jagged thin shard out there that's creeping closer. My eyes reach out to catch as much as I can. It's a wilderness of wind buckled trees and rocks and sand. One of the men from the west, standing beside me, mentions Connemara in trying to give some familiar measure to what we see.

"It's to hell or Connaught," replies another with a sigh.

"Don't be giving us Cromwell now," says the first man.

I search that distant strip for some glimmer of hope but all I see is a wild desolation. I can't see sign of village or town or pastures. There's nothing soft about it. It's fierce like a nightmare: a place for dying not living; a brute shard of lonely exile.

"Prisoners to your cells now," bellows McLerie when he sees us gawking.

We pack away the utensils then file down below. There's already excitement through the cells.

"What did you see?" they ask with their eyes all shiny with hope.

"I didn't have time to see much," I reply.

"Come on Connie, I know you saw enough, tell us what it looks like," Jimmy demands.

"Sand, rocks and scrawny trees. Maybe some mountains at a distance."

"And a township?"

"Nothing that I could see."

"Farmland?"

"Not a sign of that."

"Natives?"

"We're too far out to make out anything like that."

"Are you saying there's no sign of people at all?"

"Not that I could see. What I saw was wilderness."

"Maybe it's not the place then."

"I think it is judging by the carry-on up above."

There's boots coming down the stairs and then the guards are spreading about the cells.

"Righto lads you're back in the irons. Can't have you tempted to escape now we're nearly there. It will be confined to the cells save for the cook and the food and water fetchers."

"How long for?"

"As long as it takes to get you sorry bastards landed."

"So it is Van Diemen's Land?"

"Apparently so."

"How's it look?"

"I'll put it this way lads, I'm glad my lot are moving on to Sydney Town once we've got the lot of you off-loaded."

There's a strange flurry of hope and despair working its way through the cells. The forever forlorn almost seem delighted that their bleak anticipation seems proven true.

"Nothing but desolate wild," one murmurs.

"You can't judge a whole place by first sight of it," a young one says.

"Sure we know there's a town and that's where we're going to," says another, "and we know plenty enough from the newspapers back home. There's farms aplenty and further land to be had. There's no point getting desperate at a bleak first sight. Like the boy said, first sight is nothing."

I can feel all that's become familiar in this ship: its never-ending roll about; the constant creak of timber; the ocean hammering just a few boarded inches from where we sit; the dank smell of men; the fresher smell of salt; the shadows and the thin bands of light that weave about us. And now there's the chains again about my feet and the tyranny of their weight. As we started the journey, so we end it. I don't care what the nearby country is like. It can be rough as all hell and I wouldn't care. My first step on solid ground is a step away from these heavy irons that threaten to drown me, and a step towards whatever I can get that's close enough to a promised land.

We are alert to everything that's happening above now. Our destiny is part spelled-out in the shuffle of feet and the murmur of voices. Ears press to timber trying to catch hold of words. Eyes stare toward the light, spilling down the ladder, as though it might be laced with revelations.

We cobble together stories, anyway, about this unseen country that's sliding alongside us. The old stories of cannibal convicts and fierce natives find new life. Dark old men look to stir up fear in the young ones. The young ones put on airs of fierce indifference that cause the old men to laugh. Some swear we are close enough that they can smell the country. They say it smells of rot and misery.

Those with the tasks of cooking, bringing the food down, handing out and collecting the dishes and utensils, get to see some detail of the land. They are the lucky ones and they know it: knowing what we don't and seeing what we can't. Everyone hangs on every word they say.

"It's rough looking country," says McDonnell the cook, "We're sailing between a mainland and an island of two bodies held together by a thin ribbon of sand."

"What of townships?"

"There's a few rough huts dotted around some bays. There seemed to be a timber camp with logs piled near the water."

"And natives?"

"Nothing that I've seen, but there's heavy forest along the coast, so you wouldn't know what was in the thick of it. It's nothing like home boys. I'll tell you that much."

"How's it different?"

"It's untamed."

"Like Eden?"

"More like the wild shithole old Adam was kicked into once he bit the apple. I'll tell you it's savage country – like a mad woman's tangled hair it is. Maybe there's better to come but I can't see it."

Some are better at noticing small changes than others. The ship is calmer now. No strange sideways sliding or rapid rise and fall. There's less noise in the timber. The rolling world of ocean mountains seems to be behind us now. Thank Christ for that at least. The ship is moving slowly and then not at all. Word goes around we have crossed a great bay and have stopped downriver from a township. There is to be an inspection.

Next morning there is a clamour beside the ship, then on the deck above, and then there's unknown voices and the lilt of exchanged greetings. We can hear snatches of talk. There's rumour in the town that the ship is full of smallpox and our arrival is far from welcome. There's something more about too many convicts on the island already. There's a laugh over some muttered aside and then some further murmuring that we can't decipher.

The strangers come down with the surgeon. They are no sooner here than they're looking about at us like farmers eyeing cattle at market. The surgeon first tells us they are from the colony's board of health, and we are to cooperate with them fully. They don't look like doctors. They have the manner of government scribblers: men with narrow eyes and ink-stained souls. Before long we know that's exactly what they are: the principal superintendent and officers of the colony's probation department.

They are to go through us one by one. Haul us into one room and then another. First with the questions and then a physical examination. Soon enough, I stand in front of two of them who are sitting behind a table with their thick ledgers. They barely bother to look at me. Their faces buried in the books as they fire their questions at me. They check on my name, age, place of birth, religion, whether I can read and write, single or married, family members, the crime committed, the sentence, previous crimes, behaviour in the prison and on the ship.

I answer and watch their endless scribbling. It's as though they've got nothing better to do with their time but to write a book about me. I almost make a joke about it but decide I'd better not, given these ones will probably decide my destiny.

There's been some chat that skills are the important bit. We've heard from those, who have read letters from others, that if you get your skills right then it makes an easier life. I hear some men trotting out a story. The bad liars get well-grilled and set right. The good liars can barely stop themselves from smiling when they come out the other side. There's no greater joy than getting one over those bastards in their fine-sewn clothes and neat high hats.

Jimmy and I aren't really made for lying. One feeble attempt and our faces shine bright with it. Jimmy says it's the heavy hand of faith stirring up our blood with conscience. All I know is it's a damned inconvenience. The only honest skill that we can name is flax dresser so that's what we both decide to say.

The scribbler answers me with a crooked grin.

"I'll know who to ask for if I need new linen."

A pen-pushing prick if ever there was one. Seems we might be bound for an island full of them.

I answer all their questions and then I'm ordered to the next room. The men in there tell me to strip off everything. I give them the hardest look I can muster but there's no getting around their order. Off comes my shirt and trousers and there I am: naked as the day I was born. They set to looking at me. Every inch of me. No one's ever looked me over so intensely. I stand there praying I won't get a lamentable reaction. God knows the body has its own mind in peculiar circumstances. One man looks me over while another one scribbles. The looker yells out eye colour, height, the shape of my head, that I'm missing a finger and that another one's broken. He tilts my head this way and the other. He pokes around checking my gums, my limbs, having a thorough check for any marks or tattoos. The strangers seem satisfied, order me to dress, then out I go. I join the other well-inspected cattle. Seems we've passed muster and now we're ready for the market.

After all that business, when the strangers leave, there's the sound of scurrying feet above, muffled commands, unfurled sails then the sudden lurch as a breeze catches hold of the canvas and the ship starts up river. There's a great buzz in the air. It doesn't matter what this place is like. It is somewhere. It's a start to something. Maybe that's enough.

Munro has come down and is giving us instructions. There will be a system for coming off the ship. Of course, there will be a system. A man can't take a shit in the morning without it fitting inside a system. There will be perfect compliance or there will be serious repercussions. That's the most grinding thing. Every flicker of a flame snuffed out by the petty decrees of their noxious empire. Every ounce of strength harnessed to meet another man's needs or to be ground under the heel of a threat.

Some hope the rule-bound life might loosen once we're on dry land. Even a slight loosening would be welcome. Surely the wild of this place, at the arse-end of the known world, is enough to break the feeble reach of English rules. Maybe here we might be more ourselves than we could be back home. What a strange thought that is to have. I swear I don't even know what it means but it stirs something inside me even so.

After some hours there's a volley of orders above and then the ship abruptly shudders as it bumps and grinds against a dock. The long floating world of the Emily II is now tethered to something solid. There are more unfamiliar voices. The sound of a flock of gulls erupting somewhere to the side.

Eyes dart in all directions in the semi-dark world of the cells. Some men are braced and anxious. Some are excited. Everyone is ready to feel solid earth beneath our feet. Whatever is to come will come. Seven years, just seven years, and after that the rest of life. All good enough for us young men and boys but a harder proposition for the old ones with the lines of grief that they can never shake. Poor bastards.

I look at Jimmy as I'm ordered on my feet and start the iron bound shuffle towards the ladder. There's a constant bark. *Silence*. I move up and into that world of hard southern light. It takes a moment to readjust after days in the dark of the cells. I feel greedy to take in everything I can see when all I have seen for months has been the ocean and the sullen inside belly of the ship. I stop for a moment and take my first look at this new world. Directly across is a long row of warehouses and merchant offices and a fine, larger building along to the right, and more store buildings further down to the left. There's a great pile of timber in front of the large building and a few town people gathered to gossip with their fierce appraising eyes stabbing at us.

There are well dressed men, in tall hats and frock coats, darting in and out of offices. Papers in hand. Serious business knotted in their brows. All as though to say progress is afoot. A couple of craggy-faced ancients are smoking pipes and sharing a joke in the doorway of an inn. There are carts going back and forth: the clatter of hooves; the sweet stink of horse shit. Further up the hill, above the warehouses, there's a large windmill in motion and a nearby church tower that's half finished behind a timber scaffold.

A gang of rough-dressed weans are calling out as they race up stoney stairs. Their voices have a different sound. Not Irish. Not English. It's a kind of easy drawl that's unfamiliar to my ears. But they're weans up to trouble, all the same, so not that different from Belfast.

I come down from the boat and set foot on land. It sways as though, in my time at sea, the solid earth has become ocean and the ocean now solid earth. My eyes move ever upwards until I see the looming presence of a mountain. It's a great blue brooding thing that makes the township small. It's as though the wild has raised its hand and said this far and no more. My eyes are lost in it and I feel some unfathomable promise. It's there above and not so far: that wild beyond the Pale; the promise of some greater life to come.

PART TWO

HOBART – VAN DIEMEN'S LAND
NOVEMBER 1844

CHAPTER 14

A newsman has cornered the ship's captain. He's hoping to score a paper, from back home, before his competition arrives with a better offer. The captain has nothing but an Irish publication, The Freeman's Journal, and it's a repeal paper at that. The local shrugs. It will have to do. He takes the crumpled paper and hands over a bottle.

"Finest import I have at hand."

At a glance, the newsman sees a report of renewed tension between England and France. That's always sure to bolster the readership. Those salty old rum 'uns, who all claim to have sailed with Nelson, will be blustering in their cups and calling hoist the mainsails at word of it. Maybe something local can be made of it: some consequence of colonial significance. If there's a war, then the troublesome classes will naturally be reduced, and maybe the scourge of prison ship arrivals will lessen. There it is – a good news story then. A decent bloody war could herald an end to the probation system.

The newsman brightens at the thought. He turns his eyes towards the shabby new arrivals. There's a sight for heated parlour conversations. More ships and the island will surely sink under the immoral weight of all the wretches. How often has he heard that variety of anti-transportation sentiment? He smiles at the thought of the querulous trill that sounds in every high social gathering. How they tut and shake their heads and bluster about the blight of the probation stations. Poor-made, poor-governed, unspeakably depraved, like sores on a leper, the Sodom of the south.

He's heard it all a thousand times, over fine-china cups of tea and in the thick of smoke-filled offices. It's an island full of indignation, stirred to a roar, since New South Wales stopped taking prison ships. And never mind the dark truths hid beneath all that ruddy social bluster. The noisiest moral up-and-comers have more than a passing acquaintance with the shackles. There's so many of them desperate to prove their newborn righteous selves, there's no closet space in town for all the skeletons. Such a town as this one! He shakes his head, folds the paper, and starts back to his office.

We are lined along the waterfront. It seems we're not worth more than a passing glance in this new world. Still, we must be something of note. We are to be inspected and addressed by the Lieutenant-Governor of the colony himself.

There's fair mumble at that idea along the lines of men, and Charlie's stirred the most.

"High tea at the governor's house is it? Would someone fetch me best shirt and britches?"

"Forget high tea. Break out the finest brandy!"

No sooner is there a stir through the muster than the local peelers start barking at us. They are a blue-jacketed mob, with official-looking armbands, and bludgeons for encouragement; brawny knucklemen with little room for thinking between their ears. I know their type well enough. They have such dull, constant frowns, I'm sure they work hard just remembering to breathe. They bark we'd best mind ourselves or we'll cop solitary or the wheel. They spray curses and call us worthless new chums. One singles out Charlie and gives him a crack to the back of his head.

Soon, Eardley-Wilmott is before us in all his splendour. I suspect he gained his honour on account of the size of his nose. It's the biggest honker I've ever seen. God help the colony if the man ever sneezes. He's up there, now, blabbering about the system we're to enter and how good behaviour is our way to freedom and how bad behaviour means a longer time of hard labour and how we best pay attention to the religious ministers because the whole business is about choosing virtue and rejecting vice and embracing godliness and grace and working hard and becoming new men and good citizens for the colony and so on and so forth and so on again.

How the man goes on. I swear I've aged five years just listening to him warble. If he goes much longer, my sentence will be finished. Now there's a thought. Off the boat and home free before dinner. God knows I could eat something. I wonder what the food's like here. The hills above seem rough country for growing. Sure, but you can grow potatoes anywhere. There's a thought. A decent bowl of pratties would keep me going. Even bread and milk would stop the growling. The food here can't be worse than on the boat and those storehouses must be full of something. There's a dray loaded with a mountain of bags over the way there. I wonder what's in there: the makings of a decent bowl of stirabout. I'm sure of it. And all that bundled wool there. Somewhere there's a sheep fit for roasting.

"God, I'm hungry."

Jimmy manages a low-pitched growl in reply.

An order rings out, once the regal honker is done, and we all turn and start shuffling up a hill into the thick of the town. The guards make more noise, looking to be the big men in control. Just like the same back home. We shuffle on regardless of their ruckus.

Some, like me, are full of wonder at this new place. It's like the months at sea have left our eyes aching for sight of it. We follow the lines of sandy-yellow columns and arches that are made to look more ancient than they are. We look about for clues of what's on offer, sniffing for the promise as far as we can see along the streets, and all the while the peelers keep up their barking. Eyes front. Silence in the ranks. God help us, they're a wretched band of knuckle-draggers.

Meanwhile, the usual others among us are head down and desperate to stay faithful to their misery: the same old groaning and the same old frowns that have lasted all the way from Dublin. Jimmy has no time for it and mutters that they have a tear for every occasion.

The place is not as bad as I imagined. I half thought we'd arrive somewhere made of nothing but mud and thatch. It's not like that at all. Sure, it's not Belfast or Dublin, but it's not as bad as the worst parts back home. There's a dusty newness to it. I steal a look at Jimmy, but he's too busy looking around himself.

There are women up ahead of us. They are half hidden in their bonnets. Their billowing dresses seem faded and worse for wear. They hurry across the street to avoid us. One has a handkerchief to her face as though we might be carrying a plague. They murmur among themselves as we pass them. The way they tilt their heads hints at disdain.

The sight of them causes a stir in the ranks and then more barking from the guards.

"Eyes front and shut your mouths!"

We keep moving until we're through a gate and into a courtyard where we are lined up to be sorted. It's another round of questions and book scribbling. I've never known the likes of all this examination. I swear there's more words written about me now than I have ever read.

"The flax arrives at the mill."

I almost reply to Jimmy, part in celebration at his sudden bout of dour liveliness, but then I'm called forward and directed to a group. Jimmy soon follows, then a guard comes over to us.

"You boys are for Jerusalem."

"We must be the saints amongst the rabble."

It's the first I've heard Johnny Golrick, the fiercesome Cavan potato thief, make a joke. We laugh and figure mention of

Jerusalem is some flourish of colonial humour. One of the guards catches what we say and leans towards us.

"You new chums haven't heard, there's no place like Jerusalem for a crucifixion."

He looks us over with a twisted smirk, then winks. God, I hate a man who winks. He tells us we'll be setting off soon enough. It will be a long march, once we've made the river crossing, and there will be good behaviour, every step of the way, or we will suffer.

The guards and bookmen put a certain weight on their instructions, but they're bored with what they say to us. They've said it all before, and they will say it all again. We're no more than the latest shipload to be sorted then pushed along. Like Jimmy says, flax to the mill. If that's the case, then next comes the pummelling and crushing. And all for what? They can pummel and crush the likes of us all they like. I doubt they'll get fine linen for their efforts. At best we'll be rough hessian.

I look at the weathered faces about me. Jimmy's back to being moody in his cave, and old Johnny has now lost his taste for humour. Charlie's the same as ever he has been: peculiar with that misplaced delight of his that's never touched by trouble.

It's the early hours of next morning before a new pair of guards orders us up and on our feet. One is a stumpy cur with a scarred cheek. He has the sneer for doing evil things. I look at Jimmy, and he cocks his eyebrow as though to say, "Watch that one". The other guard's a tall bag of bones. His eyes race around, like he's unsure of everything and clueless what to do with himself, save for blindly following the orders of surer men.

"Get on your arses, you third-class dogs! We haven't got all day," says Stumpy.

I can see Charlie's going to ask something. It's as though he has no mind to know when to keep his mouth shut. It doesn't matter how many times he's beaten. He never learns. If I was close to him, I'd give him the elbow to try and keep him quiet, but he's at a distance. There's nothing I can do for him.

"Why call us third-class?"

Jimmy sighs and shakes his head, hoping the coming trouble won't spill onto the rest of us.

Stumpy gives us all a knotty look, then turns to his mate.

"Did you hear anything, Bill?"

"A question from that one."

Bag of Bones points to Charlie.

"Ah! You had a question for us, did you, sir?"

Everyone but Charlie can feel the menace in the guard's false friendly tone. A smart man would back down but Charlie isn't that. He has the gormless talent for digging himself deeper in a hole. He smiles at the guard as though they are on friendly terms.

"You mentioned third-class, and I wondered what you meant by it."

Stumpy cocks his eyebrows and nods, as though giving the question serious consideration. He turns to say something to his mate, then, quick as a flash, throws a fist crashing into Charlie's ear. Our man's near knocked to the ground. His face is hard with pain as he shakes his head. There's a trickle of blood coming out his ear.

"Third-class means you're lowest in the colony, even lower now the natives are cleared out and dying on that island up north," Stumpy says. "You are naught but beasts to serve your masters and get shit done."

He gives us a further yell to get us moving. We stumble back out the gate and start walking past a church, and then we turn northwards up a main road through the town. We are settled into a heavy silence, even as the town is busy on every side of us. I notice something that I didn't before. We are seen but not

100

seen by the townspeople who move about us. Their eyes pass over us as though we are nothing. The clatter of our chains causes nobody to pause. It's a strange familiarity that jars my soul with shame, and all I want is to be away from it.

We're soon beyond the waterside-rim of bigger buildings. Now it's simple houses with sizeable allotments. They're timber-made, though some of the better ones are red bricks. I see a woman near a house hanging clothes to dry, a man digging a field, a mob of bellowing children chasing a scrawny goat. I can hear chickens and the occasional cow. There's sheep on some of the hills at the foot of the higher mountain.

I look ahead. Farmland is spread up to a ridge. There's a brickfield and a fine mansion that overlooks the whole spread of the riverside settlement. There are church cemeteries, on smaller hills, with enough headstones to show plenty have lived and died here already. It's hard to reckon with that. This place seems raw and new, like a rough-sketched picture waiting for a solid dash of paint.

The sun is gnawing my skin. On top of that, there is a fly tormenting me. The vile beast is at me and there's nothing I can do about it. The irons make sure of that. The pernicious little bastard is free to crawl across my face, over my lips, and up my nose as though I am nothing but a corpse. I shake and growl, but it doesn't do a thing to budge the bastard, and the other men are laughing at me. I curse the lot of them. Then Stumpy is in my ear – one vile beast now at me alongside the other – and he's telling me to settle down or else.

"It's a fly."

It comes out in such a desperate, trembling way that I regret it as soon as the words come stumbling out of my mouth. The others start echoing my despair for comic effect.

"Get used to it," Stumpy snarls with his lips curled somewhere between amusement and contempt. "Here's owned by flies by day, gnats by night, especially in those piles of shit best called probation stations."

We cross the ridge. There's more farmlands spread through the upper river valley. There are mountains alongside, and a large one across the river, at a distance.

My eyes are wandering as far as I can see when I hear Jimmy draw in a rattling breath. I look at him. His face is pale with some awful shock. I follow where he's looking, and then I see it. I can't turn my eyes away from it. I can barely keep my feet moving.

We have been brought to a demon's land. There is no other way of seeing it. What else can this place be but hell, where men are bound and twisted, like that, to take the form of work beasts? It is hell turned to rough industry, and at a monstrous dusty scale, hammering and blasting and dragging at the island's rocky heart. And beneath the whole lies a dreadful silence as though men's souls have gone, and nothing but mute slavery remains.

"There it is, lads – island life in all its piss-poor glory! Isn't that right, old Billy?"

"Oh yeah!"

"Is progress you're beholden, stripping the wild 'til none's left."

"Except that wilds that we love."

"Ah, Billy, you dog, true said well enough. Proper order except when piss is to be had and whoring done and a boot laid into any bastard who deserves it!"

They both laugh at the introduction they give us to the colony, then, peering at our sullen faces, they know we've no appreciation for their words. They turn sour then, and back to the usual sneers and barking, and I'm not sure which man I hate the most.

I don't know what's worse: the weight of these irons or the

storm stirred up inside me. I'm sure it would be the death of me if I allowed it voice. I'm sure those slaves below are mute for good reason.

There's a sudden sound nearby. My muscles clench and my heart takes flight. Whistle and thud. The brute sound packs a punch, and Flannery flashes back inside my head, and in my mind it's a trail of blood and the cat made to glisten once the business is done. I feel those dead eyes of the flailed man gore a savage emptiness in me. I can hardly breathe. Panic charges through me and something buckles, and I am going down and into dark, blessed dark – maybe it's death come to set me free. I can taste its nectar. I want more. I want to suck it down to the dregs. But then the guards' faces are looming over me: all scars and rotten gums and poison air mixed into their fevered words. Is it devilish joy or pure hate they show me? It doesn't matter. I feel so far away I can barely hear their torrent, then a boot strikes a fierce song in my ribs, then Jimmy is stooping by my side and saying something. I look at him. It's like he's pleading with me. Get up, brother. Get up now. He is fierce tender about it. I can feel the dark bidding me to let go and stay forever down, and how I want it. But it is my brother's eyes would have me live, though I can't see the blessing for the curse in it.

We march until we are near narrower water where the river crossing is to be made. It's a world of mud and loneliness with a thick band of mist that snakes atop the river. The other side is hidden behind the mist, save for the very highest peaks that hover above as though resting on clouds. Even this side is brushed with it, so our every step brings a further revelation of what's about.

There's a gang of at least twenty men by the shore. They are a raggedy, hard-jawed lot and look like they are out for trouble. Some are leaning on sizeable poles and smoking. Others have heavy cudgels. They see us approaching and seem amused by the sight. They speak among themselves, but we can't hear them.

"New chums, is it?" yells out the one who seems to be their leader.

"Sure you know it," says Stumpy, "you've quite the mob yourself."

"Good enough lads, and gainfully employed at that!"

"Is that so?"

Stumpy has his eyebrows cocked as he looks the gang of river men over.

"And what's the work to do here then?"

The leader grins and peers around at his mates.

"He wants to know what we do, Wee Tommy. What do you say to that?"

A tall man, with a pair of monstrous, well-inked arms, shrugs at the question, and then the lot of them start laughing. I can see Stumpy is feeling well mocked. His face is ablaze with it. I pass the hint of a smile at Jimmy, but my brother seems tied in a knot, as though he's trying to work a thing out, and he dares not look up 'til it's done.

Stumpy musters the frown of a big man curdled by a lesser man's insult. He doesn't say anything, though. He's at least smart enough to know he's well outnumbered and he hasn't the brawn of even the smallest man among that gang. Besides they're the type who savour trouble. I'd know that eager bearing anywhere. One word from their head and they'd be on the lot of us without hesitation. Nothing for it but the glory of knuckles and blood and the tales told later, over cups, on account of it.

After a pause, their leader comes up and puts his hand on Stumpy's shoulder, like a friend, then points him towards the mist.

"Anyone who tries to cross and land here, by any means

other than our barge, is bound for nothing but a good walloping and a long trip down to Storm Bay to feed the sharks."

Stumpy nods and then turns to us and barks that we're to sit and wait.

"Where to for you?" asks the leader.

"Jerusalem," says Stumpy.

"Could be worse, could be Jericho!"

Both men laugh at that.

"The old fella over there never stops bellyaching how much he itched when he had months at Jericho. I reckon itching's in his nature, though. He's always at it. He's the scabbiest old bugger I've ever known."

Stumpy is relaxed enough now to smile at the other man's friendly banter. He has a chuckle and goes so far as to offer the man his flask.

"That itchy vermin's wicked as it gets!"

"Well, that's quite a claim," the river man replies. "See, Wee Tommy was on the gang under Bobby Nottman."

"God, the Nutman," exclaims Stumpy. "And your big man lived to tell the story!"

"Nah. You won't get any stories out of Wee Tommy. He hasn't the tongue for it, you see. But there's story enough when his shirt's right off him. Ugliest sight you're ever likely to see. Old Bobby had a taste for it."

"And Arthur loved him for it."

"Sure he did, the pious prick. His kind's the worst. Not a road carved across this island wasn't bought with poor men's blood to make the rich richer, and that bastard Arthur was always putting himself first in that line. And all the while he and his kind are lily-white in their Sunday best, saying prayers and bunging on the righteous." The river man snorts, spits at that, then adds, "Things are different now, of course. Not so much flogging these days."

"The scientific method!"

"God help us!"

Both men laugh bitterly.

"I don't know that it's better," says Stumpy. "I'd rather a quick flog than days alone in a box."

"Evil by a different name, I reckon. They lace their words with clever these days, but it's still a boot up the arse, isn't it? Just comes at a different angle. Cat or box or treadmill, never mind the how of it. No undoing the rotten in this world. No chance for the likes of us in any of it."

He looks up then.

"Anyway, here's the old man and his barge. Best get your lot ready for it. Ferryman doesn't favour those who dawdle. Are you stopping at Jerusalem yourself?"

"Probably 'til I have my ticket."

"Well, good luck to you then, old mate."

"And you!"

The ferryman stands at the back of his barge. His coat is a patchwork of rough pelts that make him more animal than man. His hair is wild and clotted, his eyes seem born from darkest night, and he has the smell about him of dead things left to rot. I swear, the way he looks at me, it's like he sees no more than meat on bones.

He grunts us onboard, grabs the slip of paper that Stumpy proffers, peers down at it intently as though he were to read, then tucks it in his pocket and looks us over.

"Lovely irons," he murmurs, "lovely irons for taming ugly pets."

He sniffs at Jimmy, who flinches. The ferryman seems delighted at that and leans the closer.

"In the end, it's all across the river thanks to me."

He pushes the barge out from the shore, and we drift into a world where half-glimpsed shadows play in the folds of a dirty-white light. A crow is cawing somewhere up above as the barge moves across the deeper water. It's still and dark beneath us, a thing more felt than seen, peaceful in some deadly way that stirs up dread inside me. As we move further, a shadow looms over us. A little further still, and the ugly shape of a prison hulk appears. The creature sniffs and chuckles.

"Can you smell 'em?" he asks.

He licks his lips, searches our faces, then shakes his head in disdain. I look up at the miserable form and catch sight of its name, Anson. It's the bleakest, darkest thing I've ever seen.

"One flick of a blade, I'd have that bonnet fair off yer," the creature says, almost tenderly, as he sets his eyes on my skull.

He looks across at the two guards. They are as subdued as the rest of us.

"Is evil makes a colony," he says.

He scratches his jaw, then stares at Stumpy. Stumpy seems full of shame at the attention. He frowns as though he's desperately trying to find some suitable word to say. He knows he can't appear to be the man he wants to be. This creature would sniff the deceit straight away.

"You been here long?"

Stumpy asks it with a supplicant tone. It pleases me to see him reduced to that. All the bluster in him and all the threats, and here he is, a petrified child.

The creature shifts around as though the question needs some space to settle. His movement sets the barge rocking, and we all grab at the sides as best we can. He grunts and stares up at the mist above, as though taking its measure, and it seems a long time before he responds.

"First come does the ugly, next come gains the spoils."

He peers back at Stumpy as though looking for some agreement. The guard straightens, thinking there might be a chance of reasserting some tone of authority.

"Wouldn't mind some of them spoils meself."

The creature raises his eyebrows at that. He doesn't laugh, as Stumpy might have hoped. He stares more intently at the guard as though the man warrants closer examination.

"What was it you said?" he asks.

"Spoils," splutters Stumpy, "I … I wouldn't mind some meself."

The creature grins and stares some more. He reaches across and gathers some of the chains in his hand as though he needs to know their weight.

"Had ones like this in the high country."

He smiles at some dark memory, spreads his legs and scratches. The mist suddenly falls away, like a curtain parted, and the rugged shoreline is right in front of us. The creature stands and sets the barge rocking again, as he thrusts his pole into the shallower water and pushes us to the shore.

"All you were is dead now."

He says it as some final benediction as we stumble off the barge and onto rocks.

The guards tell us to get going, and we are soon at a distance from the barge. Stumpy is muttering, half to himself and half to his mate, about the mad bastard ferryman and how his kind should be locked in the asylum, and that there's some evil that's beyond redeeming.

Bag of Bones seems bewildered by the rant but tries his best to nod with a vigorous sympathy. He's barely a brain in his head, that one. I'd laugh at the pair of them, one all bristles and prissy consternation and the other one dumb as an ox, but it wouldn't do me any good. Back on land, those two are back in charge and likely looking for a chance to prove it.

We make our way around the edge of a swampy cove. The hills to one side have been cleared. There's a couple of men working the land and a sizeable house atop a hill. The forest trees make a brittle hem along the line of the property as though ready to claw the lot of it back into wild. The trees grow a strange way, eking life in angled lines, and forking out like cracks in the too bright dish of the sky. There's a sweet smell. It seems odd, beside all the barren dirt and rocks around us, and it's made the stronger when a breeze stirs.

"You can take some water at the brook," Stumpy says, "then it will be hard marching up the cut."

We squat beside a stream. Jimmy makes a point of getting in next to me.

"How are you?"

God help me. He's squinting at me like I'm a problem.

"I'm fine."

"Are you sure of it? You can't be falling down like that, you know."

"Yeah."

"What happened then?"

"I don't know."

"You don't know?"

"No."

"Christ, brother, it won't go well if there's any more of it, you hear me?"

He's near spitting the words at me, but quiet enough to not draw the guards' attention.

"Those two bastards would leave you dead by the roadside. I've no doubt of it. This place is too many kinds of wrong to make any sense at all, but show weakness and you're done. I know that much. So just keep your wits about you, boy. That's all I'm asking of you. Keep your wits about you and no more of that business."

I cup some water in my hands. It has the colour of tea. It tastes a little brackish but good enough. I drink it down, then scoop and drink some more. I look up. There's a trace of soft when the trees sway. I've one hand up to block the sun and watch them: silent music in a brittle land.

"Have you heard a word I've said to you?" asks Jimmy.

I stare at his gnarled red face and hope the guards will bark us back into silence. I'd rather their bark than Jimmy's. He expects me to tell him my mind when I have no way to fathom it. All of this is nothing but strange, nothing like home, nothing like anywhere at all. I don't have a chance to say as much before Bag of Bones is barking us back on our feet and ready to march.

We are on a rough-cut road that winds through hill country. The hours go on at a sore shuffle with a hard rock face on one side and a drop to the valley on the other. The only voices are the two guards. I hear them mention the bush a lot. I look around wondering which one they're talking about. I half hope Charlie might ask, but even he is lost in a quiet bewilderment.

I listen as best I can to the things the two men say. Certain names are mentioned. Gregson is one. They talk about him like he's master of this side of the big river. They murmur and chuckle at scandals, the hate between factions of men in the township, the young girls who are known to visit the governor, and a lieutenant dead from his own hand on account of losing a fortune. Stumpy says the dead man's just one of a crowd who are trapped on the usurers' leash.

"It's nothing but debt from south to north of the island."

They laugh at the violent justice of colony life and the fall of the high and mighty, and the sorry things they've heard when drinking. Then Stumpy talks of his recent good time in a brothel.

"Such delightful depravities," he says to Bag of Bones. "My balls are still aching from the effort."

After some time they are back to murmuring about the Ferryman and then the things older settlers say once they've had a skinful. Eye for an eye. Kill or be killed. Guns and spearings and fire and bush and blood.

There they go with talk of the bush again. I almost look at Jimmy with the puzzle of it, then remember the way he spoke to me. Jimmy and his notions. Always chancing himself the bigger man. Just wait 'til he falls on his arse, then I'll be the one doing the preaching. Just don't do it, Jimmy. Just don't be falling down on your arse now, Jimmy. Why did you do it, Jimmy? It won't go well if there's any more of it, Jimmy. My brother. God help me, the punishment of being exiled with him.

"You lot just wait," says Stumpy, who has decided to level his attention at us, "Jerusalem's drier than a camel's arse come the heat of summer. None of you lot have known the likes of it and you'll be hauling rocks and pick and shovelling right through the middle of it."

"Cooked in your juices for your redemption," pipes in Bag of Bones, and they both laugh at us and all our troubles to come.

It's close to evening when the road we are on meets another. Down one way is a place called Richmond. The guards tell us we're not wanted there. They say something about roads and taxes, but I've no mind to follow it. All I want is an end to the marching.

"There'll be no stopping 'til we're at the station. You hear me? I'm hungry enough to eat a horse, so you pack of lazy bastards best get moving or, so help me, I'll see you to the station in a sorrier state than you've ever known."

Stumpy sprays all that at us, but there's no great fire to it. He's just bored and tired and sick of the sight of us. And here we are delighting in his company. God, there's no end to the wretchedness of the man.

I doubt I'm the only one with sore feet. I have blisters atop blisters from the endless miles. I see Jimmy has his jaw firm shut. He's biting on the things that he would say. I can well imagine the words he's honing on the brute old whetstone of his imagination. Words to shred the bluster of a pair of idiots

111

and put them in their place. These two guards wouldn't last a night in Belfast. I smile at the thought of a hometown reckoning for the likes of those two. The first cold cut of words to spin them dizzy, and then the follow-up rain of fists to land sweet on their jaws.

I look back at my brooding older brother. I'm surprised he still has fire enough for a solid bout of ruminating. I'm so tired I can hardly think at all. I'll be glad to sleep even if it's just hard ground beneath me. Whatever the station is, it can't come soon enough.

The sky is shot through with red and the sun's close to setting when I see a cluster of buildings just to the side of the valley road ahead. There are long walls all around the place. Two big double-storey buildings are at the back, and there's a space framed by smaller buildings in the front. There's a gatehouse and a couple of forlorn dogs sitting near a tree. There are farms in the vicinity: some sheep in paddocks; crops of wheat and the green leaves of potatoes, at a guess, that look flowered-up and ready for harvesting. The whole arrangement sits poorly on the earth: a desperate ugly scar where one should never be.

CHAPTER 15

There's not a drop of spit in my mouth as they order us to muster. Everything about me, the air, the ground, the walls of the buildings, even the sky itself, is mercilessly throbbing as I get in line with the others. All I want is to lie down and close my eyes. Just a few minutes would be enough. None of that is possible, even though the sun is nearly down and long shadows are creeping across this muster yard.

Once the guards are satisfied that we are in right order, one of the head men bellows a prayer with the reverence of a rabid dog at a bone. What god is a god of a place like this? An oily god made to keep the machinery running, a barbed god to flagellate the soul, a useful god for them that have the power. I look at Jimmy. He's standing just ahead to my right. The way his head is bowed you'd think he was praying himself. I almost whisper something but, straight away, I'm yelled at to keep my eyes front and mouth shut. There we have it then. The noose is well-tightening. The men with beady eyes will have their way.

We are instructed to call out "yes, sir" and bow our heads when the clerk reads our names. I look at those men, up front, in charge of us. There are bookmen in the finer clothes and thugs, dressed tawdry, with batons in their hands. There's something more honest about the thugs. They know who they are, and we know who they are, and we all know what they are here to do.

The bookmen have the air of those that think themselves civilised: here but not enough to be sullied by the business. They are the type who talk of Christian virtue and progress and who would raise hope, in the likes of us, only to dash it as soon as our pursuit of good hints at their minor inconvenience. And they are the ones who would expect our gratitude even as we're ground beneath their heel. Here on this other side of the earth,

113

it seems no different than back home. The full-of-shit still get the better seats.

The clerk reads the names. We "yes sir" and nod, performing at the signal as required. We're told to make another line in front of a desk. We move up, one at a time, and are thrown a uniform: a pair of britches, a jacket of coarse grey cloth, a leather skull cap with four points sticking out the sides, and a pair of unconvincing brogues.

"Change now. Sun's near down. Don't be wasting time."

Jimmy is bemused as he examines his new brogues.

"We won't be running far in these."

"Reckon that's the intention."

Jimmy puts the skull cap on. His head is squeezed into the thing and it looks close to bursting. He's a gormless fool with his big ears sticking out. I've never seen the boy look so crimson and bewildered. I swear the cap has a violent grip on his brain. I can't help myself. I start laughing. Bag of Bones is straight at me, telling me I'll know the inside of a dark cell if I keep it up.

"A few days of solitary will set you straight and who'll be laughing then?"

Humourless bastard. I steady myself and see that Jimmy's grinning now. He's mouthing "who'll be laughing then" with a mock stern look on his face. I tug my skull cap his way with my best flourish of gentlemanly reverence.

Now comes the real punishment. They start barking at us to quiet down so we can be lectured at by the superintendent of the station. What is this business with colonial life? It seems nothing other than marching, being barked at by gormless half-wits, and being lectured by pompous creatures who think they have a thing or two to say.

There he is standing in all his bluster: a man too dusty to have any real import. But he has the educated tone and that seems enough to put him above us. He tells us we are to keep to ourselves as we're now in the first stage of our time in the system. The separation of probationary classes is how further corruption is kept at bay. We will commence as third-class men on the gang doing hard labour, earning our keep by clearing nearby land for government sale. It will be hard and dangerous work and we are to follow instructions to the letter.

The superintendent's head flicks up, when he makes a point, as though he's sniffing the air for heaven's approval.

We stand and listen as his dusty lordship continues on about the wild island being tamed, made useful and productive, just as our wayward souls will be made right through grace meeting our manly efforts applied to this wilderness. He warbles that is a moral imperative before each one of us, old as the bible itself. In the sweat of thy face shalt thou eat bread. He emphasises "sweat of thy face" and casts his eyes over us as he says it.

He has the hard look of a weak man about him: nothing there that isn't close to breaking. His eyes are quick to dart away whenever his gaze is met. I wonder if, deep down, he fears the likes of us.

"Listen, lads. Listen well and take it to heart now," he says with a gentler tone as though confiding with a friend. "You will be made right, as God above would have it, through hard work and sweat, in this place and the other stations where you will spend your time. You will be made right just as this island is being made right and brought to a proper British order."

A ripple of disdain runs through the ranks on that point. Is the man clueless about who we are? I can see Jimmy has his nostrils flared: the wild bull ready with his horns stuck out. One of the men mutters "cén ualach cac!" and others stir in agreement with the curse, despite not knowing the meaning of the words.

The clueless superintendent doesn't notice any of it. He ploughs on without pause. They're all the same, those Empire boys, so thick with their proper British tone they're blind to how so many of us hate them.

"But beware, lads! Bad behaviour will mean time on the gang will be prolonged. Serious wrongdoing will mean a visit to the local magistrate, then solitary in a dark cell, or a flogging, and after that you can be sure that you will face the hardest labour that's on offer. Criminal wrongdoing will mean a likely trip to a worse place than this, down on the peninsula to the south. None of you wants that, I assure you! Murderous wrongdoing, or acts of blatant depravity, will see you dancing at the end of a rope in Hobart. I will not have depravity in this station, do you hear me?"

We bark our "yes, sir" back at the man.

"If there is punishment of any order, then no one is to blame but yourselves," he bellows. "This system is the well-designed work of the finest minds in penal science. It is justice tuned to mechanical precision. It will strip away the evil in you until you are sufficiently good to take your place as honest citizens of this fair island. Your one true hope is knowing and accepting your place here, submitting with obedience to those in charge, and learning the skills that will secure you employment when you are no longer in government service."

Someone behind me has been sniggering at mention of penal science. He mutters something about clever men scrutinising cocks, and the sniggering's contagious. The guards start their barking, and the superintendent is far from happy as he waits for us to settle.

"If you follow orders, attend to your duties, keep your bodies and bedding clean, attend to your prayers and the redemption of your souls, carry out work without complaint, then all will be well, and you will find yourselves fully restored to society soon enough."

CHAPTER 16

I am made their calloused beast, from the four o'clock rise to the bone-tired end of the day. I'm harnessed, with other men, to bring the big logs down from the hills. We've been staggering and shuffling all week, in our too-thin brogues, purple-bruised by the harness and with skin that's burnt and blistered from the sun.

The work is bad enough, but Smith, the overseer, has a knack for picking the worst paths where we are to drag the cart. I'm sure his choice is born more from dim wits than malice. He hasn't the mind for seeing what's best, that's all. He peers at us with his bovine eyes and has little to say save for "get," and "get at it," and "get on now." It's strange a man, so like a cow himself, should see us as the bullocks made to order.

Now he's pointing where he wants us to go in his usual manner. Nothing but the stab of his grimy finger and an insistent grunt. It's no surprise where he's pointing is barely a path at all. It's a tangle of bush and torturous rocks tumbling down a steep slope to oblivion.

"There's no way we're getting down there."

I like that Toby Flynn. He's been in the gang longer than most. He doesn't hold anything back. That's why he doesn't hold a probation pass, while those who shipped out with him have one and are well on their way to a ticket of leave.

He will call out a fool no matter the rank, without hesitation, and with no care for what comes next. He's gone through all the punishments on offer save for dangling at the end of a rope. He's told us of his weeks in dark cells, the endless climb of the treadmill, and more than his share of quiet beatings copped in the back corners of stations.

He tells his stories as though none of it matters. He says it's just island life and best harden up and be used to it. I admire his freedom, but not the price he's paid to get it. I doubt he's ever likely to get the certificate. They'll have him broke with madness or forever in the chains.

Smith is sizing up the protester now.

"Fastest way down."

Smith grunts it like he'll brook no further argument. He is the bigger man, but he's a lumbering sort with neither wits nor speed about him. Flynn is all sharp eyes and nimble feet. He knows his way through the wild like no one else. The two are face-to-face, and it could go any number of ways. I'm sure Smith will clout him, if there's chance, but there's a hesitation in him, and Flynn seizes hold of it.

"Can't you see, those rocks, down that way, won't make it faster. We'll be nothing but arse over tit, and half of us crushed 'neath the log. And what is it you'd be saying to the super then? Sorry, gov, at least there's not so many mouths to feed!"

We all have a laugh at that, except for Smith, who's busy frowning and desperately trying to put two words together in reply.

Smith stares at Flynn a while longer: a thick black cloud with lightning in its belly. He growls that Flynn should watch his mouth or else. That's the best old Smithy can manage, then it's "get at it, get on there" as he waves us to start down the hill.

We let out a groan, then brace to drag at the harness. I can feel catastrophe in the weight of the monster behind us.

"If you insist we go down that way, then at least let the thing go first so we can steady and slow it from behind. At worst we'll be dragged along, but at least we'll not be crushed."

We pause while Smith frowns and ponders. A few other men speak up in agreement with Flynn. This causes Smith to frown more intensely. Most of us just hold our breath and hope for the best. All our fate is in the over-strained thinking of a simpleton.

Smith finally gives a grunt of approval. I'm not the only one sighing with relief.

It's Flynn who takes charge then. He orders us to pull the cart around, so it is back end to the rim of the descent, and we are on the upper side of it and bracing at the harness.

"Dig in your heels now, boys. Once we budge it over, it will pull like holy hell itself."

He has a look of doubt about him, but it's the best idea can be made of a stupid general order.

I dig in and brace as Flynn, and one of the big men, moves up to the cart and shoulders it over the edge. We are all pulled hard, as Flynn calls "dig in, dig in." Meanwhile, Smith has settled on a stump, smoking his pipe, with barely a look our way and little care what happens to us.

"Steady on, steady on," cries Flynn as the men in front of me are pulled over the edge with little chance of slowing anything down. I'm jolted forward by the full force that's fit to tear muscles off my bones. I lean back, with all my might, as my feet skid through dirt, and I'm slashed about by sharp bushes and nettles. I try hammering my heel, but all attempts are hopeless.

There's nothing but the force of the hurtling giant that's strapped to the cart and is now looking to have its vengeance on all who wronged it. Everyone is cursing at the plight and cursing Smith and cursing heaven and hell and everything between. The cart is near flying over rocks now, smashing aside trees and scrub, bouncing from one side to the other, and tearing apart all the ancient silence with axles screeching and wheels shaking. There is nothing can be done. We are all dragged and torn in this brute, bloody baptism of bark and rocks and violence, and it only ends when the cart smashes near the bottom and the log is, once more, resting on the ground.

This is what progress is. This is how the island is cleared, how the roads are carved and laid, how the waters are conquered by rocks piled into causeways, how the wild is steadily tamed, and how the island is made a colony.

We are exhausted after the wild descent. Most are cut and bleeding. One of the big men has a broken leg. Smith is nowhere to be seen. He's probably still sitting on his stump, above, smoking and hoping those who laughed at him are now the worse for wear. But he's bound to make a nuisance of himself when he does come down and sees the cart is smashed. Never mind our injured state. He will be blustering with outrage, with spit flying out his mouth, and desperate to pin the blame on all of us.

Flynn has no concern for what's to come. He has business to get on with and is talking to a shifty man called Simons.

"Did you check they put the rest of it in the spot?"

"I did and they done it," says Simons.

"And is the drop the usual place?"

"Sure."

"Good man, then."

"Donnelly," Flynn calls out to me, "are you up for a walk?"

He's not a man to deny. I give him a nod and struggle to my feet.

"We need to shift something before Smithy's down and sticking his ugly nose where it don't belong."

We walk for ten minutes across rough country until we arrive at a half-burnt tree that's hollowed in the middle. Flynn reaches in and pulls out two sizeable bags.

"We'll be eating well tonight lad."

I look perplexed at him and he smiles.

"It's secret deals keep us alive, boy."

He gives me a further look over.

"Do you remember yesterday when there was a great fuss with the boys working the pit saw?"

"Yeah. All the yelling, I thought someone had died."

"It got the overseers out of the way, didn't it? Just long

enough for us to put some choice timber aside, in the bush, for a farmer who was desperate for it. And this flour is our payment. Highly illegal, of course. Settlers aren't meant to feed the likes of us, but bugger all that. There's surviving to be done."

"Could there be trouble?"

He laughs, and I feel shame burn my cheeks.

"Have you come across anywhere here that isn't marked for trouble?"

I shake my head.

"If they find out about this, then they'll make sure someone pays, but their finding out is pretty unlikely. See, there's more of us than the government boys can manage. Every shipload just makes it worse for them. The system is a pox-mad bastard pretending to be a man of reason. Nothing is what it seems here. There's none of it made but by crooked lines. But you can be sure there's no hint of crooked in their fine-written lines back to London. All of this is just a wretched game, boy. That's all it is. The part we play is doing what must to survive it."

I nod at him, but he doesn't seem convinced that I understand.

"Look at it this way. We're meant to be fed a decent meal according to their books – they got it all laid out there, the portions and all the bloody rest – but tell me something, have you had a decent meal since you been here?"

"Best I've had was nothing but bone swimming in thin gravy."

"Exactly, lad. You score yourself lucky if you manage to get a maggot in the bowl. And don't get me started on that shit excuse for what they call bread. Sawdust and floor-sweeps and mouse turds is most of what's in the mix. There's not a thing that lands in front of us that hasn't been well-picked over by every man and his dog above us. So we do this thing instead, yeah, and get a belly full of something decent when we can. Fair enough?"

"Yeah."

"So tell me, Donnelly, are you hungry?"

"I was born hungry."

He laughs.

"I thought you had that look about you. Come on. We'll plant this closer to the station, and later we'll make decent coal-baked bread of it."

I follow him as he jumps over holes and cracks and dodges under branches. He flows across the crackling ground while I stumble along behind him. We have the station in sight when we stop by a mound of rocks half hidden behind some trees.

Flynn pushes some rocks aside and uncovers a box that he opens.

"We put it in here for now," he says as he puts his bag in, then takes mine.

Stumpy catches sight of me when I'm back at the station. In recent days, he's gone cold and quiet in his menace. His nostrils flare when he's sniffing for the scent of others' fears. His eyes stab as they look for some tender point in a man: an unconvincing smile, a tremble in the lips, a quick drawn breath, a nervous hesitation. These are the moments Stumpy seizes, at every chance, so he can prove himself a man of power.

"Where's your jacket, prisoner?"

His hand is flat on my chest. He doesn't push. It's just there long enough to stop me.

"I took it off, sir."

His eyebrows cock at that. He tilts his head and his eyes dart to the side like he's pondering some deeper meaning in my words. He turns his silence into a blade, then hones it as he stares me down. He lets the menace linger just enough for me to feel the edge of it.

"So where is it?"

"Back where we brought the cart down."

He has what he wants now. His lips tighten in a brittle smile.

"Her Majesty's Government has clothed you, and how do you show your gratitude?"

He waits to see if I'll respond. I know that's a trap. The best I can do is keep my head down and wait.

"This is a serious matter, do you understand that, prisoner?"

I nod.

"Look at me when I'm speaking to you."

I look at him directly.

"You have lost a government provision. Do you understand the gravity of that?"

"Yes, sir. I'm sorry, sir."

He echoes my sorry and shakes his head with mock pity.

"Sorry doesn't make a damned difference, prisoner," he pokes me in the chest, "This is a matter for a magistrate. You're in all sorts of bother now."

***

I wake and sleep, then struggle between the two, in this fevered solitude. They'd have me cower in the dark of this box until I'm broke with remorse: the penitent monk in his cell. I'd rather strike this black flint with a curse. I join my hands. I kiss my knuckles.

I saw one man, in the barracks, singing the old songs until he spun himself into madness. His words came all undone. He started sobbing like a feeble child and rocked himself until his head was pounding at the wall. He went again and again with bone crack and the wall painted in his blood, and there was no amount of pleading that could stop him. His eyes bulged, like a beast knowing it's soon to the slaughter, when the guards dragged him away.

I will not sing any old songs in here. Whatever words I knew are close to faded anyway.

123

I curl on the earth to sleep.

I wake howling from a savage rain of spears and Mary standing in flames and Jimmy dressed as a magistrate and calling me a fool. I fall into a world of animal stench and heat and hooves. I'm half-buried in mud and shit. Faces I know can't tell me apart from the beasts. I'm lost to them. Lost to all the world. I haven't the voice to make them hear me.

Market day and Da is up there. God man, can't you see your own son? Why can't you see me, Daidí? Why can't you hear me?

He turns, and he is gone.

I am worn down to an unseen ghost, prodigal son with no boots to see me home. I climb, but the gravel is loose beneath me. My feet are raw from the effort. There is no grace to raise me up. Any hint of it is well-sailed out the door.

Where have you gone and hidden, you bastard? Where have you fled? I thought I saw you once, those birds at evening light above the Lagan, that sweet taste of better days to come – pressed between the mill and violent nights – all the promise has slipped away from me – and my old wonder is swallowed by the dark.

There is the cup, Mamai's best cup, broken to shards in the mud.

It's treacherously broke.

She comes, as she did, as she never will again. My belly is full of ache at what's been done. It cries and writhes like a steel-trapped beast. Her hands press my cheeks. Her fingers lace my tears. I am gathered into the once was: safe home in a crumbling world.

My boy, can't you see it?

That tender whisper of hers. She holds a shard on her palm. Blue lines are writ over mud-splattered white.

I broke it. I've ruined it.

Sorrow sets me trembling, and I am raw to her gaze. She

smiles that melancholy smile.

Can't you see? You can never break the beauty. No one can.

I see the shard has cut her, yet she smiles.

She is long gone, and all the grief has flown down to nestle in my bones. There is nothing but falling from birth to the grave. Nothing but an endless shredding descent. I spin and my heart is dashed at my ribs. All the falling world is rushing past me.

I jerk awake just before I hit. I am trapped in a black box, on an island, in a demon's land. This is my nightmare and it is no dream. I hold my knees to my chest and I sob and I rock but I keep the door held fast enough to make sure that I do not sing.

CHAPTER 17

Sunday is prayers, then, on a good day like this, the bets are on when there's a decent fight in the back yard in the afternoon. Religion might separate the sheep from the goats, and the Catholics from the Prods, but the spectacle of a good thumping draws us back together.

It's a truer communion than anything on offer in that chapel. For one brute moment something honest and unmuted happens in this miserable place. There's a strange peace nestled in that brute honesty. Two men might be at it, but we are all in it, and awake to ourselves in seeing it. It takes hold of all of us as we move to the hooks and the blocks and feel the slam to the side of the head and the belly; as we get a holy spray of the flying blood in passing; as we curse the outrageous low jab, bellow at the torrent of answering blows, and finally savour the bloody end when one of us owns a victory no bastard can take away.

The authorities are too deep in their cups to care about any of it. I daresay, they think it's better we're distracted by violence, in the station's vicinity, than that we've gone bush to cause trouble with the local settlers.

I've wagered a good wad of baccy on a monstrous English boy, from Bristol, who's snorting like a bull. He's got the wild look in his eyes, crubeen-thick fists, and I'm hoping he will bring me a winning.

"You're on the wrong horse there," says old skinny Davey Maguire, "He's a glass jaw that one. You mark me words. He'll be down and finished soon as he cops the first blow."

"I'll have none of it," I reply. "My man's got homicide written all over him. Can't you see it? Fierce as a demon, he is. But then, being a man of such certainties, Davey, how about you line up to go agin' him next and you can prove your theory?"

"Nah, Connie. My brain's too precious for the brutal art."

I laugh and then call out to the snorting answer to all my

misfortunes.

"Step up and at it, boy!"

The opposing fighter is a real jig-about, bouncing around and darting. I figure he can't keep that up too long before that English brick wall falls right down on top of him.

"It's like seeing a rabbit dance with a tiger," says Jimmy. "Get at him, Bristol Boy, and get it done."

We're all given over to it now, like a pack of furious dogs, as Bristol Boy has a swing and a miss and exposes his ribs to a jab from his skittish contender. There's no great heft to the blow, but it fires our man with a good dose of outrage. He has the devil in his eyes as he swings a furious backhander that grazes the jaw of the other and brings a splatter of spit and blood through the air.

I give that one a cheer.

Jig-About staggers backwards as Bristol Boy drives his fist fair into the other man's belly. The winded man doubles up and all the crowd surges forward, tightening the ring around the fighters, with lusty cries to get in and finish him off. But Bristol Boy has some measure of fair play about him. He stands back, despite the yelling and jostling, and lets Jig-About get his breath back.

The mountainous English lad has no interest in putting on a show. There's no great sign of passion in his face. He has nothing to prove outside the plain art of fighting. He stands to the side as Jig-About straightens up, then motions to recommence.

Jig-About has lost his sprightly manner. His feet are heavier on the ground. He throws a half-hearted left hook that Bristol Boy swipes away. One man's arm is around the other, and they're dancing about in a clinch.

"We're here for a fight, not a fuck."

"Save it for tonight."

There's a swell of laughter through the crowd as Jig-About tries a couple of kidney punches. Bristol Boy replies with a rabbit punch before he pushes his opponent away. They stagger around for a bit, then our man closes in and drives a fist straight into Jig-About's face. The contender staggers backwards like he's drunk on the blood that is streaming from his eye into his mouth.

"There goes your pretty looks boyo," cries a voice at the back. "You'll have no visitors tonight!"

Everyone laughs at that.

Jig-About goes at it with his last good effort and manages to clip Bristol Boy's ear. It's all intent with no great value save for stirring our man to finish the business. He goes at Jig-About with a torrent of blows to the belly and ribs. The poor contender has all his breath slammed out of his body. He staggers back, but Bristol Boy keeps closing in. He drives a straight punch to the head, then another. It's all a blur of our man's arms doing the vigorous work, first to the head and then to the belly, while the other man's head and torso are tossed back and forth like a puppet jerked about on strings.

Jig-About's face is now nothing but bruises and blood, but he has a look in his eyes that I've seen before in this place. He's now in the fight with a lust for his own demise. He wouldn't be the first man killed in a Jerusalem fistfight. He makes no effort to block the blows but, all the while, he spits out taunts to stir Bristol Boy's ire and make the punishment harder. It's the pity in Bristol Boy's eyes is most likely the hardest blow for Jig-About.

"Is that your best, you son of a whore?" the bloody man spits at Bristol Boy.

Our man then lines him up, with more regret than anger, and drives his fist up under Jig-About's jaw. The man flies, spins, and lands face down in the dirt. He is as still as a corpse, but not dead. His mates drag him off to the doctor while I collect on my

128

bet.

"Well that's it for Sunday entertainment," says Jimmy as he starts stuffing his pipe with his winnings.

"Man would be a fool to go up against Bristol Boy," I say.

"Sure, but maybe you haven't noticed, we're not among the smartest company here, brother. Dimwits make good cannon fodder."

I grin at that, then all the ease is shattered by the clang of the station bell.

"Here we go again," I say as we join the mob who are making their way to the muster yard.

As soon as we're in the yard, we're back to being herded animals. We don't need to guess why. There's an out-of-sorts farmer having words with the superintendent. The cranky culchie's shaking his bald head and throwing his hands about, in exasperation, as though some great catastrophe has been unleashed on him and now he's out for justice.

It never takes much to bring his kind to the gates of the station. They've a wad of tobacco astray, or a misplaced bag of flour or a sheep missing. It doesn't really matter what it is. Something goes wrong in their miserable lives. And here we are – a station full of the ready-to-blame – lined up straight in ranks, eyes front, waiting to be offered up for their appeasement.

The superintendent has a brittle look about him. He has no time for a little man like this one. He can barely keep the sneer off his face as he looks down on the other man and listens to his interminable bellyaching. The farmer has interrupted his Sunday rest. All he wants is to get back to his brandy and cigars. Why did he ever accept this wretched post? It's nothing but a godless world of scrub and dirt, the charge of a prison mob that's good for nothing but to swell the ranks of the island peasantry, and always the constant nag of Hobart bureaucrats saying get busy and clear more land. More fool are they thinking land sales will save this colony. The only sure thing in this place are the endless waves of convict arrivals and the desperate plummet of the island economy.

The super's cheeks are flexing with impatience, but the farmer's too busy blustering to notice. We watch in silence. The sight would be amusing if we didn't know it's our misfortune waiting to meet us at the end of it.

There are some in the ranks frowning as they tally their wrongdoings to see if any tie in with the raging farmer. There's been good takings moved around the station recently. We all know that. There was that young lamb nabbed two weeks ago. How tender was the meat on that thing, and the smell of it roasting on the coals. Was it from that man's farm? Surely, he would be familiar if that were so. He's no near neighbour. Maybe a new arrival?

He has an uncertain look about him. He's trying to hide it underneath the outrage. His eyes betray him, though. He doesn't spend too long looking our way. The old lags say the island's small and memories are long. It seems he's been here long enough to know that much at least. But the way his arms are flying about, whatever was took must have been enormous. It's more than a newborn lamb that he's making a fuss about. That's for sure. It's something big. Something that matters. If someone's swiped such a thing, then it's well hid. There's been no talk of such. But there's always talk when sizeable deeds are done. Pride always gets the better of a man, and then he crows despite himself. But there's been no noise like that and that's the troublesome thing. If no one's been seen doing whatever they're talking about then anyone is up for the blame.

The overseers are gathered to the side. They've been drinking. They're rowdy and now excited by the dark opportunity that's laid before them. They're bristling with thoughts of payback. Stumpy is whispering in Smith's ear. That snake-eyed bastard's plotting something. His eyes are darting along the lines of us. He's sizing options up. He leans back towards Smith, whispers something more, and the dim man nods in agreement.

Meanwhile, the super has had enough of listening to misery guts. He's gesturing towards the overseers. He wants one of them to come over and sort it out.

Stumpy pushes Smith forward, and the big man lumbers across. There are more words said, and then Smith and the farmer start walking the lines. Smith has a gormless smile planted on his face. Some deal's been struck, no doubt, and it's much to the dimwit's pleasing. He makes a point of stopping in front of some men just to see them squirm. They'll not be mocking him anytime soon. He knows that much. He's relishing the moment as he and the farmer stop in front of Toby Flynn. Smith whispers to the farmer. The farmer gives Flynn a nervous glance, then nods. The sacrificial victim has been chosen. Our man is hauled off to the cell as the brandy beckons "come home" to the super. He has no time for final words. He leaves it to Stumpy to dismiss us with his usual bark.

I walk back to the barracks beside Jimmy. There's a general murmur through the crowd. Things are always unsettled after that kind of business, but this time it's worse. Toby Flynn got things done in the place. He was brave enough to push back at the bastards and smart enough to make things happen for the better.

There's no one around who's likely to replace him. The overseers know it. The racket they made at the end of muster. Now they will be looking to pay back those boys who rode on Flynn's coat-tails. The days ahead are looking ugly.

"Did you know that farmer?"

I turn to Jimmy and shake my head.

"Any idea what it was about then?"

"You know as much as me. Whatever it was, it wasn't Flynn. He's been in the box for most of the past week. God knows the man can pull a trick, but even he couldn't conjure it from the box."

"Smithy's been after him since the wagon."

"For what that's worth."

Jimmy looks around and scratches the back of his neck.

"Stumpy's the one to sniff an opportunity."

I tighten at mention of Stumpy. He has become the worst bastard in the place. The other overseers do his bidding. Some say he has a network of spies in the barracks. He knows things he shouldn't know. Words said in private. Deals made in secret. Sometimes he'll make mention of a thing, almost in a friendly way, just to let you know that he knows it.

"I'm tired of this shithole, Jimmy."

My brother looks me over and sees trouble is heavy on me. He has concerns. God knows I wish he'd keep them to himself. He tells me every day that I haven't been right since I got out of the box. He gives me the uncertain eye, night and day, as though I'm cracked and close to breaking. He's in a panic at what he'll have to do if it should happen. I swear if I do go mad, it's him who'll be to blame, banjaxing me with that sideways look of his.

"I hear we're due for moving soon."

I skip a beat at that. Anywhere that's away from that Stumpy bastard is good enough for me. I ask him if he's heard where we're likely to be sent. He gets the crooked grin. I haven't the patience for it. Not at the best of times, and sure not now. He's overbearing care one minute and mockery the next. That's always the way with Jimmy, round the bend and back for more, and here we go again with it.

"Well, funnily enough, I was discussing it with the super over drinks in his dining room the other night."

"God, you're a horse's arse."

He clips me behind the head, and seems happier for giving me a bash, and then he settles back to being serious.

"Flynn told me we'll be moved around a few times before we get the pass. They don't like us being any place for too long. That's what he said anyway. Could be to anywhere. Probably somewhere not too far."

"Anywhere is better than here."

"Maybe. We'll see."

CHAPTER 18

Word has come through from Hobart. Flynn has had his trial. He's been found guilty of burning down a barn. The only good in barn-burning is settling a score, and Flynn wasn't one to hold a grudge. He'd always make a point of that. We all know he didn't do it. The authorities know it too. But someone must be hanged to give this world its balance, and a man who is troublesome to this system is forever marked for heavy irons or slaughter.

One thing is for sure. There will be a crowd, in the town, to see him take the short drop. They will watch the life choked out of him, his poor body twitching on the rope, then they'll be off to drink and tell others of the spectacle.

I'm sure there will be little said here, when the day comes, save for those dark bastards who feast on all the ugly in the world. Truth is the station is already washed through with melancholy. Flynn seemed the one man able to withstand anything the system could dish up. He dared live to his own full measure. What hope is there for the rest of us, who stumble along clueless and largely muted, when a man like him is brought to such an end?

I see Charlie sitting in the dirt beside the chapel wall. He has been quiet since we came to Jerusalem. I can't remember the last time I heard a laugh from him. No more jokes. No more gormless questions. No more wonder at the world about him. He has sunk and become one of the subdued. Maybe I am one too, but I can't see it, and I refuse to concede it.

He looks up and gestures me over. I go across and sit beside him. He sighs, and there's a rattle to it. I wonder if he might be ill. He prods me with an elbow, then leans across to me.

"Connie, I need a favour."

I swear his eyes are empty as a corpse.

"What is it?"

He looks at me and doesn't say a word for a time and, when he does speak, it's barely a whisper.

"I need to know I can trust you, though."

He digs his fingers in the dirt and stares towards the surgeon's place. He has the look of a desperate, trapped creature. It's not a look well-suited to this world. If some get a sniff that he's lost that way, they'll be quick to finish him. A boy like him wouldn't have a chance.

"Well, only you can tell that."

He keeps digging with his fingers for a time. There's something fearful desperate about it. I sit and wait, but I don't feel easy at all. It's a real foreboding that's getting hold of me now.

"Toby got a letter through to me."

I raise my eyes.

"Toby Flynn? Did he now?"

"Yeah. I got it here."

He pats his chest, then leaves his hand resting on the place.

"What's he say then?"

Charlie seems wounded by my question.

"Ah, Connie, you know I can't read it. I've been carrying it around, trying to think who can help me."

"Most who read would."

"Sure, but I think it needs be someone I trust." He looks at me again. It's like he's searching for something in me. "Can I trust you?"

It's not a common question in this place. Not the way he asks it. There's an ominous weight to his words. I could easily walk away. It might be the safer thing. It would be the smarter thing. I know that much. But there would be a treachery in doing that. Surely if there's anyone in this place who is my friend, then it's him.

"Of course you can trust me."

135

I feel good saying it and he looks relieved. He reaches beneath his jacket and brings out the letter and takes a deep breath. His hand is shaking as he passes it to me. I unfold it. The writing is rough, but I can make it out enough to read.

"My Charlie. How my heart is broke that I write your name knowing I will not see you again. The one good thing I take to my grave is knowing the times we've had. I dread thought of you with another man. I can hardly bare it. I wish you safest years ahead, tho, and freedom, dearest one. Make the most of it for both of us. My heart forever yours. Toby."

I don't know what to say. Words like that, from one man to another, are peculiar beyond my fathoming. And yet such tenderness is something in a place so starved of it. But from Toby Flynn. I'd never have guessed he'd have the inclination. Not the soft way it's written in this letter. There are men, sure enough, who are at it or talk about wanting it. Any hole will do. That's the thing that's said most days. There are times in the barracks, at night, when there's no mistaking the rutting. But I'd not seen hide nor hair of Toby and Charlie getting together like that. Yet here's Charlie staring at me with the red eyes and panic of a widow. God help us. This peculiar world. I doubt I've seen a more pitiful sight. One thing's for sure, this letter is the end of him if it gets in the wrong hands. I hand it back, and he quickly puts it away.

"I'll tell no one, Charlie. But you'd best get rid of that letter for your own sake."

"I can't," he starts crying. "It's all I've left of him."

I can't help but shake my head at the boy's wretched state. I can't see any good for him ahead.

"You need be careful. That's all I'm saying, and I'm not saying any more about it. Never again. But I tell you, if Stumpy got sniff of something like this, I don't know what he'd do to you. There's men been hanged for it. You know that, don't you?

136

That letter would be proof enough to have you dead."

"I know. Thank you for reading it."

"We'll speak no more of it. I think that's best."

Charlie nods. I get up and walk away.

I think I've come to understand this world, but then a thing like this happens, and I've no clue at all. I won't talk about it, not even with Jimmy. Word spreads too quickly in this place, and it would be the end of Charlie. I won't have his blood on my hands. At least I can do that much for him.

I wish they'd just move us on from here. This shithole will have us all mad. It's already getting that way. Any longer and it'll be worse. I don't care where they send us. Flynn said there's no stations that are any good. But he's as good as dead now, anyway, so what's it matter what he said? Now I think on it, I think the man's a fool. Why would he write that letter and send it to Charlie? What good did he honestly think it would do? I swear I don't understand the man at all, that he would do that. I thought I knew him. I thought he was the one to find a decent way through all this. He didn't know a thing. There's no wisdom in this place. There's no deep, true thing that's waiting to be read. We're all just animals in a pen, exactly what they'd have us be, animals to be pushed around and used, and with no end to the misery.

I see Stumpy over by the gate. Smug bastard. I can just about feel my fist meeting his jaw. If only this was Belfast. If only I was free. One good crack to put him in his place. Fist or brick or blackthorn. Whatever was at hand. How I'd be at him 'til there was nothing left. How I'd revel in his blood spilt to the ground. Never again that look on his face. Never again the poison stare and the surly manner.

All this thunder is brewing inside me, but what's the good of it? I drop my eyes, as I always do, when he looks my way. If he had a sniff of what I'm feeling, he'd be over to provoke it. Just to get the better of me and have me dig my own hole. Then all the miserable system would be on top of me to kick and grind me down the more. If nothing else, I have become a beast well-trained to play it safe. I hustle past him and don't dare give him a look. He's too busy eyeing Charlie off to bother with me anyway.

HOBART – VAN DIEMEN'S LAND
FEBRUARY 1845

CHAPTER 19

Anger over prisoner arrivals is a powder keg in Hobart. Thirteen thousand have landed in three years to overwhelm a free population that's less than thirty-five thousand. Campbell Street is now ringing with a chorus of outrage. The slurred vitriol of those who stumble out of the Dorchester Butt, the Tasmanian Inn, the Union, Labour-In-Vain, Hope and Anchor, and other hotels, mixes with the level-headed passion of temperance leaguers.

A few more years and it's more of them than us. A few more years, there will be no freedom from the tyranny and taint. This island will be cursed forever. It's already polluted near beyond redemption. The only sane choice is to leave and be done with it, leave it to the damned prisoners, lock the gates and throw away the key.

Now they're talking about increasing taxes. It's outrageous. They send us the plague then tax us for the gift. Where is British justice in any of this? What, in God's name, are they going to throw at us next? We are taken for granted as a colony. I'll tell you that much. Outsiders are always looking to squeeze us for the little good we have, and what do we get in return? More prisoners and increased taxes! If it goes on much longer, they'll have us sunk.

I know some already reduced to a beggar state. There are solid free workers, came here in good faith, and now they can't compete with all these cheap probationers. They fill up the prison boats and send them here and the bastards take our jobs.

Shame. Shame.

And there's not even a skerrick of benefit now. At least a few years back we had assignment. A man could clear land and get in crops and get ahead with a decent head of workers. Now it's the hire fee for every convict's work and more than half the time its money wasted. The ones they're sending now are no good at all. They'd sooner steal coin from a dead man's eyes than do an honest day's work.

There will be no taxation without representation. The Americans had that right. To hell with Lord Stanley and his damnable impositions. No taxation without representation.

Is there anyone who would claim they're fairly represented with this current arrangement? The Legislative Council is a joke and Eardley-Wilmot has neither mind nor balls to take care of our interests. We need decent leaders – genuine anti-pollutionists – who can stand up to those, outside this island, who would impose their will on us and have us thoroughly crushed under heel.

The rowdy crowd shuffle into the theatre. Some are well charged up, and still shouting their views, while others are caught in wonder at the great number that's pressing into the place. It's as close to a monster rally as the colony has ever seen and it generates a raucous charge of hope. When a township gathers, as loud and bold as this, surely something will come of it. Something must come soon.

Eyes turn towards the stage. Joseph Allport is up there, ready to propose the resolution. He looks at the gathering, draws in a breath, and raises his hand for the crowd's attention.

"It only required an attempt at taxation, such as is now proposed by the government, to unite colonists as one heart and one hand."

The crowd erupts with cheers and feels the stronger for the volume of their noise. Boot heels are hammered on the floor. The noise shakes the theatre, and some say it must surely be heard across at the governor's residence above the cove.

"I will show those taxes that have been called for are not for the benefit of our colony but for purposes purely British."

He starts reading Eardley-Wilmot's own minutes to illustrate his point. All the increase in public expenses, on policing and judiciary and health, is due to the monstrous rise in prisoner numbers. Britain's gain, in purging itself of trouble, is the colony's loss. Britain's wretched export is driving the island into financial depression and moral bankruptcy. The injustice is intolerable. It's enough to turn the most reverent British subjects into people compelled with a raging revolutionary doubt.

"Pauperism is an evil that has but recently come upon us. We knew but comparatively little of it in this colony, until the swarms of prisoners drove those who were either free emigrants or free by servitude and good conduct to ask for alms."

The theatre fills with cries of "shame" and "we will not tolerate it" and "no more."

"It's impossible that the colony can maintain, and usefully employ, this vast number. What can we do with thirteen thousand prisoners arriving in three years? But, they say, in due time the numbers will be winnowed. A description of prisoners will be sent to neighbouring colonies. And what do you think will happen then? All those who are useful servants, who have decent conduct, and have proven useful will be withdrawn from our colony and sent to the others."

Shame! Shame!

"And what then? All who are worse than evil – men who could not comprehend right from wrong – the ones for whom crime is second nature – these, and these only, are the ones who will be left here as servants to the unfortunate settlers in Van Diemen's Land."

CHAPTER 20

The main road, south to north, is a savage slash through country. The hunting tracks and paths of seasonal migration, from highlands to the east coast, are now cut through with a conquering hard line. The journey between the two major towns is a relentless sight of probation stations and their gangs: chains and picks and shovels, dust and carts and rocks, bodies put to task to make and repair the island's one sketchy claim at progress.

Robert Smith is furious at the whip. He's been at it since the four in the morning departure from the Ship Inn. He has the four horses thundering northward, and he will have the record broke, and Mrs Cox proud, and that bastard Hyrons and his Comet smothered in his dust. He knows how far to push the team from start to end of stage. A vigorous run but never enough to break the beasts. He lets rip a yell to show his mastery then flicks the whip again.

The twenty-shilling outsiders are desperate gripping anything they can. It doesn't stop them whooping and hollering to fuel the driver's bid for greater speed. The thirty-shilling insiders are less enthusiastic. The one female on board is desperate with her fan.

"Can't the man slow down?"

The opposite passenger smiles at her, as if to prove his manly forbearance, even though his bowels are in a knot and he's desperate for the stage to end, so his cranium can have some rest from rattling, while drinks are had and the driver attends to the change of horses.

"The faster he goes, the sooner we're in Launceston."

The woman frowns at him. She will have none of it.

"I'd rather arrive late and alive than dead in a ditch and done over by some convict."

She looks out as they pass a gang, just outside Jericho. It's as wretched a sight as any that she's seen. They are bedraggled ghosts: creatures more of dust than flesh. No sign of hope in any of them and no great sign of industry in what they are doing.

"When will this business end?"

"Soon enough if we follow Sydney's lead. The end of transportation is an inevitability. A matter of a couple of years at most."

She looks back at him. He's one of those ruddy fellows. They're all the same, guff and bluster, snorting out their never-ending opinions. They're the type who would be nothing back home but presume they're proper establishment here. There are so many of them. It's tiresome. She closes her eyes to be rid of him and sets her mind on her Launceston arrangements.

***

We see the dust thrown up from a mile off then stand aside as the coach passes. It's rocking along at a cracking pace. We're meant to drop our gaze, but I look at the well-to-do inside the carriage. They put on such airs. The lot of them all tight-clenched, in their rocking little box, and tangled close to suffocating in their frippery. The poorer ones, atop, are all white knuckles and clamped teeth and pale precarity. I'd almost feel sorry for them, if I had an ounce of sympathy, then I remember they likely have no sympathy for me.

I see the judgement of those, inside the coach, who watch us sweating and straining to make their journey smooth. I suppose we jar their dreaming with our grim charms, and remind them of their own rough colonial truth. There's no escaping it on this island and how they hate to have it put right in front of them.

There is a woman, inside the coach, wielding her fan with spiteful vigour. I think she might take flight and soar above us.

"Look at the consternation of that one, she can clearly smell

143

the stink of you, brother."

"No, she's hot and bothered at the sight of this fine specimen of manhood. Mark my words Connie. She'll be restless all night at thought of me."

"So says the humble man."

"Never mind humble. Fortune favours the bold, Connie boy."

He scoops some gravel, plants it in a hole, then tamps it down.

"I had chance to talk to a pass-holder back from Hobart yesterday."

"Oh yeah. What did he have to say for himself?"

"Said he was glad to be done with it. They had him play the servant in a house of up-and-comers. It didn't go well. He took off, drank what he could, slept it off down at the wharves, and was nabbed in the early hours."

"Did he say anything of the town?"

"Said it's as desperate as any port town he's known. And he said they well and truly hate us."

"Do they?"

"That's what he said. They've taken to calling us an evil plague. He left service on account of it. He said if he'd stayed, being lorded over that way by people no better than himself, he would have taken a knife to the lot of them. Better to hang with honour than be ground down by a pack of uppity arseholes. He said the lord of the manor came out a prisoner himself, though you wouldn't know it now from the way he carries on."

"Desperate."

"He said the whole place is built on lies and secrets like that, and the only hope for our kind is the bush. Keep as far away from those judgemental bastards as you can. That's what he said."

"But was he, you know, wrong in the head himself?"

"What do you mean?"

"Ah come on, Jimmy, you know. There's some of these boys you'd give a peach, and they'd call it a rotten egg. There's some so broke they can't see anything straight."

"Sure, I know it but this one wasn't like that. He was as plain talking as me."

"So wrong in the head then."

"Watch your mouth, you cocky little bastard, or I'll leave you wrong in the head yourself and then some."

"Sure. Sure. But all I'm saying is it can't be all that bad, Jimmy. I can't imagine everyone in the town is playing the pompous game. I mean there must be down-to-earth types just like back home. And, besides, getting hired out's our way ahead. We've got to make it work, at least 'til we have our freedom and there's enough saved for some land."

"Maybe it's not as easy as that, brother. That's what I'm starting to think. Let me put it this way, how would you fancy being someone's servant?"

"You know well enough I'd hate it. But if it got me ahead and it was only for a time."

"You couldn't hold your breath long enough, brother. God imagine the sight of it. You'd be busting your buttons with the aggravation. Don't get me wrong. I'd be the same. No doubt about it. You and me aren't made for that sort of thing."

"Maybe. But what else is there?"

"Your man said the bush."

"And what does he mean by that?"

"The kind of work we're doing now, but for a wage. They've got us at this for a reason, Connie. We're doing the thing they need. And if they get what they want, and the prison ships stop coming, well they'll still need land cleared and wood for building and the roads will still need repairing."

"So that's it, is it? A life of slave work for a pittance. That's all that's ahead for us, nothing better than the mill back home. It's giving up, Jimmy. It's giving up and staying stuck in the place they'd have us stuck while they live in their fine houses, in that town, thinking they're better than us and making profit from our sweat and toil."

"Honest to God, Connie, would you listen to yourself? What did you expect, boy? Did you think we were on our way to paradise? Did you think we were going to strike our fortune? It's like you're still up Cave Hill looking for Da's treasure. You go on about me having notions, but you're so crammed full of them they're coming out your arse. This world isn't made for our kind. How is it you don't understand that yet, after everything we've been through? I know you think you're the clever one, but you're not really. It's stupid expectations will be the end of you, Connie, mark my words. You will be forever bitter with wanting what you can't have and getting yourself in trouble trying to get it. Isn't it enough we got transported for the likes of it? Are you looking to get sent somewhere worse than this now?"

I look at my brother, hard-knotted in his resignation. All I know is I can't be like that. I'm damned if I'll settle to play the lifelong slave. I wouldn't have it back home in the misery of that mill. I sure as Christ won't be having it here. There's got to be a better way. I look at Jimmy. He's already moved on and is thinking of other things. Sometimes I can't fathom we're born from the same mother. Up never down. That's her words. I swear I'll see they count even if my brother has no mind to it.

"Anyway, did you hear about Charlie?"

It gives me a start to hear Charlie mentioned.

"No."

"After we were moved on from Jerusalem, he took off to the bush. No one's seen hide nor hair of him since. I tell you now. He was one with notions and what's become of him?"

"No, he wasn't Jimmy. In his better days he was excitable. I'll grant you that. He'd make some noise and cop a clip for it. But

146

there were never many notions in him. He wasn't one for that. But he had more heart and innocence than anyone I know. Maybe too much of it for this place. All the good in him was smothered by the time we left Jerusalem."

Jimmy looks at me as though every word I've said is odd.

"What makes you say that?"

All the things I could tell him, but I won't. Not even now that Charlie is likely dead. I told Charlie I'd keep his business to myself, and I will. It's one good thing that I can do and Jimmy doesn't need to know it anyway.

"There's some cop more bashings than the rest of us. Charlie was one of them. The boy we met in Dublin was long gone. Couldn't you see the spirit was dimmed in him?"

"Can't say I noticed, but you know I could only ever take that one in small measures. Didn't have much to do with him at all."

He says it in a carefree way that I find hard to take. I can almost see Charlie broken at the bottom of some cliff.

"He's probably out there, dead somewhere, getting ate by God knows what. It's a lonely place to die. He deserved something better."

Jimmy frowns and shakes his head.

"Notions, Connie. Give them too much mind and they'll lead to no good. That's all I'm saying."

CHAPTER 21

Jerusalem, then Jericho, and now Rocky Hills. My feet have turned to leather on this coast. I think my soul has turned the same. Words dry to salt on my tongue, and I am left with little to say to anyone. I swear the day will come when I'm no more than a broken shell, tossed atop a midden, left lonely, ringing in the wind where no one lives to hear it.

Men made a bridge, up the way, two years ago – a splintered, spiky bridge, a monument to all our miserable days. I swear that bridge is the truest thing made by any of us. It doesn't bury the brutal under sandy curves and smooth arches. It shows progress is nothing but a mound of what's been broken, and all the jagged shards are left to cut those who get too close to it.

We are presided over by a fat Prussian superintendent called De Gillern. He fancies being called the Major on account of claiming to fight at Waterloo. I find it hard to believe. Just look at the man with the hooked nose and the sagging, sallow jowls. I'd say the fiercest battle that one's ever seen is managing to get his britches on in the morning.

Sure, he gets about when he has visitors to impress, with the easy air of a pipe and slippers man. We ill-kept rabble know the truth, though. That's part of why they hate us. That one's a fallen man. We know the special scent and sound of them: that stink of debt beneath the pompous surface; that bluster with the crackle of despair. This island has more than its share of them. There'd be no officials to run the stations without them. They are all desperate to gain the funds to climb back to a respectable height, and we are the stones they clamber atop to get there.

Once they're back in the good graces, taking brandy with the Governor and all the rest, they'll get on trying to forget their lowly days in government service. And how they hope they don't cross paths with the likes of us who, they know, will well remember the worst of them.

The Prussian occasionally deigns to wander around the station, swinging between indifference and irritation. He barks mangled English commands as though still on some battlefield. Most of the time the man's not to be seen though. He has no great concern for the ruinous state we are in here. We are so far out of sight no one who matters cares, until some of us escape, and then there's nothing but a torrent of vehement caring and finger-pointing and general baton-wielding retribution.

Some boys have traded their boots to nearby settlers for flour. Knowing the state of those hopeless brogues, worn close to nothing, makes me wonder which side of the trade is in worse weather. I've heard the starved boil old leather for a meal. Poor toothless bastards will sure struggle at that.

It's the poverty of the free that needles me. The rich have carved the mutton-fat land in the midlands among themselves. The poor are left to eke a pittance from the edges. What hope is left in freedom when it's freedom that knows nothing but being poor? Seven years of government servitude and that's the promised land!

I've kept away from Jimmy lately. There's only ever aggravation when we speak. Everywhere my mind wanders ends in desolation, and anything he said would make it worse. I'd rather have no thought at all and no talk to arouse it, but even thinking that leads to further thoughts, and then I'm sunk back in the mud and struggling to find good reason to go on.

I often do field work alongside Fingers McGinn. He offers me distraction with his endless chatter. He's like a hive of bees stirred to a frenzy. It makes me think of Charlie in his best days, back in Dublin, when he still had life inside him.

Poor Charlie. There'd be nothing left of him now but his

149

unburied bones. No prayers for him, no blessing, no sacred earth scattered atop him. Nothing but flies and ants and devils long done dragging at his flesh. If ever he's found, they may well find that letter. But what does it matter now both men are dead? There's no one left to hang. Those bastards who need squeeze moral lessons out of others' suffering will say Charlie was drove mad by what he'd done. At least he's free from cruellest judgement now. Maybe the treacherous wild is a salvation. Saved from the evil righteousness of towns.

"Hey Connie," Fingers pants in that over-eager way of his, "have you heard the latest?"

His eyes are dancing with the mad pressure of whatever news is swirling in him. He's one who likes nothing better than to be first to know a thing. Some say he's good as a newspaper, though we're yet to fathom how he gets informed: a shot of facts in a tankard of imagination. Any news comes slow to Rocky Hills and the overseers don't tell us anything. Most haven't the brains to think enough to care.

"I suspect you've a need to tell me, Fingers."

He breaks into a grin then flaps his hands about.

"You remember me saying about Jacky Jacky?"

I pause just long enough to see him hop about. His news will drive him mad if he hasn't the relief of saying it.

"The one who escaped Port Arthur with the other boys?"

"Yeah," he vigorously shakes his head, "He goes by Jacky Jacky but no one knows why. It's just the name he's got himself. That's all. Jacky Jacky. There could be a reason for it. Nobody knows. That doesn't matter though Connie boy. No it doesn't, does it? Well, hmm, the thing is this, he's been at it, at it again, at it again at a place called Redlands."

"Where's Redlands?"

He shakes his head at me as though I've distracted him with some irrelevance.

"It's near New Norfolk, that's all, Redlands. Anyway Jacky Jacky and his gang bailed up to this estate, you see, and who do you think was there?"

"Well Fingers, you might be surprised, I wasn't in the know with the guest list."

He stares at me and blinks. The boy has no sense of humour at all.

"The Chief Clerk of the Police, of all people, was there, a man called Tomlins. There were others, too. And what do you think old Jacky Jacky did?"

I shrug as Fingers is near jumping out of his skin with excitement.

"He had this Tomlins and the rest locked up in a cupboard. In a cupboard! Can you imagine Connie? Boots on the other foot eh? Bout time though, bout time. All of them pushed right in. In a cupboard, Connie! Bastards. Pack of bastards. And then Jacky Jacky and his boys helped themselves to everything, like kings, like kings in their own castle, eating the fat land and all the rest of it, and off they went back to the bush before anyone could catch them."

He pauses, expecting some response. I raise my eyebrows at him. He doesn't seem to notice my indifference.

"Jacky Jacky's the best of them, you know. They say he's a gentleman. Fleece you and you'd thank him for his kindness. Chrissy said that to me. He said exactly that. He said that Jacky Jack is not like the mad-as-a-meat-axe boys. You'd thank him for his kindness, the way he fleeced you."

"He told you that, did he?"

"No, Connie. I haven't met him. Did you think I met him? No, no, no. How would I meet him, Connie? You gone a bit mad, Connie? Me meeting Jacky Jacky? But, another thing, Connie. He's the smartest bushranger that's ever been known. Ever. Gospel. That's not just me. It's everyone says it. He's escaped every prison between Sydney Town and here. Did you know that?"

"No, Fingers."

"I heard he fought off sharks, with his bare hands, when he escaped an island in Sydney. He was swimming with one arm and punching the teeth out of the sharks with the other. He can't be pinned down, you see, not anywhere. He's got the better of everyone of them, even down at Port Arthur. And you know why that is?"

"Because he's clever."

"No, well, yes, that too. But it's because true justice is on his side, Connie."

"True justice?"

"Yes. Yes. I'm not talking about court justice. That's just shit. It's shit. No chance with arsehole magistrates for us. No, Connie. No, mate. But ..."

He stops and seems to have run out of words. He peers at me like a forlorn creature.

"Well, that's all a thing now, Fingers, isn't it?"

His face has sunk into a serious state as though he's dragging some deeper consideration out from under a mental rock. He leans into me. I really wish he wouldn't. His breath is like the dead raised up without a hint of glory.

"Do you ever think about bolting, Connie?"

"No, Fingers. No, I haven't."

"But Connie ..."

"I had a mate who took off. And you know what became of him?"

"Is he with Jacky Jacky?"

"No."

"Does he have his own gang?"

"No Fingers. He's out there dead somewhere, probably cut right through by a mantrap. That's what's likely to come from bolting. Bushranging is a thing to imagine. I'll grant you that much. But they always end up dead, Fingers. Even your Jacky Jacky will end up dead."

"Don't say it."

"Well, you're talking to me, Fingers, so I'll say what I want to you. Bushranging stirs us up. No doubt about it. But it doesn't end with being free. It ends with being shot or hanged or coming in half-starved and mad and bound for the asylum. Did you not see the six brought in last week? They had nothing to show for their grand escape but skin and bones. The smart thing is to do your time and get it done."

Poor Fingers slinks away from me. He's full of hurt. The boy just wanted the pleasure of imagining, and all I could do was knock the wind right out of him. Why did I do that? Why not let the boy imagine whatever gives him delight and gets him through the bleak days? I swear I'm getting as curmudgeonly as bloody old Jimmy on a bad day. Everything irritates, nothing consoles. I am sharpened on too many edges now.

I don't know what freedom amounts to here beyond a piece of government paper. Sure, I'll be certified free, but then what? Some miserly scrap of scrub and sand and praying for a potato crop? Or worse, being stuck as a servant to some bag of wind? There's some can tolerate that. They fit the livery well and are happy enough prancing under harness. Not for me. Jimmy was right about that. We're not cut out for that sordid, soul-dead caper. I've already endured too much bowing and scraping and minding my words. Dress me up as a servant and I'd be clawing the papered walls of their fancy salons. I'd be having words with little provocation needed. Too long too close to those you loathe is too much of a temptation.

Besides, it's foolish going down that road when the law makes servants near-prisoners. What's a government pardon mean if life is then imprisonment in servitude to a master? If freedom isn't real, then what is there to hope for? I swear the endless gnaw of wanting, and not seeing any answer to it, is more punishment than anything that's happened up 'til now.

Maybe I'll find something in the township. I hope to go there once I have the pass. Hopefully I'll not be hired as a servant. Maybe I'll be hired for the docks. Maybe muscle work is good enough for me. It wouldn't be so bad. I've an eye for the ships arriving and the bustle. I'm most alive when there's life about me. And there'll be ready drink, if nothing else, to ease the burden. I hear the streets are lined with hotels. At least there's one freedom I can have, letting rip and letting roar, everything I've been through piled to burn in one hot blaze of glory, and all the world aflame with my savage, splendid judgement of it.

CHAPTER 22

We are moved again, this time by boat, from Spring Bay to an island off the coast. It's the last station before we can go out as hired men. The fields near the Long Point station are spread across an arc. There's cattle and sheep, a bullock team for clearing work, and more than a hundred acres of scrappy wheat. There are a few acres for potatoes, turnips, barley and flax. But this station is a careless-built place. There's just one room used for eating, praying, and schooling, and men sentenced to solitary are kept in wooden cages. The hospital is nothing but a thatched hut and, when a doctor's needed, he has to come across from the better station. The whole place is perched at the end of the earth and made to crumble to oblivion.

One of the overseers is a Donegal boy. He has not been corrupted by the role. He will gladly speak of home and I'm always glad to hear it, but something has changed in him in recent days. The way he's standing now, it's like some terrible weight has fallen on him, and I feel sorry for the boy.

"What's up with you?"

He turns and looks at me.

"Did you know they're starving back home?"

"I didn't."

He's looks down, with a scowl, and kicks a rock.

"They're saying it's famine but it's hard to call it that when there's boats full of oats and bacon and butter leaving Ireland every day for delivery to London. I heard that read from a paper last week. They said three full boats came into London from Ireland in just one day. Just one day Connie, can you believe it?"

He looks around, as though to check that no one else is listening, then drops his voice to a whisper.

"They're taking all our food and leaving us to starve and saying the starving's all our fault. If you ask me, they want us dead so they can have it all. They'll not be satisfied 'til there's not one native Irish left to live on our own land."

He gives me a sharp, wounded look.

I know that weight of grievance, the way it sets hard in the jaw, eats at the edge of every thought. I know how it torments the soul with the need to do something but with no clear notion of what there is to do. It's such a wretched impotence to suffer and doubly so being where we are.

"I've no idea what's happening with my family. They could all be dead and I wouldn't know it. I heard there's so many dead they can't be given a decent burial. The lot are tossed in a hole together. You wouldn't know who's buried where. You wouldn't know where to stand to grieve and say your words."

He confesses all his troubles as he stares across the water. There's nothing I can say to him, so I don't say a word. My mind goes to thinking of Da and Mary and the boys. Belfast would be alright. I'm sure of it. They couldn't have the mill and factory workers starving. That would mean the rich are out of pocket.

I sit beside the boy and look out on the waves. A slight breeze clips them at their peak. The salt is gathered in the air and I can taste it.

"Do you know uaighneas an chladaigh?"

I shake my head.

"It's the lonely felt at the edge of the water, the whisper of those gone to God. It all makes sense back home, you know, the thin places. But here."

He screws up his nose then gestures towards the water and the rough land across on the other side.

"Our people aren't here. I can't make any sense of the whispering of this place."

HOBART – VAN DIEMEN'S LAND
DECEMBER 1846

CHAPTER 23

Tommy Mollor is one of us, though he won't speak of it to me. This town is full of men like him. Their truth is hidden underneath their shirts. Their permission-to-marry wives all share knowing glances whenever there's mention of trouble up at the factory. The memory, in all of them, is whetstone. It's when they're brooding in their cups, they show their scars, and flash the sharpened blade.

Tommy made it clear to me, on my arrival, that I was only hired because his wife insisted. He scrutinised me with a wary eye then and said he had no interest wasting hard-earned coin on a useless probationer. I'm sure his eyes drifted to my mangled finger. He said he knew the likes of me and, if there was any trouble or drunk absconding, I'd be booted back to the depot before I knew it.

I was a breath away from saying something sharp. Better to be back at the depot, doing close to nothing, than lorded over by some bastard who's no better than me. No hire pay is worth that grief. I felt a ready tightening in my joints and thundering my heart. I was just about to launch right in and let him have it when his wife stepped in.

"Never you mind my cranky husband. It's good to have you with us. There's no end to the work that needs be done. I'm sure you'll earn your keep well enough."

She was close enough for me to feel the warmth of her and smell the clean of her. All that firm tied hair, so full of loose and lively promise, and the soft line of her neck near enough to touch. I lost my breath just long enough to forget the better points of my outrage. The way Joanna Mollor looked at me, I

157

knew it's a woman's kindness that could get around my guard and have me weak and shamefully undone.

God, how I've been aching for it and against it ever since. I've been ripe to a fever some nights and cursing the too-close walls of this place. Strange that in a town that offers the best that life might offer here, I find myself dreaming of the bush as though it's the only place where I might breathe and maybe make a life that's free.

Something has changed in me and I've no one to tell. Jimmy was sent miles away to Pittwater. He wouldn't have helped even if he was here. Talk of feelings just gets him aggravated, then it's hard work managing the moody bastard and his murderous, sharp looks.

I take my strange feelings to the work I have to do. It's all I've got. I've swung the axe so fierce they've a mountain of firewood, and even the smallest faults in all their fences have been brought to order. Their stock are well cared for and their yards are in good order. Anything Tommy tells me to do, I do. He has nothing to complain about save for if he knew what was in my head. There'd be no end to the complaining then.

She's on the back step now, calling to me.

"I've an errand for you, Con."

I walk across the yard to where she is standing. She has a hand raised to her head to block away the sun. She gives me a smile, God help me, then passes me an envelope and tells me a name and the likely place I'm to find the man.

"Make sure you've got your pass with you."

It's a relief to get away. I'm quick down the Murray Street hill, past the Duke of Clarence on the corner, then into the brick and rough-hewn world that's pressed along the rivulet. It's all a freshwater promise, on the way to being a typhus-clotted mess, as it winds through town down to Wapping, then the river.

Grubby weans are everywhere, the raggedy mud-splattered

white firstborn of the colony. They roam around, bound together in gangs, and launch themselves into trouble wherever they can.

Just ahead a boy is charging across a horse's path in Liverpool Street. The beast rears up and nearly throws the rider, whose fine hat is flying and soon trampled under hooves.

"I'll have you flogged!"

The bullish man is red cheeks and flaring nostrils as the boy responds with dropped britches and a bare arse. Then there's a string of curses, sharp as barbs, directed at the man who's near falling out of his saddle with the outrage. The boy sprints down to his mates, at Elizabeth Street corner, and the lot of them are yelling up the road.

Come get me, bloody old pig! Lucky I didn't shit in your hat and plant it on your head! Look at him! Look at him! Old pig's fallen off his horse! Old bluster guts! C'arn come and catch us then! Come on old pig!

I watch it with amusement, as I pass, but then I'm stopped in my tracks by a gormless peeler. He gives me the up and down. Government permission is grabbed from my hands as I humbly drop my head. The peeler squints his eyes, and mumbles, pretending he can read. Never mind. I see the dimwit is all at sea. I play the well-trained probationer before his solicitous frown, knowing that I'm smarter than the likes of him.

After his bout of playing the big man in control, and keeper of colonial good order, he tells me to get on my way. I give the fatuous blue-clad clown a nod then get going. I go across to Collins Street and pass two boys, perched on steps and sucking on their pipes, with their eyes darting about for sign of any peelers.

I can smell the chicken shit and blood before I've set foot in the Commercial. My ears are soon rattling with the roar of bets being laid as men push past me to get through the bar and out the back to the action. I follow them and see a chubby man, in a waistcoat, taking centre-stage and holding up the fiercest red bird that could be imagined.

"Behold, The Annihilator! Fiercest cock in the colony and ready to shred all-comers!"

There's whooping and hands flashing about with money as another man comes forward with a bird that's black as a moonless night. The bird seems more formidable for its cool lack of aggravation and its eyes have a stare that's steady like death in the waiting. The other man speaks up but he hasn't the theatrical flare of the first one. His voice is gravelly-flat without a hint of passion.

"Here is Satan, Lord of Darkness, Master of Death. Prepare for such savagery as would bring the hardest man amongst you to tears."

There's further yelling, and laughter at the showmanship, as glasses are raised then quickly emptied while the two men squat in a circle.

They start waving and shaking their birds at each other until the creatures are in a violent frenzy. There's a flurry of feathers as the two men launch their creatures. The cocks' feathers bristle about their necks as they circle, each looking to loom larger and sharper than the other. And then both are at it, all at once, flying up to land a ripping slash across the belly of the other. The lethal gaffs, fixed to the back of their feet, flash in the dappled back-alley light. That glint of steel adds fire to the blood-lust, and the crowd roars as the birds are back to circling. One charges to mount and ground the other from behind but fails to take a hold and only manages a few hard pecks at the other's neck as the creatures twist and turn about each other. There's blood in the feathers of both contenders as time and again they fly at each other, all wings and sharp squawks and flashing blades.

The savage spectacle soon has a grip on me and I'm barking alongside the other men wanting the brutal release of seeing one bird's murderous domination of the other. Before I know it, I'm forking out my meagre money for a drink. The fire down my throat and into my belly stirs me further. I'm ready to be right into it, but feel a hand on my shoulder and turn expecting trouble.

It's a jolly enough looking man standing beside me.

"You're the man working for Tommy Mollor?"

"So I am."

My back is turned to the action just as a final roar goes up. I missed the moment. I'm none too happy about it. I turn around and see the Annihilator is dead on the ground and black Satan is strutting and cawing his victory along with the raucous sound of the men who have made a winning.

The man beside me leans towards me to be heard.

"And do you have something for me?"

I frown at him on account of the presumption.

"You're Robert Radford?"

"That's me."

I give him the envelope. He takes a cursory look at it then pats me on the shoulder.

"Come aside, I'll buy you a drink."

I'm suddenly not so bothered by the interruption. Another drink and it will be fine sailing for me. I follow him back into the bar. He orders beer and whiskey for both of us, and we go and take a seat. He raises his glass.

"All strength to you, lad. Tell me, what's your name?"

"Con Donnelly."

"You been off the gang for long?"

"Yeah, a few months."

"And how are you finding the Mollors?"

"Good enough. Are they friends of yours?"

"More business acquaintances. Maybe not even that as yet."

He waves the note that I delivered as though it should mean something to me.

"I have an establishment, up north, and have an idea that I think is better suited to Hobart. If Mollor gets his licence, well then, we'll see."

He narrows his eyes and looks me over.

"Has he told you his plans?"

The man's after something. I doubt I have it, but it could be worth another drink to keep the hook well-baited. I tilt my head and give him a puzzled look before I show a glimmer of remembering a thing.

"I've heard him talking to people."

He's eager at that point. He leans right in and murmurs.

"And what have you heard, lad?"

I figure he's paid me well enough with the drink to give him something to keep him interested.

"He's keen on getting the Bath Arms. Says it's the pick of pubs, a real money winner."

"Indeed. It is ideal. It's the room out the back that makes it, you see."

"The stables?"

"Well, yes, certainly, there are good stables. That's not a thing to sneeze at. There's plenty you'll hear, around town, bellyaching about the lack of accommodation for the horses. An establishment with decent stables will never be short of clientele. Mollor's right on that score, I'll give him that. But, as good as those stables might be, and I've no doubt they're fine enough, they are far from the most appealing thing about the old Bath Arms, young Donnelly."

He pauses and looks at me with a face that's close to bursting with a strange enthusiasm. He really is a most unusual man but there's something about the bustle of ideas in him that makes him strangely compelling.

"It's the additional room in the back of that place that I have my eye on. That's the thing that matters. Give me an adequate space and I will realise a grand vision the likes of which you have never, in all your short days, seen, young sir. And I'll tell you something more, I'll put this island ahead of the other colonies with what I will have on offer."

He raises his glass again and knocks it back, then orders another round. I make a point of telling him I have no cash at hand. He waves away my concern and says he'd expect as much for a poor probationer.

"So what's this grand vision of yours?"

He's pleased to hear my interest.

"Well, tell me now, are you a man well-acquainted with horses?"

"I know as much as any."

"No fine equestrian skills to speak of?"

He gives me a level gaze. I can't tell if he's being serious or mocking me.

"What skill is there, Mr Bradford, save for keeping the reins tight in hand and your arse planted on the back of the creature?"

He breaks out with a belly laugh and claps me on the shoulder.

"The gang hasn't knocked the spirit out of you, lad. Well done. Well done. No. If you had some finer skills I'd be well tempted to grab you from the Mollors. I do need a dab hand, you see. I have such fine horses. I'm busy training them just outside Launceston."

"Training them for what?"

He raises his eyebrows, looks around at the crowd in the bar as though checking for any spies, then leans towards me.

"The future, my good sir, is popular entertainment but of a

163

respectable variety. This rough business of cockfighting and dogfighting, and the like, might draw the rowdy crowd – with a decent enough thirst – but a man risks his licence putting on these sorts of shows."

He leans back with a look of satisfaction.

"But legitimate entertainment, an honest to God spectacle that's ripe for all to enjoy without any tricky legal repercussions, well that draws a fuller crowd and, if what's on offer is half decent, it will keep their thirsty selves captivated and happily imbibing for a sizeable portion of an evening."

"Is it racing you are talking about?"

"No. Not racing. This goes beyond the stolid old business of plonking around a racecourse. All due respect to the racing fraternity. I'll grant there's the excitement of winning a bet, but that's as far as it goes. Once the racing is done, the crowds go home and there's no further commerce to be had. No, that's not my caper. Not at all."

He pauses, leans forward, and spreads his hands apart as though revealing something right there between us.

"Imagine, if you will, an arena that's large enough for horses to raise a good canter but tight enclosed enough to allow a close-watched spectacle such that the audience feel they are in the excitable thick of it. And I can see you wondering what the crowd would be witnessing. Good question, lad. Imagine – extraordinary feats of riding skill and acts of humour and bold daring."

"Oh, you mean to start a circus here."

"Indeed."

He scrutinises me with a sharper look.

"What do you know of circuses?"

It's clear the man presumes I'm a fool.

"Well, there was Batty's back home in Belfast. I never had chance nor money to go to it but I think it was like your idea, horses and fancy performances. They'd get a decent crowd – I heard that much. It's been quite a thing for many years there."

"Batty's, you say? I'm sure it's fine enough, but what I offer will have the genuine colonial spirit, and that's the new thing. Age-old riding skills but with contemporary spunk. Entertainment is deliverance, you see lad, from all that's mundane and oppressive in this world, and it's a double-deliverance where there's a drink in hand."

He looks around at all the people at the bar, then leans back towards me.

"I doubt there's a place on earth more eager for such deliverance than this one."

I nod my head. It's true enough. This place has more demons to escape than any I've known.

"And what part does Tommy Mollor have in this grand vision?"

"That pub, that Mollor is after, is the one best-suited for bringing the act down to the south."

"And what of that?" I ask, nodding towards the envelope I delivered.

"I imagine it's some assurance of his commitment to the plan. Now let me buy you one more drink and then I must be off."

***

The streets are awash with a softening glaze when I stumble out of the Commercial. Something of Radford's bold confidence has got right into me. It's like a door has broken open and there's nothing but bright light spilling through it, and the future is looming large again. I feel such joy there's tears streaming from my eyes. I tell a woman, passing me in the street, that the future is looming large. She looks at me. There's such a strange abhorrence in her eyes, I wonder what her problem is. She scurries away before I have the chance to ask her. It's a most peculiar thing. I want to tell Jimmy, but he isn't here. More's the pity that Jimmy has missed this moment. I'd have let him know the future is looming large again. Maybe he would have liked to know it. Who can tell with him, though? He can be such a cranky bastard. He's more likely to turn sour on a thing than sweet.

There's a couple of uppity boys ahead of me. They're a pair of shiny-buttoned geese striding along as though they own the world. Pompous pair, warbling queer birds. Just look at the sight of them. I strain to hear what they're saying just for the laugh.

"God helps those who help themselves," one crows.

"You know the lazy Irish," his friend adds, "always ready to complain, despite all England has done for that wretched country. And when is there a year when they aren't starving anyway? There's no helping that hapless lot."

They're prattling and guffawing, with one man thumping the other's back, and I don't like it one bit.

"And, besides, it's the fate of primitives to die out. It's as true back home as it is here. You know old Reverend Malthus. He was right about the Irish. What was it the good man said again? A great part of the population should be swept from the soil."

"Swept from the soil, indeed. One can only wish they would stop sweeping the dross in our direction! Doesn't your heart sink when the flags are up, signalling another boatload of brain-addled Paddies and Biddies making their way upriver?"

"Never mind. The half-starved ones are finished off by the roadworks and you can be sure the others will drink themselves to an early grave."

Again they laugh, the hawing donkeys, and look around half-hoping to see their words have stirred some outrage in the passing. They see me, then turn to each other and laugh some more. I'd have words if I could find them or let my knuckles do the talking if I could just catch up.

166

"Speak of the devil!"

One raises his eyebrows and I feel such a stir in me to knock him off his feet.

"You're a pair of donkey cunts. You hear me? Donkey cunts ripe for a fucking belting."

It's the best I can manage. They walk all the faster now and I just wish I had some of the quick boys from back home with me. We'd sure give that uppity pair a walloping, a good old Belfast one, and leave them sad and sorry. They'd not be speaking ill of the Irish again, that's for sure.

There's too many of their type in this town: all bristling with their tawdry stabs at being the big blowhards. God, how I hate them. Despite all England has done. I swear I can hear Da stirring in my ear at that one. The broody head on me. I'm dizzy with it. Steady now. But still. Donkey cunts. It was a good one, wasn't it? As good as could be managed in the hour.

There's a squealing peeler up ahead. I'm sure he hasn't seen me. I wouldn't put it past the likes of them to have got in his ear. I could hold my own. I know it. But best not. But still there is an injustice and I've a mind to have words about it. The great injustice, old as sin itself. But a peeler like that one hasn't the brains for fine points though. Look at him: the knuckle-dragging sod. Barely a glimmer in answer to a thought. I best not. I'll take a left at Murray and go up past the Prod church and down towards the waterfront. I might lay down a bit. The Mollors won't mind it. And if they do? To hell with them if they can't grant an allowance for all the efforts I've made.

CHAPTER 24

That sorry excuse for a governor, Eardley-Wilmot, is dead and buried. He couldn't even manage to return home before dying. His replacement is already riled with loathing for the hopeless people he is supposed to govern. Denison's contempt extends from the troublesome senior judges of the colony through to the bellyaching horde of free settlers. His ears ring with the tinnitus of ill-bred whinging everywhere he goes on the island. The democratic spirit. Every fool and his mangy dog think they have a place to voice opinion here. The mob muster in their vulgar American style of town hall meetings and blast their presumptuous demands at him as though they were his equal.

If he had known the half of what this place was like, he would not have taken the commission. He would have seen the offer for what it was: a backwater insult wrapped in a tawdry approximation of vice-regal splendour.

He feels the aggravation every day as he stares across the cove and wishes he was anywhere but here. His every military instinct demands he put some stick about and get things rightly-ordered. There's such a satisfaction in that thought. But they would have their ways of payback. He's gleaned that much from his predecessors. A man's good standing is easily demolished by those pernicious settlers who have the ear of the right people back home. The greatest tyranny in this place is in the arrival and departure of the mail sacks. Sure, Franklin vanished into the frozen north just to escape the savage aftershocks of his unfortunate days here.

Denison turns his mind to Earl Grey, puts pen to paper, and pours his scorn across the despatch page.

When we consider the elements of which society here is composed – when we see the low estimate that is placed upon everything which can distinguish a man from his fellows, with the sole exception of wealth – when we see that even wealth does not lead to distinction, or open the road to any other ambition than that of self-indulgence – it can hardly be subject of surprise that so few are found to rise above the general level; or that those few owe more to the possession of a certain oratorical facility than to their powers of mind or the justness of the opinions which they advocate.

***

I've been called to load the kegs onto the dray at sunrise. The cold is gathered to an ache in the shadowy folds of the mountain. It's nothing but frost underfoot and a sharp air that's so fierce it's painful breathing. The man who makes Degrave's deliveries is familiar enough to me. He nods at me as I approach then looks at me with a keener eye.

"I know you from Rocky Hills."

"Yeah. Frank, isn't it?"

"It is. It was you and your older brother. Jimmy's the older one isn't he?"

"That's right. He's down Pittwater way."

"Oh, I know that much. I saw him not that long ago. And how are you managing with a brother gone to the other side?"

There's some game afoot. I can see that much. It's too early in the morning for it, but I'm in no mood for trouble, so I ask him what he's talking about.

"You know, him being a constable."

"Jimmy?"

"The one and only."

The man's a fool and presumes me to be one too. If he keeps it up, I'll have no choice but have words with him and more than that if needed.

169

"Tell me now, did Jimmy put you up to this? He's never been one for cobbling a convincing story. Even he could have done better than this, though."

"He didn't put me up to any of it. I've no cause for telling you any stories."

Frank frowns at me as though I'm the absurd one. I don't think he is lying. The furrows are too thick on his forehead, and he has the look of a man who won't take kindly to being contradicted. But what he's saying is well beyond my ken. Jimmy in the livery of the constabulary is like a donkey dressed up to be a priest. Nothing but shit all around and an awful lot of nonsense to behold.

"A constable?"

His frown smooths away when he hears that I believe him.

"Either that or he snatched a uniform and was putting on a performance. Mind you, he'd had a bellyful when I saw him. Could barely manage one foot in front of the other. It was quite the sight."

"That's one thing that isn't a surprise. If there's a drink to be had, Jimmy would be at it. Sure, putting on that uniform would drive any man to drink and doubly so for anyone in our family. Poor old Jimmy, what the hell was he thinking? God help us all. Were you talking to him? Did he have anything to say for himself?"

"He said he'll be longer getting his ticket. Something about getting caught pretending to be someone's servant. But, like I said, there wasn't a lot of sense coming out of him."

"Pretending to be a servant! Who pretends to be a servant?"

"I don't know. He's your brother. You tell me."

I wish I could say I couldn't imagine Jimmy as a constable but, when I stop and think about it, I suspect he'd have it in him. At least he'd try it on, hoping to get ahead and be well-seen for it. What madness is it to expect to be well-seen as a probation constable? The free loathe the sight of them and the authority they're given.

How the rich mob squawk. Probationers as constables: foxes made to guard the henhouse; cutthroats trusted to protect the innocent. Yet another instance of this island's inordinate depravity.

It's well against our grain, to go and get caught in a desperate uppity business like that, and Jimmy drinking to oblivion is a sure sign he knows it. Out of his depth, that's what he is, out of his depth and desperate drinking to escape it. He won't last in that uniform. I'd put all my wages on that. They will have him kicked out and probably back on the gang for good measure.

Imagine if the shoe was on the other foot. I'd know no end to the grief from him if I'd put on the peeler uniform. How he'd go at shovelling shame on top of me 'til I was buried six foot deep in it. But how sweet will it be when I see his sorry face and let him have it. I can feel the vigorous stir at just the thought of it. He'll be crotchety, of course, or sheepish, or a bit of both. I can see that startled, red-faced look on him – backed into a corner with no sure way to go – and me with the good boot on and ready to swing it.

Imagine what our Mary would say if she knew the half of it, or Da for that matter. Sure, he'd probably go looking for excuses for the boy, though. He was always like that with Jimmy. God help us all – my brother and his notions – there's no end to the wonder of it. What is it that's got into him since he's been far from me? Pretending to be a servant. Where's the ambition in that? If you're going to take a risk, then at least make it one worth taking.

I watch the loaded dray leave. It's one part in the daily moving business of the township: kegs to hotels; flour bags to bakers; pork to butchers; timber to shipbuilders on the point. An

171

industry of cheap probation hire is moving all around me – behind the cool stone of the brewery, beside the endless creak of the millwheel, and in the steady trudge of timbergetters up to meet the tree line. Soon the mountain will be set ringing with the endless strike of axe to wood as stones grind grain to flour and fast blades cut straight lines through timber.

"Donnelly are you looking to be docked pay? Quit your dawdling. Where are you meant to be?"

"Just finished loading the dray."

"That's long gone. Get where you're meant and on the double."

So much for being closer to freedom. All I want is a life where no one's barking at me. There's no end to the barking and the orders in Degraves' mechanical mountain kingdom.

I've known his kind plenty of times before: crooked men made rich by wage-slavery. Like all the rest, he knows enough to give small blessings: a nod of recognition here, a happy slap on a probationer's back there, a round of drinks to show some fellow feeling. The old man has played the game and won himself this empire, and we are his probation-hardened servants.

He struts around Hobart, when he goes down there, as though he owns the place. He sure owns enough of the political class. That craven mob handed him the town water supply, then thanked him when he seized it with a chokehold. Now the water runs through the bowels of his mountain empire: the sawmill, the flour mill, the brewery, the piggery. Protestors complain but it makes no difference. Letters are written to newspaper editors, but they make no difference. Degraves sits up here on his mountainside throne. He looks with contempt at all the ants below.

If a publican makes the audacious choice of selling someone else's brew, then down come Degraves' bullyboys to pay a visit, or up goes a competing hotel at great speed to drive away the renegade publican's profit. If a government inspector begins to make a fuss then along come Degraves' well-paid lawyers to stitch him up. And if a government contract needs the addition of further benefits, then there's Degraves' political lackeys taking their place at the table to see all's done to gain the big man maximum advantage. He has friends everywhere that matters.

"It's the likes of Degraves who will make our township prosper," they crow with their eyes brim full of desperate dreaming. "It's his kind will put this colony on the map!"

And who can put up an argument that makes a difference against the man who is producing beer and bread and well-sawn timber for the colony? Who would speak evil of the island's great industrialist who has fine ships, in construction, down at the point beside the river? Who could level a crass accusation when the island basks in his incomparable engineering genius: designer of Her Majesty's splendid theatre; inventor of rapid-fired ovens; builder of the hydraulic flour mill; man who envisioned a ground-breaking cooling system?

"Surely there's nothing the man can't do," they trill and squawk in their over-stuffed sitting rooms, "and God help the colony if the man finds cause to leave."

He makes fine bread for the fine people down below. They have nothing to complain about. He saves the lesser loaves, made of rough ground husks and floor-sweeps, for the voiceless incarcerated in the factories and stations. But, for the whole riverside population, the shackled and the free, he carts down that one thing that they most need by the dray load. Those troubled by the devil in their past, the sad and mad, the scarred old lags and madams, the high-born who have fallen off the edge, every sad and sorry inhabitant, are ready for his mountain-brewed salvation. Raise a toast and never mind misfortune. Always beer and never mind the water.

I go into that raucous world of timber and sawdust. Men are positioning a log for the frame saw. I go across to help and feel the bark-stripped smooth of the wood just as we're about to move it forward. I'm glad I'm not stuck down a pit to saw the thing. That blade ahead is a force all on its own. I'll credit Degraves that much for his machinery. There's nothing done that isn't better done with the force of water driving around a wheel or the piston-push of iron-channelled steam.

The log moves forward, then the high screech of blade to timber starts. We keep it on track, mindful of the blade, until it's through the first time. Soon we have the log cut down to decent flitches and ready for the circular saw. I breathe the sweet air and push aside the dust and see old Roddy Murphy is standing to the side.

"How goes it, Con?"

"Well enough, Roddy. You know, I heard the damnedest thing this morning."

"What was it?"

"My brother Jimmy has made himself a constable."

Old Roddy laughs as though this is the best joke he's ever heard.

"Well, it's probably easier than this. Maybe your brother's the smart one, Con."

"Nothing of the sort! I don't know what's gone wrong with him that he would go and do a thing like that."

"Well, plenty do. We all need to get ahead some way. How did you hear about it?"

"I was helping Frank Watts with loading the dray for deliveries."

"Damn, I meant to go with him."

"You're always down to the town. I don't know how you manage it without landing at the magistrates."

"It's legitimate business, Con and, besides, I do certain things

174

for Mr Degraves that keep me in the good books."

"And what is it you do down there anyway?"

"I get appraised of matters. It's the most important thing a man can do, to be appraised of matters."

"Whatever you say, Roddy."

"This is the great year I'll have you know, young Con. The world is about to turn and there will be no turning back now. Did you know that?"

"I had no idea."

"Breathe deep, lad. Revolution is coming. The bells have rung in France and soon they'll ring across all Europe and, from there, throughout the far reaches of the empires. The workers are finding their voices boy. The shackles are being thrown off even as I'm talking to you. Mark my words, this fine year of '48 is the beginning of the decent world to come. A new order is on the rise, and the old order will be finally thrown asunder."

"And this is what you go and get appraised of?"

"That and other matters."

"Well, I don't see any signs of any revolution here."

"Not yet. Not yet. But a man must have the mind to imagine it. Till the soil, ready for the seed lad."

"You're wasting your breath on me, Roddy. I've heard it all before. Look, when it came to changing the world for the better and all of that, there's no one loved the Liberator more than me. I would have died following Dan O'Connell and I know plenty felt the same. There were so many fine words, and all that promise, but where's our man now? Dead and buried, isn't he? And where's his repeal movement but in the grave with all the famine dead?"

"And yet Young Ireland is on the rise."

"Young Ireland, Old Ireland. What difference does it make, Roddy? You talk about the promise of '48. I bet the long-dead rebels said the same of '98 and how did that go for them? And,

175

anyway, what difference does any of that make for us? I'll put money on the fact that tomorrow I'll be working like a slave, dragging timber to the mill or shovelling pig shit at the piggery, just the same as today and next week and next month. But maybe you would like to make a wager, Roddy? How much are you prepared to bet on your revolution coming to Hobart anytime?"

"How is it you're such a cynic?"

"Seven years transportation, old mate, and knowing enough to know how this world really works."

"Ideas can make a difference, Con, when they agitate and provoke men to act. Believe me, that's what's happening in the world out there right now. Men like you and I are getting moved by ideas and taking to the streets to demand change. The change is real."

"Maybe it's real somewhere else, but I don't see it happening here."

"Not yet. It will come and you will see it."

"What makes you so certain?"

"It's hunger makes me certain."

"Well it's hunger makes me want to eat and, on a good day, I'll get a pannikin full."

He laughs.

"You know as well as I do you're hungry for more than food, Con. I know that restless in you. I can see it a mile off. A man like you can try and damp it down inside himself, and God help him if he succeeds. It's the restless hunger for something better that shapes a life into something that matters."

Roddy says a thing like that, then leaves me to stew in my juices through the long work hours. I like the man, but not the way he stirs me. It's the one thing I don't need here. All this pain of wanting, and what am I to do with it? All I have is marking off my days. Sure I might ache for tomorrow, but I curse it too. I curse the sour hidden in the sweet and the treachery that I know is up there circling the dreams. I curse the lethal strike that's bound to wait until I let hope come right back through my door. But most of all I curse my heart that beats too hard when I hear grand visions.

Once work is done, I clamber up the mountainside looking for I don't know what. There's nothing but a murmur over wind-twisted scrub and mossy rocks. Still no Danish gold, Da. Still no wealth to gain me independence. Still no more than this mad hunger that presses me against the nothing that they would have me be.

I am raw in the roar of the mountain. I stand uncertain in the pummel of southern gusts. My soul is prized open in all its fearful loneliness. And down below is the sprawling splendour: land spread to fingers pressed about by water. All the elements are woven, and struck by light, from Hobart Town as far as coast and peninsula. The known world is before me – spun through with some impossible lovely grace – and, on the mountain's other side, the long unfolding promise of the unclaimed wild, the holy hellish more, the all that's waiting there beyond the Pale.

CHAPTER 25

Jimmy's face is twisted in a crooked grin when I meet him in the town. I know that look. He has some half-buried aggravation on the brew and there will be trouble ahead tonight. I've no doubt of it. He punches me in the shoulder, then tilts his chin at me as though he's ready for a dust-up. He's joking and not joking. I shake my head at him. I'm not in the mood. A couple of drinks and that will be enough for the night.

"Are you ready for a hooley, little brother? It's not every day you get your ticket, you bastard. All these years and here we are, set apart by the system. You the ticket-of-leaver and me still the probationer slave. I'll tell you one thing boy, you're the one buying the drinks tonight."

"It's not my fault you got yourself in trouble."

"Oh don't bother me with it."

I look at him. To hell with it. If we're to be at it then we might as well get on with it.

"Anyway, constable, I was expecting to see you in the uniform. Where's your baton and your shiny peeler buttons?"

His eyebrows arch at the provocation. He takes measure of me, for a moment, thinking about what might come next. But the night has only started, and he's yet to get a drink in him so he packs his other ideas away and conjures a sour smile instead.

"Don't be starting at me boy. It was a mistake. Enough said about it."

"I couldn't believe it when I heard."

"Jesus, how did you find out anyway?"

"Frank Watts."

"Useless flog that one. Anyway, it didn't last and I'm better

178

for being done with it and we won't be talking anymore of it. You hear me? There's no place for it anyway when we're here to celebrate a thing, so let's stop wasting time and be at it."

We wander into the Commercial. It's more crowded than usual, and there's a mysterious excitement in the air. There are men gathered around a few who have newspapers. There are boisterous calls across the bar for the drinks to keep coming and hopes expressed there's enough beer to get through to sunrise. Faces that are normally made for nothing but scowling have stirred into broken-toothed smiles. The whole sight is writ with a strange, ugly joy that I have never seen in this town. It's as though some holy wild thing has swept upriver and taken possession of everyone all at once. Jimmy looks at me and asks if I know what it's about. I shake my head.

There are two boys over in the corner holding forth to a crowd gathered around them. I ask a stranger what it's about. He says the two are off some boat and have been to California recently enough, so they know a thing or two about it. The name means nothing to me, but the excitement draws me and Jimmy closer so we can hear the boys.

"The climate is like here. It's warm and healthy. But the whole place is pretty lawless and that was before. It's hard imagining what the place must be like now."

There's a ripple of chatter through the crowd. A man near me says that law or no law, it would be worth it and it would be good just getting away from this miserable colony. He says if you've enough wealth, you're the one to make the laws anyway. There's a grumble of agreement among others. Another man is seated at a table with a copy of the Chronicle spread open. I've never seen such a look on so many faces as he reads the story out for all to hear.

"All the seaport towns are deserted. Out of a population of nearly one thousand, San Francisco only contains about fifty or sixty souls, and these would leave were it possible. The news of the gold discoveries has spread with lightning speed, and the minister, merchant, artisan, mechanic, farmer, labourer, and loafer have all gone to seek their fortune."

There is a cacophony of calls and hoots from men, like us, who have never known a minute of good luck in their lives. The word gold is being tossed about as though it's close enough that we could reach down and claim it here and now. There are emptied ships in some distant, foreign harbour and gold thick on the ground there. Rivers that shine with it. Mountains afire with it. A true equality born from nature's golden bounty. Poor are becoming rich. Servants are taking the master's seat. The whole wretched order of this world is being turned upside down.

I am struck with a fierce wonder with every word I hear. Imagine it. Men like us are seeking their fortune. Not just seeking but gaining. Not just dreaming but having. I grab hold of Jimmy and shake him as though to stir the joy up in him, too. He brushes me off and puts his hand up to stop me doing it again. All this joy, and there he is nestling back into one of his moods.

"How far is it?" asks an old lag.

"Seven weeks sail from Hobart."

The crowd is now stirred with an urgent need to do something and get across the seas to the place as soon as possible.

"We need ships now!"

"Here, here!"

"To hell with this island. It'll have us slaves forever. All we need are ships to this California to make our fortune and a life worth living and genuine freedom at last!"

"Here, here!"

The hotel is bursting with a working-class passion now. Everyone is struck with the fever, wanting a ship organised, scribbling their names on a list. There are at least one hundred ready to go in a fortnight and I am eager to be one of them. To hell with the ticket-of-leave conditions. I join the shuffling line to get my name down on that list, but now it's Jimmy who is grabbing hold of me and dragging me away and yelling at me.

"What do you think you're doing?"

His face has turned fierce red, and he looks like he's ready to savage me. I push him away, and I'm ready to drive my fist into his jaw. I won't have a decent future ruined by whatever stupidity has taken hold of him. The publican has a baton out and he's come around the bar and is yelling at us to take it outside. The crowd is so filled with excitement they barely notice what's happened. Everyone is eagerly lost in their own newborn dreaming.

"What the hell, Jimmy?"

He looks at me and shakes his head with a disdain that makes no sense to me. It leaves me wanting to be at him but he's taken to walking down the road so there's nothing I can do but chase him.

"Do you not comprehend what is going on, you thick bastard?"

He doesn't stop to answer me.

"Once rich, no one could touch us and, besides, we would be in America and beyond the reach of this place. Jimmy, imagine the freedom of that. It's in the air. Can't you taste it? It's close enough to grab."

He stops in his tracks and turns to face me.

"Close enough to grab, eh?"

"Yeah."

He shakes his head.

"Just like Ballynafeigh? Close enough to grab. You know what Da had me promise when he came down to see us before we shipped out?"

I don't want to give him anything, so I just stare at him.

"He said I was to remember I was the older one and I was to look out for you no matter what. It's what an older brother does. That's what he said, and don't I know the truth of it."

"Don't bother me with your stories, Jimmy. Look out for me! God help me if you think that's what you've been doing these years. The way you see yourself. The ever-watchful older brother is it? Anyway, what the hell has any of that got to do with this?"

He shakes his head again.

"You always think you're the smart one, don't you? Always the one with the better ideas and the nobler thinking. You've got no idea, none at all."

"Jimmy, just listen to me. There's a chance for something real and good tonight, the likes of which we will never see again. All that news can mean something for us. We can make our lives a different thing – no more being trapped and made to play the servant of the rich – and the first thing we need do is get our arses on a damned boat. I'm not saying there isn't risk in it. I know it as well as you. But the thing that's there to gain with just a moment's daring. God help us, Jimmy, can't you feel it in your blood? Don't tell me you don't want it? If you don't want it, I don't know who the hell you are or how we could be brothers at all."

He stares at me with such a dead look it near smothers the passion in me.

"If they get ships here that are bound for California, do you not think every inch of every deck will be scrutinised before leaving? Do you not think they know well what every old lag on this island will be thinking? One moment of daring, you say, and then what, Connie? What do you really think comes next? Is it the golden promise of Port Arthur? Is that what you're after? The joy of another year of gang labour? God, boy, I thought you'd got the foolish out of you, after all these years. Seems I was wrong. I'll happily wager a bet when there's a decent chance of a win. You know I would. But there's no chance of a win for us here. All well and good to get excited, and good luck to those who are free enough to leave, but that's not us, brother. We're not there yet, and it's nothing but a grave mistake to act like it's otherwise."

There's nothing for us to do but go and drink in silence, but every hotel in town is charged with the news. It aggravates me hearing others full of the joy that my brother has torn right out of me. His cadaverous common sense has laid too cold and heavy a hold on me. If I tried to claim that joy back, I would lose it before I had a chance to plant it.

All the while, he sits there with his face gone dull. All the world is spinning around him, and he's not touched by it. Not one bit. How is it that he's become like that? It's not the way he used to be in Belfast. He was nothing but surrender-to-the-fierce back then. He was daring to the marrow of his bones. I never thought I'd say it, but I miss those fiery ways of him. If he just had an ounce of it in him, our names would be on that list. But that Belfast brother of mine is dead and buried and now old furrowed-brows is here to take his place. How I hate the sight of him with his hunched-up shoulders and brooding eyes: a man who's made compliant enough to forever fit well inside this colony.

I could put my name down and be done with it and done with him. That wouldn't be such a bad thing, would it? He could join me once he got some sense into his thick head. Maybe Da and Mary and the young ones could come across to America and we'd be together again. Imagine that. Our broken family made whole again, with gold to bind the fractures.

"I know you're disappointed. I know you think the less of me for this."

He says it like some wounded creature. His eyes are wet with feeling. What has become of my brother that he has become like this? I don't know what to say to him, so I buy another round and settle back to drinking until the world is made soft by it and all the care is bled right out of me.

"I've forgotten more than I remember here."

Jimmy frowns and thinks about what I said.

"It's easier to forget Connie. There's too much pain remembering."

CHAPTER 26

The town quickly forms two tribes: the few who are set to leave and the many who are resigned to stay. The luckiest ones have a place on the clipper brigantine John Bull. It's offering seven weeks direct passage from Hobart to California. That's faster than the poor man's wagon trail across the American continent. It's faster than the long sea voyage, around Cape Horn, from east to west America. It's even faster than the short trip from New York down to Panama where there's less distance to trek across to the Pacific side where another ship can be taken north to San Francisco.

The schooner, Eliza, and brig, Marianne, are also bound from Hobart to San Francisco but they are stopping at the Sandwich Isles. The hint of any delay feels perilous. Better a direct passage than a broken trip, but better any passage than none at all. The door to a better life is open now, on those gold fields up in the Californian mountains, but how long before the gold runs out and the door is shut again?

The thought of lost opportunity makes men restless. They pace the docks with an urgent need to be away and digging for a new life. They check the signal station and stare downriver and pore over the shipping news. Every hotel has the buzz of men who would be diggers. Even those with no near chance of leaving seize every skerrick that's reported in the papers and feed their imaginations with the details.

They talk about the way the gold is found, debate the way a pan might best be utilised, and theorise about the workings of the new-invented rocking box. The usual characters peddle bombast with an air of expertise, crowing insights based on spurious presumptions. They are soon cut down by a mocking chorus of drinkers who are happy enough with gold talk but have no time for blowhards and their bullshit.

Some quieter conversations extend to broader topics, even the nature of America itself. There's news that goldfield lawlessness is now being met by lynch mobs. Seems even justice is a wild thing over there. Maybe this is what it means to be beyond the control of England. Surely, it's the stuff of Chartists' dreaming: a kind of raw and ready democracy in the making. Many toast that country's independence. Its rough ways are bound to suit a working man. Just hearing this causes men, at the bar, to vow to redouble their efforts to secure passage. Better there than here, even if the gold runs out. A poor man has more chance where there's some true equality.

Others adopt a cautious view. A country fuelled by youthful independence is surely always skating near disaster, and a country that leans towards the rule of the mob is bound to be a honeypot to all that's worst in the world. A place like that is never as good as it seems. Say what you like of this colony, but surely there's a certain strength in British order. Lynch mobs are the stuff of savagery. There might be gold, but secured at what cost? The smart critics keep their reservations to a murmur. When men are in their cups, best not disturb their dreaming.

People all through town are sniffing with a renewed spirit to get ahead. The next round of ships is at the wharves in April: the fine fast-sailing schooner Munford, the clipper schooner Vansittart, the packet schooner Martha and Elizabeth. The cost of passage is increasing. Fortune is favouring the wealthy yet again. Some give up. Some get angry. They curse the isolation of the colony that seems well-placed to crush a poor man's opportunity. Some choose to live at a distance from the town before the river-pressed restless gets hold of them and curdles them to madness.

CHAPTER 27

Jimmy is at me again as we're walking through Franklin township. He's got the niggle in his voice, and I'm trying to ignore him. I look out on the river. It's calm this evening: a long straight line pushing up the valley to the backside of the mountains. There's no interruption to its peace except a squawking gull above and a squawking brother beside. I feel an ease despite them. It ripples over the water and breathes right through me: the rightness of this place for my new-gained freedom.

The valley is christened with enough soft days to keep it green. There's moss and the sweet smell of damp and rot in the deep forests and the fern-thick gorges in the higher country. There's timber work and small crop plots near the water, and there's plenty like us, living here, all looking to bury the near-past and make a new life.

Those mountains are helpful. They separate us from them. There's too many in Hobart always ready to see the worst in us. I doubt that will ever change. The uppity will always have need for people they can blame for things gone wrong, especially when their own failings are nipping at their heels.

I look to Jimmy to tell him what I'm thinking, but realise he hasn't stopped his blathering. He is a dog at a bone. He's playing the wiser older brother again, twisting his brows in a judicious knot, trotting out his tired old song as though he has the voice to carry it.

"You'd have had us on the wrong side of the ocean brother. And not able to return without fear of being captured as absconders. Just admit it's good you've got me, isn't it? The wiser head prevailed."

The wiser head prevailed. He's been going on with it, since the other day, when he heard reports of gold discovered in a place called Bathurst, somewhere in New South Wales. It's given him cause to wonder if it was divine inspiration that had him thwart my plan to escape to California. He's cocky with the godly idea and carry-on with all his notions now wrapped in a new guise: once a peeler, now a half-mad prophet and always a pain in my arse. If the man comes out again with – if you wait, then the good surely comes – I swear I'll throttle him to an inch of his life.

But I know he will keep on this point: bunching up the tinder and striking at the flint to try and get a spark. The thing the man always forgets is that I have thicker skin than him. He's a fish that'd jump on a hook before it's baited. Poor old Jimmy's the easiest catch I know. It takes nothing at all to set his cheeks ablaze, his eyes set small and tight like a desperate mouse, his voice all trembled-up to a blustering crescendo. Then all I need do is reel him in. Just the thought of it gives me delight. I can't help but interrupt his speech.

"That's no way for a ticket-of-leaver to be talking to a respectable freeman."

His nose curls at the reminder. I've got his attention now.

"You should mind yourself now. You're not the right reverend constable anymore, old lag. That ship's long sailed."

He emits a snort. I brace at the well-known sound. I'm ready to duck his fist and tackle him to the ground. He stops in his tracks, catches my eye, then nods up the road.

The dim-witted district despot, Philip Stanley Tomlins, is marching from the watchhouse with his constable. He's the magistrate everyone in the district hates: a man who thinks his appointment has delivered him a world that's ready made for his personal benefit. His constables are a local joke – good for nothing but drinking beer and playing skittles – and they're not even convincing in their execution of those duties.

They strut towards us with their noses in the air, sniffing the wind for their tinpot share of empire. We keep quiet as they pass but that's not enough for Tomlins.

"It seems to me you don't know the proper respect for a gentleman when you meet him."

Jimmy is quick to fire one back at the blowhard.

"I don't see you deserve more respect than any other man."

There's a fearful beauty to the way that one lands. Tomlins is jittery like a kettle about to boil over. I look at Jimmy. He's lit up, with a shot of good old vigour in him, and smirking at the outrage he's provoked. It seems the Belfast boy has risen from the dead. God help us both for what comes next.

"Who are you?"

Tomlins asks it with the old imperious trill: a pompous little songbird looking to be cracked. Jimmy has turned to face the man with his arms crossed and his eyes levelled at the man.

"Free men."

The magistrate's chin goes up at that.

"Where's proof that you're free?"

"We haven't collected the certificates from town."

Tomlins grins as though he's caught us out.

"Then I doubt you're free at all."

He gives his constable the nod. The baton-wielding cur grabs Jimmy to take him down. Jimmy braces himself, eager to shake the man off, looking to throw his fist and make his mark, barking at the injustice of it all. The constable relishes the chance to put him in his place. He twists Jimmy around then kicks the legs from under him and shoves him onto his knees. Once Jimmy's down his arms are pinned and he's left kneeling on the gravel.

Tomlins doesn't forget me, though he seems to have forgotten seeing me in his courtroom days ago. I assert that I am also a freeman as he well knows. He demands I prove it. The constable is at me, grabbing and shoving, as though I'm a wayward beast to be controlled and I'm down on my knees beside my brother. They keep us there just long enough for the magistrate to strut about and crow, then we're dragged to our feet and shoved down the road to the Franklin watchhouse.

CHAPTER 28

We tried to reassure ourselves at first. Surely our friends will hear what's happened and speak up for us. We imagined a wave of local outrage at our wrongful imprisonment. It would be the talk of all the boys drinking sly grog down on the banks of the Kermandie. Tomlins has finally gone too far. He's crossed the line. It's those Donnelly boys will take the bastard down now.

How the excitement would build with toasts made and stories being told and laughter echoing right along the river valleys. I conjured the whole thing in my mind: the fine times, nearby, waiting to be had; the backslaps and the bottle pressed into my hand; that first hot guzzle and the heady buzz and then a raucous song breaking out and rising to a rowdy chorus. I was so charged with all those thoughts the cold and gloom couldn't lay a hand on me.

Jimmy's excitement faded before mine. Now his face is settled into stone and his eyes are lost in the poor man's sullen stare. He looks at me as though to sort me out. He needs to see me rid of foolish dreaming. I wish he would stay quiet. There's nothing he could say that I don't know.

"It might take some time before they let us out. There's no higher authority to put Tomlins in his place down here. Word needs to get to Hobart and then back again. Might be days then, hopefully, we will be alright."

"Hopefully? Surely in this colony, where every inch of our lives is scribbled in their books, the truth about us can be easily proven."

"I know it. It should be like that, but the right thing coming out relies on people who think nothing of us, doing something for us. There's no easy bet in that, brother. When have you ever known the system to work to our advantage? It doesn't happen. Not on this island."

I have no answer to that, no answer that I want to voice. His saying not on this island rubs me raw, though. We wouldn't be in this trouble if I had had my way. There's no point saying it, though. The cell's too small for fighting. Jimmy lays down with his back to me and curls into his defeat. The moody brother is back in his cave and I'm left keeping watch again.

I sit and watch a stream of sunlight creep around the cell. Hours darken into claws that start to dig, unearthing desperate thoughts, then letting rip a fevered dream in me: the gavel falls and we fall again, always falling, together and apart. We are all at sea, Jimmy and me, all at sea and riding the wild above the dead abyss: the feeble rise of hope, stupid hope, the plummet of despair.

If I can't hold something, I will drown.

I find hate. It's solid in my grip. Solid in this monstrous rolling nothing. Solid enough to raise and swing. Blackthorn-hard and well-knotted at the end. I've still enough in me to set it loose to break this world and break the likes of Tomlins. I taste the satisfaction of it. It burns like liquor down my throat. It tastes like home. These walls are nothing to me. I am not a man to be contained. I am a powder keg ready for a spark. I am wild justice come to visit. No threat of hell can stop me. No system can break me. Let the well-to-do throw their judgements down on me. Let this wicked island dish out the worst it has got for me. I'll meet it all with a tenfold curse twisting at their bowels in dead of night. Sweet insatiable hate: the only power a man like me can own.

Jimmy is woken by my agitated mumbling.

"Settle down," he snaps.

"We could have been somewhere else. We could have been far away from all of this."

I stab it back at him. He stares at me, incredulous, then shakes his head as though I'm nothing but a fool. I turn away from him and stare at the wall.

Night breaks into day then fades to another night. We gnaw at the meagre rations they give us. Our bellies ache because it's not enough and our demands for justice are ignored. Tomlins is nowhere to be found. He's busy persecuting others somewhere else.

The dark hours have smothered all my fire. My rage is now pathetic to me. Wild justice. God help me. I am nothing. How easy was it, for the likes of them, to do this thing to me? Even if I'm free again, I will never be truly free. Not in this colony and, maybe, nowhere on this earth.

Cold is in my lungs and pressing through my veins. Freedom. The cruelty of that word. The emptiness of that word. Seven years' desperate living for the promise of it, and what was it ever really? Bait on the hook that dragged me where they wanted. Freedom. There's no such thing as a poor freeman. I can see that now. It takes money to make freedom secure. Poverty and guilt are one and the same in the eyes of the likes of Tomlins. I have no doubt that's how it will always be. The guilty poor are made to be kicked and controlled by the likes of them.

And what of God?

It's barely worth the thought.

But, maybe, where there's gold there is a genuine freedom. Enough of it and it couldn't be taken away by some pompous bastard at a whim. Isn't that what I hoped when I heard of California? Isn't that the thing I put to Jimmy and that he smothered with his caution? And where's your caution landed us, brother? Damned fool.

There's nothing foolish about the golden promise though. It is more than just dragging shiny rocks out of the ground. There's a benevolence in something being buried in the wild that can make things right for us. Maybe that is the only genuine gift, from God, on offer for those of us he tends to forget. And, maybe, I still have it in me to believe I might find my way to that benevolence. Maybe. The only prayer that matters is every step that gets me closer to it. But none of that means a thing when here I am caged in a cell that's made to snuff out hope.

It's eight days before the door is opened for us. We expect to hear all is well and that we can go but there's no such thing. We are ordered out of the cell, shackled, and set marching to the beat of the distant Tomlin's magisterial whim. We're told he wants us relocated to the Brown's River watchhouse. It's more than twenty miles away. I emerge from the shadows. I am knotted and aching from confinement. I stretch, as best I can, and take a deep breath, but the air is laced with lead. The sight of this valley, where I'd travelled freely little more than a week ago, is heavier to my soul than the irons that drag me.

Poor wretch who thought himself free. Joyfully drunk on his ignorance. I shake my head at the thought of him. Idiot.

Jimmy shuffles beside me in silence. We share the predicament but we're alone with our share of it. No one has come to protest our miserable procession. No one has bothered to establish that we are free men falsely imprisoned. Now any who might have cared are left behind as we shuffle up the valley and into the hills.

What's to become of us? A return to the grinding injustices of the probation stations? Another seven years for no crime at all?

Better to be dead.

I have a taste for that dark nectar. It adds a beat to my sorry pulse as we struggle along the track. Surely it would mean a final end to all this pain; maybe the only free act I might truly know. But pressing up through the mist-laced bush, watched over by a constable, there's no means to do the grim deed. And besides, there's Jimmy to consider. He might be silent, but I hear him in my head.

If you wait, then the good surely comes.

The guileless hope of that hopeless man. I shake my head at him. He gives me a frown then raises his eyes to the skies as though this is nothing at all. It's all just a foolish story we're caught in: an occasion that's made for a future joke. In this moment, looking at Jimmy, there's nothing but him and me – always just him and me – the bare bones of us thrown together time and again – and, despite my better instincts, something close to hope is sparked on that fragile note of tenderness between us.

We walk on.

There's no consolation in this country now. Nothing speaks to me. We are pressed to walk at speed and so we do. I walk for miles in thoughtless rhythm. Not thinking is my only liberation. I am here but I make myself not here. Let the well-to-do see me as the dull mute beast they expect. To hell with them. I can't afford the thought-busy freedom that they have. All I have is my mind gone somewhere else while this dull body is left to do some other bastard's bidding. My mute eyes stare ahead. There's nothing but the tangled tracks of mud and the easy trip of roots underfoot. Nothing but the hammer of my heart and the winter chill fingering at my lungs.

We're not far from the southern coast. I can see the long stretch of Bruny Island on the other side of the channel. That was the way we came when we first arrived. I almost say something to Jimmy but I don't. It's hardly a happy memory. It feels a long time ago. I had managed to hold onto dreams in the belly of that boat. I was blessed with ignorance.

No sooner do I remember the boy I once was than here he is. He is mocking me with his dim colonial dreaming. I can't abide it. I want to yell at him. I want to shake my shackles at him and see how well he dances to that tune. I want to drive his

195

clamorous hope right out.

Freedom is a lie. Do you hear me, boy? Freedom is a lie. I chant it like a monk's prayer in my mind to silence him. I shake my head to shake him out of me. But still, he lingers in the shadow of the trees. He whispers tomorrow, tomorrow, tomorrow, like a prayer. He tries to catch my eye with some consoling speck: the good light-dappled sea, the good high-flying bird. I can't bear his tricks. He taunts me with his wonder. Treacherous ghost.

Closer to Hobart means closer to proof of your status as a freeman.

The boy persists. I push back. He whispers all the louder. But here, I tell him, here is evidence of what this world truly is for me. Your tomorrow is nothing more than these irons. Free or convicted doesn't matter. Here's our destination. Save your hope. Better still cast it to the wind. Be done with hope. You hear me. Hope is mockery to a poor man, and freedom is a lie, and I will not punish myself with those notions anymore.

We arrive at Brown's River in the evening and are locked up again: just two more convicts of no consequence entombed in the familiar dark. There's no word about determining our status as free men. There's no hint of any judicial hearing that's to come.

Justice is as great a lie as freedom. It's one of the words people say to show themselves as civilised and reasonable. It's nothing but a dash of paint over rotting timber. Justice. Freedom. I start muttering the words like a mad old woman until Jimmy barks at me to shut up.

We just sit in the dark then, and in silence, until we lay down to sleep. We wake and eat the meagre rations. We stretch our limbs as best we can. I feel the day, outside the walls, begin and end through the movement of the shadows. I read the dark, like a night creature, even though there's nothing there to read. We lay down to sleep again. Wake again. Wait again. Sleep again. We have been three days at Brown's River, and eleven days imprisoned in total.

The doors open and light spills into the cell.

"Get out," barks the silhouette of a constable standing before us.

I stagger out alongside Jimmy. We're both in a bad way and feel all the worse for the violent sunlight that now blinds us. We don't know what's coming next. We don't really want to know. We brace ourselves for the worst. It's better to expect the worst.

"Seems your claim to being free men was right after all."

The constable says it with a half-amused tone.

I take a sharp breath at the man's attitude. Jimmy puts a hand to my shoulder to steady me. That's all well and good, but I wonder who is steadying him. Even now, after being wrongfully-imprisoned, it would take nothing for them to twist circumstances, so we are made the villains to suit their needs.

"The good magistrate is generous enough to offer this for the minor misunderstanding," the constable adds.

The bastard's enjoying himself. He's probably been practising that mocking twist he gave to the words – minor misunderstanding – all morning. He will say it again, later, when he's drinking with his constable mates. I can imagine the jackals making their noise. How they will all laugh at the predicament of those Donnelly boys who were left stewing in the box for eleven days.

The constable is shaking the money at us, the way a boy dangles a scrap of meat at a dog. It's a pitiful amount. He knows it, and he can see we know it too. There's just a hint of a tremble in that disdainful stare of his. A pair of well-whipped dogs can still have it in them to deliver a savage bite.

We stare at him, in silence, just long enough to see that

tremble grow. A threatening silence is our meagre ration of power.

"Keep your money, we'll see real justice done for this," I finally tell him.

CHAPTER 29

Everyone says the same thing to me – settle down, Connie, stay steady, boy. I guess they see the murder in my eyes and know I've got fair taste for it. They bring their common sense to meet my ancient grievance, as though a cup of sand can stop the tide. They tell me everything will be alright now. I tell them I'll believe it when I see it.

I walk up the land we're leasing and find Jimmy sitting on a stump and drinking tea.

"I've a mind to get on a mad one, brother."

He presses his lips like an out-of-sorts old woman. His jaw is hard-clenched, trying to hold the beast back. His face takes on a constipated heat at all the effort. He pauses long enough to give a gravelly measure to his words.

"You need to simmer down old cock."

He says it like he's ready to belt me one. I ignore his sullen tone and rub my chin. I stare across the valley, looking for the thing to say. I let out a sigh when I find it.

"Do you know the one thing this island has taught us?"

He gives me a cold stare before he finally shakes his head.

"Even when the likes of Tomlins is far away and there's no likely threat about, it's us who play the prison guards to ourselves."

He frowns and shakes his head again, as though what I have said is nothing but foolishness.

"Sure, you act like you don't know what I mean but you're not telling me you're not as angry as I am. I can see it in you, but what are you going to do about it, brother? You look at me like you want to belt me one but I'm not the one you're really itching to be at, am I? But there's that voice," I tap my temple, "always with the grubby little whisper. It isn't worth it. It isn't worth the grief. Simmer down and be quiet. There's no point making a fuss now. There's nothing can be done that will make an ounce of difference. Cause trouble and you know full well it's you who will pay the price."

I look at him to see if there's any understanding. He's dropped his eyes to the ground. He is kicking the dirt and making a rut. He looks up at me, angrier than before, but doesn't say a word.

"You know what I'm talking about, Jimmy. That pernicious pissy whisper comes, the cell door slams and locks, and we're forever prisoners. There's no certificate in all the world can undo it. It's what this place has done to us, and not just you and me, every one of us dragged here in the chains. They've pressed defeat so deep in us I swear it's buried in our bones and writ into our seed. This place will have us prisoners, kept low, until the day we die."

Jimmy looks at me with a frown.

"And what would you have us do Connie that doesn't end with us hanging on a rope?"

I don't have an answer for him. I don't have an answer for myself. No matter where a thought goes, it always ends with that whisper.

"We've got to do something. That's all I know. We weren't born to be cowards in this world brother. I can't believe I'm the one telling you that, when it was you who led the pack back home, you who was first to take the fight to them and wear the bruises like a mark of honour. Sometimes I feel like I'm remembering a dead man. But that thing you had, the thing we both had, isn't dead, is it? It can't be. I feel it, more often than I want, charging through my veins so hard I swear my skin will burst with it. Maybe it's better to let loose and run to the fierce beat of who we truly are, even if we end up hanging from a rope. Better to live and die that way than live the slavish life."

"Enough speechifying, boy. I haven't the patience for it.

While you've been plotting your half-baked revenge, I've been doing something useful and talking to John Thorpe."

"What's he to do with any of this?"

"He has an interest and that's plenty good enough for me. He says he wants to help us, not just for our good, but for his own good and the good of the whole Huon. The way he put it to me, I trust him, and he's been honest with leasing us this land. We haven't had any trouble, have we?"

"Well, no."

"Exactly, and that's good enough for me."

"What kind of help is he proposing?"

"He said he'd loan us money to take Tomlins to court. Now, if we add what we get from him to what Da sent us then we could get a good man on our side and do it right. We could get paid a decent compensation for the wrong done, and that horse's arse, Tomlins, would be brought to a public shame. Now there's a thing worth imagining, brother. Public shaming's worse than a broken leg to a man like him. It's better revenge than anything you've thought up, with your hot air and bellyaching, and we're not left the worse for wear for doing it."

I look at my brother and I can't help but grin. The bastard has actually conjured up a plan. Who would have thought it? He looks at me and flicks his nose in the air with his cocky pride on show, and I well know what's coming next.

"The wiser head prevails again, Connie. Just admit it."

"All well and good, but who are we likely to get to make the case?"

"Thorpe says he knows Edward Macdowell. There's no one better in the colony."

"The Wicklow man?"

"Yeah. How do you think Tomlins would go facing up to him?"

I snort, and we're both laughing at the thought. They say

Macdowell has a legal mind as lethal as a knife. Sure he and his brother Thomas, the newspaper man, go back a way in the colony. They were friends of old Governor Arthur. They say those boys know how to get things done in Hobart. But none of that politicking means a thing to me. The only thing that matters is there's no finer barrister to argue our case on this island and we have funds enough to have him enlisted to the cause of achieving Tomlins' annihilation.

We go to Macdowell, in Hobart, and lay out our story. He listens and scribbles notes as we talk. I tell him that I was known to Tomlins, before this business, on account of being drunk and abusing the peelers in Franklin.

"So he dealt with you as though you were a freeman?"

"I was free, and he dealt with me as such."

Macdowell raises his eyebrows at this. He scribbles a further note. He says it is a key point in the prosecution of our case, but the previous instance of being drunk and abusive to the constables might nevertheless prove a problem, depending on the jurors. Temperance men are sometimes inclined to pass judgement in light of their higher cause rather than the specific facts of the case before them.

"Then where is our hope?" I say.

"You're looking at him," Macdowell replies without a hesitation.

He says in this matter I will be the plaintiff. Donnelly versus Tomlins. Macdowell stares at me to take my measure. It's as though, in his mind, he is in the court already: looking at me there, and then seeing me the way others would. He frowns at some thought that passes through his mind but doesn't say what it is. I suspect he's adjusting the terms of his presentation; playing out one argument then another; polishing choicest words that would strike the killer blow.

"Your aggravation will not be your friend in the court," he

finally says to me. "Your brother's a calmer one to take the stand."

I frown at that, about to speak, but Jimmy weighs in.

"The thing is, we want to see Tomlins found guilty for what he's done to us. And, once this business is behind us, Con, you'll be on a boat to wherever gold might be found. There's talk of a rush in Victoria now. That's not so far. You can strike a fortune for us both of us, brother. Make us rich. Just think of that. Haven't you been nagging me about goldfields for two long years? Well, now the chance has come so lets make the path smooth for getting there, like your man here says, and get this business over with."

"Sure," I say to Jimmy and then I turn to the barrister, "and we want two hundred pounds for the hardship that bastard Tomlins has laid on us."

Macdowell smiles at that and says it's unlikely we will get that much. He keeps scribbling and then tells us he has what he needs for now. He's satisfied that we have a case. Not only that, but it has a significance for the colony. He talks of respect for man's freedom with such eloquence that I almost dare believe it.

There is a good, heavy feeling in this moment. It's in the leather of this seat and the rows of books behind the man. It's in the good-smelling air of the room and the fine suit he is wearing. It's the good heaviness of mattering to a man like Macdowell, who was once the colony's Attorney-General. Sure, we are only here because we have the money to pay him but the likes of him can pick and choose his clients. Sitting in this office, right now, we are men that matter to a man like him, and we matter as much as anyone else. And if men like him can talk this way about the predicament faced by a man like me, then maybe hope has a chance to grow despite the darkness of this island.

CHAPTER 30

Memory stirs whenever I am in Hobart. Too many moments linger in the shadows here. I set foot in Murray Street and feel that boy I once was. I see him pass me with his quickened pulse and those hungry eyes searching for any signs of promise in the town. I can feel and hear the steady stomp and clatter of that march up from the New Wharf. Everything is ahead for that boy: Jerusalem, Jericho, Rocky Hills and Maria Island, old Tommy Mollor and his wife, the mountain kingdom of Degraves.

All those years have laid down scars. I'll not be rid of them. I am not a man of easy forgetfulness or forgiveness. I envy those who are. A better life needs some measure of forgetting. But the only time I feel close to it is when I'm in my cups and close to passing out. I'm sorely tempted now. A quick walk to Victoria Tavern would steady my anxious nerves. A drink beside those Young Irelanders, who gather there to argue and gossip, would set me right for the legal business at hand.

I say as much to Jimmy, but he won't have it. Not before the trial anyway. So we stand before the sandstone world of law and government as a pair of clueless sober men of questionable standing. We look about at buildings chiselled as though to conjure some ancient thing: all grand columns and porticoes like a new Rome made for this bedraggled island. The whole of it is made to cast men like us in the shadows. But here we stand, anyway, as two free men demanding justice in the light of day.

I'm not as convinced as I pretend to be. I'm certainly not as convinced as Jimmy, who is already planning how we will spend the money. Any confidence I have begins and ends with Macdowell's reputation, but even that dims in the shadow of these buildings.

The judge is another matter. I'm glad I'm not before John Pedder for a hanging offence. Some say you're no sooner in the door with that one, than the noose is around your neck. Others say the man is known to sob when he's passing sentence, but not when it comes to men abusing boys. Then he brings a righteous holy vengeance to the matter, or as close to it as an old Prod can, and that's no bad thing for those wickedest men. But I've also heard he is no friend of us Catholics, though I've never known a judge, of any persuasion, to be a friend of mine.

We take our seats inside the place. Macdowell is there in his robes. He has a glimmer in his eyes: excited at the prospect of displaying his fine powers of argumentation. He leans across and whispers that it is well that Tomlins has decided to defend himself. The man can barely manage a civil greeting without fumbling his words. Our man insists Tomlins' foolish choice is all to our advantage.

I can see our persecutor's beet-red indignation creeping up his tight-collared neck. He looks my way and sneers. I nod my head, then smile and wink at the feckless prick.

We look across at the jury. They are the well-polished men of the New Wharf precinct; importers who promise deliverance to the colony's well-to-do through whatever finery the world has to offer. There's no one like me or Jimmy amongst their number. I doubt any of them knows the nature of our disadvantages or has much care for our kind beyond the service we can give them. I am not comforted at the thought our fate is in their hands. I whisper as much to Macdowell. He says their general view of us is neither here nor there, but best keep a pleasant demeanour, when looking in their direction, to help the cause. The law is on our side and that's enough. He does have some concern about the temperance man, George Washington Walker. He says it could be a problem as he had mentioned to us before. He doesn't have to say anymore. I am the epitome of a temperance man's concern.

The court stands as Pedder, in his wig and gown, enters and takes his seat above us. The business commences with legalistic chatter, then Macdowell lays out the story of our false imprisonment. He presents what we went through as a matter of pressing importance to the whole island colony and, when he turns his attention to the character of Tomlins, I can barely control the charge of delight that's thumping away inside me.

"There never was a more gratuitous act of despotism practised by any man holding Her Majesty's Commission of the Peace."

Tomlins turns crimson at the charge. He starts blustering a protest to the judge, who cuts him short. He sits there stewing in his juices as our man, Macdowell, continues. He has hit his stride and is drawing the jury to think about what might happen, with the convict population, if Tomlins gets away with his despotic behaviour.

"The reason why the convicts in this colony are held in restraint is that they have a confidence in the administration of justice. But if they are taught that there was one law for the rich, and another for the poor, and both equally maladministered, the jury would soon discover the likes of Captain Rock with his banditti gang at work across the island. For if the prisoners in this island are led to have no confidence in the administration of justice, then I would say there was no security for the peace, the prosperity, or even the safety of the country. I am not endeavouring, in any way, to overstate the facts, but it is because I feel strongly that I express myself warmly. If these things are done in a corner, the jury might rely upon it, that the time would come when every one of us – when every peaceable citizen in this island – would have deep reason to regret it."

The faces of the jurors are hard-pressed by the calamity that Macdowell has conjured. He has called up the greatest fear amongst the wealthy of the island: the ever-present threat of a convict uprising. It's a wonderous thing that Macdowell has made the future of the whole colony rely on the jury's judgement of what Jimmy and I went through.

Our man concludes his comments with one final blow.

"I trust that your verdict will teach Mr Philip Stanley Tomlins that he is not, with impunity, to molest the liberty of a free subject."

Tomlins is on his feet to make his case. His cheeks are still blazing at the charge of being called a despot. His words come stumbling out. His tongue is all thick and twisted. He is a man intoxicated by his own vehement outrage and a sorry spectacle in the wake of Macdowell. There's more than one crooked grin among the jurors. Who says duty can't include some entertainment?

Jimmy is called to the stand. He has arranged his eyebrows in their most grave setting: a serious man ready to get down to serious business as he's sworn in.

Macdowell starts with his questions.

"Can you recall where and when you encountered the defendant?"

"It was in Franklin. My brother Cornelius and myself live in the Huon region. We lease some land from James Thorpe just upriver from the Franklin township. We were walking through Franklin when we crossed paths with the local magistrate, Mr Tomlins there. It was the 10th of June."

"Did you recognise him?"

"Oh yes. Everyone in our region knows Mr Tomlins."

Jimmy says it straight, but there's a snigger among those sitting behind us.

"And did anything untoward happen?"

"Not at all. He passed us by with no trouble at all. The next we knew he was calling out to us, so we turned. He said "It seems to me you don't know the proper respect which is due to a gentleman when you meet him.""

"Strange. And did you respond?"

"Well yes. I said I didn't think he was entitled to any more respect than any other man."

"And what was his response?"

"He said 'We'll see about that.' He asked me who I was so I said I was a freeman. He asked for how long and I said since the 9th of last October. Then he asked how long I'd been living in the Huon and I said about eighteen months."

"What happened then?"

"He asked if I had proof that I was free, the certificate. I said I hadn't taken it up. Next thing I knew he was ordering me taken to the watchhouse. He did the same with my brother. Asked him who he was. Asked him if he had proof he was a freeman. As Cornelius also did not have the certificate, he was taken to the watchhouse too."

Jimmy goes on to tell the story of the imprisonment: eight days at Franklin and then three more at Brown's River. Macdowell prompts him to flesh out the details and then our man is done.

Tomlins is up to cross-examine Jimmy.

"So where is your residence?"

"My brother and myself lease eight and a quarter acres of land from James Thorpe. It's just upriver from Franklin township."

"What is the cost of the lease?"

"Five pounds a year."

"Where did you get the money to bring this action?"

The judge reminds Tomlins that it's me who is bringing the action not Jimmy. Tomlins is flustered at being set right by the judge.

"Oh! So it is. Well. Where did your brother get the money from to bring this action?"

"Part from my father."

"Where did you get the rest?"

"Borrowed it."

"Who from?"

"From Mr Thorpe."

"When are you to repay it?"

"When we are able."

"Any amount of the produce of this eight and a quarter acres?"

"Perhaps not. We might give him shingles."

"Did you either write, or cause to be written, a letter to the Government complaining about this matter?"

"I did not write nor cause one to be written."

"But you know there was one written?"

"I was told so."

"You were told so. Oh! Very good indeed! You were told so! Capital! But you did not know anything about it, eh? Very good! Now what I want to know is – how is it that you do not bring this action as well as your brother?"

Our man Macdowell jumps in.

"He thinks, probably, that one party to the action is quite enough for you."

There's a ripple of laughter, even from the judge, and Tomlins is even more flustered.

"Oh! Well! But. Never mind. By the bye, have you got your certificate yet?"

"I went yesterday for it, to the Comptroller-General's office."

"Ah! You went yesterday to the Comptroller-General's office. Very good! You say you have been living, if I remember rightly, down at the settlement for eighteen months. And, of course, you are cognizant of the occurrences that have taken place there. Do you remember Mr Thorpe, who has kindly lent you this money, having been fined for illegal selling of wine?"

The judge starts laughing at Tomlins and tells him the question is completely irrelevant, and then our man Macdowell jumps in.

"Oh, Your Honour, let him go on!"

Tomlins cheeks are blazing and I swear he's near to tears as he slumps back in his seat like a sorry sack of potatoes.

The proceeding goes on with other witnesses. Tomlins continues to make a fool of himself with irrelevant questions, fired-up aggravation, and general bluster. By the end of it all, Tomlins pours out an apology to the judge for his lack of knowledge of the rules of cross-examination.

"Then you should fee some counsellor to plea for you," says Pedder.

We know we are heading to victory when the judge makes sure the jury has it clear that there is no law to compel a man to take up his parchment certificate of freedom.

It takes no time for the jury to reach the conclusion that Tomlins is in the wrong. But the damages that are offered are insulting. One farthing for eleven days of false imprisonment. Macdowell is in my ear telling me it's no surprise. Two hundred pounds was never a likely outcome. The courts rarely give a sizeable damage payment for these sorts of matters.

I leave the court. Two opposing thoughts are slugging away inside me. The system found Tomlins in the wrong, so there's some measure of justice. But the system also found the hardship of the likes of me and Jimmy of no worth whatsoever. Their token of money seems aimed more to insult than to compensate. It's rich men telling poor men like me that we best know our place and stay in it. I am four-parts wild with anger to one-part satisfied as I stumble towards the waterfront with

Jimmy chasing after me. A farthing. The insult of it. I know Jimmy's not happy either. How could he be? But he's still set on playing the reasonable man. He takes me for a drink and levels his eyes at me.

"One lucky strike, for both of us, brother, and none of this will matter. None of it. Do you hear me, Connie? Then we'll be rewarded more than any jury could ever have granted us. That's the thing to be considering now. Not Tomlins. Not chasing some impossible measure of justice. We'll be getting your arse on a boat across that strait and you'll be making our fortune and then we'll be grand with our own land and masters of our own lives and servants to none. That's the only kind of justice I'm interested in, Connie, and you should be too."

He raises his glass to me and gives me a nod as though to seal the agreement.

"To the future, Connie, and to hell with servitude."

PART THREE

CHAPTER 31

Hope has returned to me, but it's an ugly reborn thing. It's made more of chaos and sweat than any pure spirit. Hope is the fevered thick of more than two hundred souls crammed into this boat. It's alive in the endless chatter: things gleaned; things dreamed; things reckoned to be a providential sign. Hope is in the bruised weedy boy, in the shadows, who can barely keep his skin on for all the excitement that's coursing through his veins. It's in the bawdy laugh of a ruddy old madam who knows a soft eager welcome is sure to be demanded at the goldfields.

Hope sparks through the constant churn of names of places in Victoria: Clunes – but didn't you hear that place petered out to nothing months ago; Ballarat – well yes, mate, but there are mixed opinions about its future; Mount Alexander – well now you're talking son – gold nuggets the size of a fist ready to be collected clean off the ground.

I see faces lit up everywhere with the promise. They're counting their riches long before a pick is swung or a cradle is rocked. Some can't contain their dreams of splendid houses, bountiful land, and servants aplenty. They gaze as though the dark of the ship's groaning belly has fallen away and splendid wealth is now laid out before their eyes: fine silverware and china, tables so heavy with banquets that the wooden legs tremble, and decent pianos for belting out all those best tunes that can set a room dancing with a fierce, gay abandon.

Some bung on the manner of the well-to-do and bark instructions to imaginary servants to pour the finest brandy and polish the silverware while they are at it. They crack up at the preposterous, prissy manners of the masters and mistresses they've had the misfortune of serving under. There will be no more dipping the lid to the uppity back on the island. That's for sure. Now every Jack will be made master, and the masters will be made servants. Ring the bell for tea my dear! Ring the bell for beer and oysters! Ring the bell for the bloody hell of it!

There are some who have settled away from the raucous crowd. They are focused on plotting the details for the business to come. Some already claim a dubious expertise. These know-alls have read all they can from newspapers and feel fit to proclaim opinions about the Californian techniques and the best equipment for the business.

I listen to them with a grain of salt. It seems I've been listening to their kind for most of my life. It's tiresome how they gabble away, playing the desperate game of one-upmanship and passing sharp judgement on others' ignorance.

"Did you hear talk of gold in Melbourne itself?"

The weedy boy's voice has settled into his best stab at a man-to-man manner but his darting eyes prove he's no more than a child. There's plenty of times I'd put one like him in his place, but I don't want to be like those plotting blowhards. Besides, maybe the days of dampening dreams and not hoping above the scraps is over. I smile at the boy and ask him what he's heard for the sheer pleasure of hearing the full sweep of his wild imagining.

"There's wealth in the gutters of the streets, they say. Children are finding flakes of it in their mud patties. The whole place is filthy with it."

"Let's hope they leave some for us."

"I am going to be rich and I'm going to go home."

I can see the hope and heartbreak that's waiting ahead to meet the boy. I'll not say a word of it to him. I tell him that I hope he strikes it lucky and that his journey back home is a good one. He nods as though all of that is well assured, and he says he hopes the same for me. I bite my tongue. I know I'll never see home again, but enough gold could well make a good life here.

There's a sweet edge to this desperate brotherhood. How long's it been since I've felt anything so strong and bright? That I might rise above the depth of all my falling. That I might rise, secure in my life, and stay up there tomorrow and for all my days to come.

"I've heard they don't want us coming over the strait."

The old lag, who proclaims it to the crowd, has eyes agleam with the chance of causing a stir. There's plenty who choose to ignore him. They're too busy feeding the fire of their dreams. But a voice from the shadows asks what the old man means. He smiles at that, pleased someone took the bait, then takes a swig from his silver flask before elaborating on his point.

"They are getting anxious about the lot of us coming."

"The lot of us?"

"Vandemonians!"

He's already delighting in the outrage that's bound to erupt and, soon enough, a tough man gone to fat is shaking his head.

"Is that what they'll have us be? Never mind we are free men. Never mind Melbourne was settled by that old butcher Batman, and his lot, come across from the island to grab what's there to have, just the same as us, no better, probably worse. Cut from the same cloth, we all are, and to hell with any bastard that says otherwise. Whatever's wrong in us is wrong in them."

There's a general mutter of agreement in the crowd who have now decided to take an interest. A raggedy philosopher, who has the learned tone, jumps into the fray.

"Ah but it takes no time for people to favour themselves in their thinking. To them, we're criminals, by virtue of where we most immediately come from, and never mind that most of them knew time on the island themselves. It's the anxious way of the newly respectable, you see. They're all in a rush to distance themselves from shameful truths. Ah, but climbing is a most precarious business. One foot wrong and there's nothing to do but fall."

The philosopher's words seem to have stirred the outrage further. There's indignation all around me, and I've a share of it myself.

"There are some leaguers over there would have closed their border to us even before the gold was found. They talk of us like we're a contagion, worst evil in all the world."

"Anti-transportation league, my arse. They're just anti-us for our not bowing and scraping to the likes of them."

"Well, if they talk that way about us, then too right they should have a fear. We will knock them off their perch."

There's further muttering in the crowd.

"I heard some of them reckon they can spot one of us a mile away. Reckon we've got a thick criminal shape to our heads."

There's a ripple of laughter at that, with one man elbowing another in the ribs, and there's a flurry of suggestions that some onboard have thicker heads than others.

"Sounds like they've been listening to that cur Gregson."

There's moans of exasperation at mention of the island's politician.

"The poor man's friend on the council," replies the old lag. "I've heard he said no man of true virtue would be found in company with the colony's scum – that's all of us mind – who are on our way to Victoria."

"Ah yes, the peasantry should know their place in the world and have no desire to ascend above it," adds the philosopher who lifts his flask to the crowd, "so here's to all of us ignoble scum and our sure and vigorous ascension despite the bastards!"

Some respond to his toast with their own flasks and bottles raised.

"I'd rather be named scum than be a lifelong slave to Gregson's kind. Let's see how those poxy bastards treat us when our pockets are close to breaking with gold. Enough wealth and the worst Vandies among us will be worshipped by those money-greedy bastards."

"If that bastard Gregson came cap in hand to me, I'd have him lick my boots!"

"I'd have him kiss my arse!"

"I'd have him bend over," I chime in, "so I could plough my boot right up him."

I get more than my share of pats on the back at that one.

The hunger on the ship is for more than the gold itself. I can hear it in the voices all around me. It is hunger fired by all the injustices of our crowded past and the worst the island has dished out at us. And now it seems there's judgement and persecution yet again, waiting for us in Victoria. As if they are any better than us. But if our convict reputation causes hearts to race with fear, well, good. Let the Victorians entertain their fears and get out of our way. We'll let rough manners smooth our road ahead. We'll claim our stakes and play the convict-hardened part if that's the thing that helps our cause today. And we'll gladly take whatever name they throw at us: Vandies, Derwenters, Old Lags, criminals and whores. Let them have their words and petty games, and we will have their gold. Then they'll have hell to pay if they try to lord it over us.

We come through the inauspicious heads and into a wide bay. It takes forever to get across the waters and we think there's still a way to go when suddenly they let go the anchor off a beach. There's general irritation through the crowd. What's this? Where are we? Where the hell's Melbourne Town? Most of the crew scurry, avoiding the growing inquisition, but then the captain makes an appearance above us. He says our tickets are to Port Phillip not Melbourne itself and he has fulfilled the contract so this is journey's end: some place called Liardet's Beach.

"And how are we to get to shore?"

"Row boats. They charge three shillings."

No one is happy with that news.

"Three shillings for that little distance. And they say we're the bloody criminals!"

I don't have much and I figure what I have will float well enough. At least the bay is a mellow thing. There's no wild surf to contend against. I secure the money I have in a tight pouch tied around my neck and jump off the ship without much thought. Some other men do the same.

We set the water flying with our paddling. I have one arm cradling my possessions while the other desperately claws at the water. My legs kick me towards the shallow and I'm hoping I'll feel sand against my feet soon. I tell myself it's not so far but my heart is pounding madly and I'm sucking in as much water as air with every breath. I have such a fit of coughing I feel a sudden terror. Surely this is not how the whole show ends. I hammer at the water all the harder.

A hairy man beside me is spluttering, worse than me, and cursing.

"I'll not be bloody dying before I see the bloody diggings you whorish bastard!"

He says it with his eyes raised up to some heaven beyond the clouds. I'd almost laugh at his impotent fury if I wasn't busy avoiding drowning myself.

We keep going, with desperate splashing and occasional fits of blasphemy, until we stumble through the shallows and onto the sand. I collapse like a bedraggled survivor of some terrible wreck. My heart is so panicked it seems the earth itself is throbbing with its pulse. I turn over on my back and stare up at the sky. My chest is heaving and I'm coughing up half the ocean.

I could laugh or cry. I'm determined to do neither. I know I'm fit to live another day and that's enough.

I turn to the side and see the hairy man has his eyes fixed on something.

"What is it?"

"The first sane thing this colony has to offer."

I turn around and look. There's a hotel nestled on a rise just above the sand.

"First a drink and then the diggings."

The hairy man's desperation has turned into a soggy smile. We stagger back on our feet and are soon at the door of the premises. Well-soaked new arrivals seem to be no surprise here. Drinkers look up with bemusement then get on with their business and the publican gives us directions to make our order and then drink outside until we're drier.

I'm soon toasting our impending fortune with the other men. Now we are in Victoria there's good cheer all around. We are on the road to our fortune. That's a thing to savour, so we continue with the rounds until our spirits are well elevated and our funds are well reduced.

I figure it's time to go. A man nearby instructs us to take the bush path until we reach a main gravel road, and then we will find Melbourne is to the left and St Kilda village is to the right. We're told to watch out as there's often trouble on St Kilda Road. A coach was held up yesterday by two men who made an easy escape. The hairy man laughs at the suggestion that we might be in danger.

"Look at us, can you not see we are the trouble, sir?"

The man laughs in a nervous way. He gives us the up and down, then waves us on our way with good wishes that we make our fortune.

We are soon walking through the kind of bush that's familiar to me: nothing but scrub and sand and the stab of the afternoon

221

sun. It's a narrow winding track, sometimes interrupted by tufts of grass and tree stumps. As far as I can see the land is mainly flat and made for easy walking. It's a relief after all the hills and mountains of the island.

There are clusters of people who have set up camp along the way. Tents have gone up in a great variety of styles. Some are free-standing things with a neat military look. Others are scraps of canvas tied to trees at one end, then staked to the ground at the other.

We pass a group that has a well-guarded pile of supplies and equipment for the diggings. I ask them why they are waiting. My words are left hanging in the air. Their faces are tight with distrust and they barely glance in my direction before turning back to examining a map.

No matter where I go, it seems there's always judgement waiting. It takes great effort not to give those uppity bastards an earful. I let out a grunt instead then race to catch up with the hairy man, but he has spied friends in a crowd and he's eager to get to them. He punches me in the arm, in a friendly way, and says he'll no doubt see me later in the town or on the way to the goldfields. The other man who was with us has also disappeared. Seems comradeship is a short-lived business here.

I make my way over a bridge, across some falls. It leads straight into a wide road that pierces through the town. All about me is a wonderland half-risen from a swamp, not twenty years old but already thick with history and blustering self-importance. The streets sound out a raucous dream: one lucky strike upcountry and a whole new life is born. I can feel the promise as I walk along the street that's ringing with the sound of merchants.

"Pans, picks, cradles, barrows, buckets, canvas, compasses, and axes. Come in and equip yourself for diggerdom. Everything you need under one roof for your convenience, and all at the most reasonable price in town. We'll have you sorted out and on the road before you know it. He who lags now regrets later."

Another storekeeper seems set on lecturing about the dangers and depredations of the bandits, somewhere on the way towards the diggings, in a place called the Black Forest.

"They say men go in there and never come out. Unimaginable horrors. Terrifying criminality. Only a fool would travel to Mount Alexander without dependable armaments and generous ammunition. So happens I have the very thing on sale now for one day only. Finest guns money can buy in all of the Australian colonies. Bullets guaranteed to travel straight as an arrow. Buy from me and you are assured of a safe journey to the diggings and a sure and safe return home with all that golden bounty you'll be hauling back."

There's a great mix of people on the streets and in the shops. Soft men in fine clothes – the kind of men who flinch when you call them mate – are quibbling over the price of items. Rough customers, with every mark of poverty on their faces, hand over great amounts of money as though the expense means nothing to them.

The normal world is planted on its head here. I see nothing of the convict hate that was talked about on the boat. The derision doesn't seem to be directed at us at all, but at the high-born and their ilk. Fancy words are mocked. Lordly manners stir nothing but laughter. The old superior sneer is likely to meet a bruising interruption. It's as though the air itself is full of a law that no man is better than any other, and anyone who claims superiority is destined for a fall. God in heaven, it seems I've stumbled into a poor man's promised land.

I walk on and see hotels full to bursting with the happy and ferocious drunk. There's a dingy place, called Flinders Lane, that offers gin and beer and flea-riddled lodgings. Somewhere a piano is getting the life pounded right out of it, as a motley choir

223

butchers the better qualities of an old song. In every street there's clouds of dust. Everywhere there's constant movement. Wild carriages rocket past me carrying former servants now dressed grand: women with their pipes and painted faces; men with drunken exuberance singing Californian songs.

I swear this place is nothing but a dream. I tell myself I'm bound to wake up, any minute, in the clammy dark of the bark hut by the Huon with nothing but the sound of Jimmy snoring and nothing ahead but another day of splitting. I can't fathom this place, and I'm not sure I can trust the thing I feel. I barely dare to say it. Where's Jimmy when I need him? He'd kick me up the arse to get me out of my head. I know that much. Imagine what he'd make of this. What would this place make of him? If there's anywhere to undo the island's worst, it's surely here. Made new. Made free. Made equal. There, I've said it. There's no denying the feeling of it. This town is like no other.

I plunge into a criminal den that's otherwise known as a shop. Every store clerk is eager for the little money I have. I've never known the likes of it. A craggy-faced character, in a suit, is peppering me with "yes, sir" and "no, sir" as though I'm Lord High Muck himself.

"You'll soon be one of the New Aristocracy."

I've no idea what he means by that, though I like the ring of it. It suits me just fine. I feel pride ripple through me, and I straighten up a bit to fit my new status.

"Better to buy here than at the over-priced stores at the diggings, sir."

He wins me over with his unending praise, and general tone of concern for my well-being, and so he soon claims a generous portion of my money.

I emerge dressed in the full digger manner in a bright flannel shirt, a pair of moleskins, and a shiny buckled-belt. I've decent brogues on my feet and a cabbage-tree hat on my head. My bag is full of spare clothes for the months ahead. I still need food and tools and the means for getting there but that's for tomorrow. Tonight I'll have another drink, celebrate my new aristocratic nature, and savour this new beginning. Tomorrow I'll start my journey to my fortune.

CHAPTER 32

I have everything I need in a long canvas bag slung against my back. There's a shovel and a short-handled pick hanging off a rope by my side. I've no set plan for getting to the diggings. The carters' fees are too expensive and there's no great guarantee they will get to the fields any sooner. They say the northern roads are barely passable in places.

I just start walking, like most others, through the town and up the long stretch of Elizabeth Street. I'm used to walking. I have the leathery soles to prove it. Most times, on the island, it was a heavy walk from one dismal prospect to the next. There's nowhere there not riddled with the poison of the system. But today my stride isn't heavy at all. I could walk from furthest south to furthest north and feel nothing but contentment. I swear the air I breathe tastes bright as sunlight. For the first time in my life, I'm bound for somewhere that offers a genuine promise.

I'm told Flemington Road is the way to glory. An old Hobartian advised, over drinks last night, that I make sure I take that road and not the other. He told me Sydney Road is a trip back to hell. There are convicts up that way, penned in prison wagons, at a place called Pentridge Stockade. He told me you can see the sorry lot of them on the roadwork up there. The same sight as from Hobart to Launceston: just another colony making progress on the back of slaves. They say this is a freer place but there's no getting away from that old savage song: the blistered swing and ring of picks with no concern for gold. We've known enough of that misery haven't we – we need see no more of it.

He said it with such worn-down melancholy I couldn't find a reply. The miseries we've known. God help us all. Even saying it brings it back, and anger soon comes nipping at its heels. My mind gets rocking with the thought of all the things I might have said and all that unspent anger that's aching in my fists. But it's always a swing and a miss when the enemies are ghosts.

I wanted to be away from all that trouble. I wanted Bass Strait to be the knife that cut the cord to it. But with a few words from the old man, it all came back as though I'd not made the crossing at all. I steadied myself, and bought another round, and we quietly sank our drinks in hope of banishing the devil from our thoughts. It was worth a try at least. The old lag just sank deeper as the night wore on. I almost went down with him, but managed to get away. I walked awhile, just to try and shake it out of me, then slept down on the riverbank and woke at dawn.

There's a well-seasoned wind, coming from somewhere ahead, that sets my guts churning. Someone says there's boil-down places on the nearby Saltwater River. All that stink for the tallow for the candles and the soap. The smell brings me home to Belfast, at low tide, and the noxious bite of the old Blackstaff Nuisance. The smell of home, enough to make a man gag. I smile at the ugly, tender thought of it and imagine telling Jimmy for a laugh.

There's no way beyond this miasma than to plough right through it, so I press on alongside others who have taken on a jaundiced complexion. Some hale and hearty type spouts that it's a minor test on our path to fortune and that it's not much worse than the stinking mounds of rubbish on Flinders Street and down on the Yarra banks. The glories ahead trump the discomforts of the present.

The man means well by it, I'm sure, but his words do little but stir up aggravation in a mob where most have sore heads from a raucous night in Melbourne and trembling bellies from the stink that's all around us.

"We've no need for preaching on this road! There's enough of that nonsense back in the town!"

There's a general swell of murmured agreement on that point and the man now seems embarrassed that he spoke. We are all folded into silence then, alone with our thoughts and general aches and with no sound but the grind of our boots on gravel.

There are all kinds, all about me: bushmen and government clerks, sailors who abandoned their ships in Port Phillip, and merchants hungry for faster wealth. Every kind of man who can be imagined is committed to this adventure.

Some young lads are laying it on thick. They've dusted up their faces to look the part of hard men, tried and true, real diggers, the genuine article. They're boisterous but betrayed by their uncalloused hands. I laugh, when they side up to me, and I wish them luck. They don't know the half of what's ahead but nor do I. We are all trudging towards the unknown.

Bullock drivers regularly roll past. The drays are piled high with supplies for the diggings. The grizzled drivers curse their plodding teams. They curse and swear with every jolt caused by the treacherous ruts and bulging roots along this road that's really more a bush track. The sound of their long whips crack the quiet air. A man beside me flinches at the sound. He spits as though it's poison in his mouth. He meets my eyes. I catch sight of the cut he hides. I give him a grim smile and nod: the silent trade of the scarred brotherhood.

"The diggings is hard work. Most think they're in for an easy ride. I'll tell you now, they'll be back in Melbourne before the month is over."

The man beside me sounds friendly enough but it's not always easy to tell. There's plenty who seem friendly enough but they're just looking for a score, ready with a quick flash of blade to the throat when you least expect it, or just plain cracked in their chattering head and with an appetite for trouble. This one has a dark complexion that's more than dirt and sunburn. He has the colonial drawl, and an easy manner walking on the land like he belongs here.

He looks me up and down with one eye squinting and the other one wide open.

"I reckon you know hard labour, though."

I nod and figure he has me labelled a Vandemonian and probably with a cartload of judgement to boot. I can't say from the look of him, though, that he's got any claim to be above me. Maybe he's just friendly. I take the measure of him just in case. He's taller than me, has a barrel chest and thick arms, and I figure he'd have speed if he put his mind to it. It would be better striking friendly terms with him, even if he's a schemer, and see what comes of it.

"Are you familiar with Victoria?"

He smiles at the question as though I've asked him something bigger than I have. He looks out towards the horizon, like he's gathering something in, then he turns his gaze back to me. There's a decision planted somewhere in that look. He pauses a while longer before he speaks.

"I was in Geelong when they were making a fuss about Ballarat not that long ago."

He gives me another hard glance before he goes on.

"The big towns make most noise about the diggings that are nearest to them. Did you know that? If there's a strike nearby, then there will be a crowd and if there's a crowd then there are sales to be made and if there's sales ..."

"Then the shopkeepers are happy."

He grins and tells me I've got it in a nutshell.

"So have you been to the diggings then?"

"Yeah, I went and had a look around Ballarat. I figured it was better to go and get equipped in Melbourne though. The cost of anything at the diggings is criminal. Anyway, by the time I was in Melbourne, all talk shifted to the prospects at Mount Alexander."

"What's it like then?"

"The diggings?"

I nod.

"You're familiar with an ant nest?"

"God knows it. I've landed in plenty and been bitten places I wouldn't want to say."

He smiles again.

"Well, that's the diggings. Men turned into ants, fast-clawing the bush to mounds of gravel, and making dirty, desperate holes. The whole country is upside down now."

"And how much trouble is there?"

"You've got a stir of ants; you know yourself there's going to be a bite or two. I've seen men near kill each other over claims and others fighting for the drunken hell of it. I've seen lifelong mateships broken up for good over one piss-poor scrap of a nugget. The diggings is naught but rocks and dust and violence and made all the worst by this never-ending drought."

"How's drought trouble?"

His forehead creases at that and he gives me a quick up and down.

"You haven't studied the business too well, have you?"

My cheeks fire up at his accusation. He has my measure, no doubt about it, but I won't give it to him save for a sheepish smile.

"I know some, and I figure I'll find out more when I get there."

He frowns, then grins, then shakes his head.

"Alright. Well you need water for the panning and the

cradling you see. When the nearby creeks dry up, and they all are now, more than half the work is carting water to your claim. I've heard a lot have cleared out from upcountry already for lack of water and the summer's heat has barely started."

"I know about the heat."

"No you don't. You see the burnt country around us? That's from summer past. I was in Melbourne when the flare-up happened. There was so much smoke you could barely draw breath in Swanston Street. It was 117 in the shade with fires the likes no one had ever seen. Then a hot northerly came blowing through and filled the sky with flames. A good quarter of the colony is turned to charcoal. And the dry has just kept on ever since. And here we are back at the start of another summer."

He pauses and looks around.

"Point is, you have to be ready to work hard for whatever fortune you make. Half the time you're battling with nature and the other half you're battling against bastards who'd steal the little fortune in your matchbox without a hesitation."

"The way you're talking, I don't know why you're on the road to it."

"I'm not saying there aren't good strikes. Of course there are. They're the stories that fill the newspapers and set the streets of Melbourne ringing. They're the ones that have people clambering onto ships to get here. It's all people want to hear about – the easy chance of a better life. They pile on their boats and come here expecting it. They haven't got a clue. They've got no understanding of the country."

"And you do?"

"I had good lessons taught me."

"About the gold?"

"About what really matters."

He's cagey, half-saying things, and I'm not too sure I like it. There's something brewing not far below his surface. I'm not sure if it's close to boiling over and I'm not looking to get scalded. But he's not unfriendly to me and he knows far more than me, so I'm not ready to shut the door on him.

"So what's the best thing done when we get there?"

"The easy surface stuff along the creek, where we're headed, will be exhausted by now. Whatever's left is waiting down below. They don't call it diggings for nothing."

"Are they having to dig deep?"

"From what I've heard it's not too bad at Mount Alexander. I've heard they're going deeper now at Ballarat. One thing I learnt from seeing what I have. There's more success working in a team: four men with three working the diggings and the other minding the tent and doing the cooking. There's some who go at the business on their own, but more is gained with a trustworthy band of mates."

He pauses and he looks me over again.

"Would you be interested in joining a team if I put one together?"

"How would the gold be portioned?"

"Equal shares to all for all that's found."

"That sounds alright."

"What's your name then?"

"Con Donnelly, and yours?"

"Adam Murphy."

He offers me his hand and we shake.

We continue across the Keilor Plains, aiming to camp at a place called Diggers Rest. It's hard-dried grass and sheep for as far as eyes can see.

"Not many years ago it was still good hunting here."

There's a hollow ache in what he says. He looks at the sheep as though they are wretched creatures. He looks at me, with a bewildered grief, and shakes his head.

I remember drinking alongside old settlers who came out in

the twenties and before. Enough drinks, then there would come the shadow stories: a worn remorse hung dark around the eyes of one; a brittle volatility in another; a trickle of angry, shame-sharp words about the war, soon building to a torrent like hot piss from a near-to-bursting bladder.

I spent my share of hours listening to all that dark reminiscing and the dry laugh that comes from brute remembering. I breathed in old men's tales and fell into that drag of loyalty, and the staggering comradeship of the bottle, and the kill-or-be-killed talk that makes men animals, and the dark gaze of old chums ready to strike at the vaguest whiff of others' scornful judgements.

But now, alongside this man, I feel a wound of forlorn brotherhood I dare not name: that boot heel grinding down on everything that's precious, that savage wound of loss and dispossession, and that hard knuckled not-forgetting in our core. Everything that matters has been stolen. I know that much. My father and his father knew that much. The sight of Adam brings it home to me again, but I can't have his measure of grief in me. There isn't room for it and there's nothing I could do to make it right anyway. If I'm to make a decent life there's nothing to do but grab the best I can.

We settle for the night at Diggers Rest. I gather kindling and larger wood. The heavenly dome is all above me. It's a different one than I knew as a boy, though the moon's a constant wherever I've been. Its light presses soft across my eyes and makes me think of you, Mamai. I don't know where you got to in my mind. Maybe I didn't want you near me when I was on the island. Of course, I know you saw it anyway. I've no control of that. You've always been the one to see it all.

It's quiet here. There's a murmur of others settling for the night around a great spread of campfires across this country. There's a kind of beauty in the sight of it. It's like stars have

233

come to settle on the dust and grass: heaven above and heaven on earth. It's not some well-polished heaven here, though. It's one that's rough and made from men like me. There's a coarse good woven through the whole of it: the pockets of laughter, the occasional moans, the shouts of over-excitement. There's good in the humour and good in the ache to get to where we want to be.

There's little to do before I go to sleep. I set a fire that flicks at the starry cross that's hanging just above us. The heat sets my cheeks glowing and brings ease to my muscles and peace to my mind. I lose myself, for a time, in the dance of those holy tongues of flame that are flicking and tossing ember trails to the sky. I watch the red sparks drift until they're folded into the dark. There's a wounding beauty in the sight of all that vanishing. It leaves me with the strangest thought. Nothing touched by glory is ever lost. It's all just folded in and held inside the dark.

I come back to myself when I hear Adam fussing about the camp. I go and add my share of flour to his. He kneads the damper mix and makes a place to bury it in the coals. I soon smell the burning wood and baking bread. I hadn't noticed my hunger until now. The beast is awake and growling in me. The billy's on the boil and mugs will soon be filled with tea to round the evening out. What more could a man need on such a night? A final pipe and a nip from my near-to-empty flask.

I'm close to falling asleep when there's a volley of gunshots. I'm up like a bolt, expecting I'd be in the middle of an attack, then Adam calls over.

"Best get used to that, Con. The mad bastards fire their guns at night just to let the world know they're ready for anything. Those couple of bangs just now are nothing compared to what you'll hear every night at the diggings."

Morning comes with heat and a cloudless sky. My bones

have an old man's creak in them after a night on a bed of leaves. I roll up my blanket and then boil up the billy. I have a skerrick of damper, from last night. It's already hard and crumbly. I shake off the ants then dip it in my tea to soften it. It's enough to get me going on the road.

I give myself a moment, sitting under the tree, listening to the quiet of the bush. I can hear a breeze in the leaves above, and other men clawing their way from sleep at the nearby camps. I see them stirring up the embers of their fires and getting ready for the day. I can smell mutton frying nearby. It sets my belly trembling for a decent serve of meat. I put the hunger aside and kick dust onto the fire and take up my bag and gear.

We're back to the grind of boots on gravel and mud. The whole of us are a strange, bedraggled army, though each is about his own advancement. We're together and alone in the adventure. It's as true for the rich who ride past, on their well-groomed horses, as the poorest man hobbling along the road. We're all hungry for our betterment and we'd march as far as hell to gain it.

Yesterday's excitement has fallen away. There's no more cries of eureka or mad chants about boundless wealth and buxom women. Those who charged ahead, thinking they could be at the diggings in a day, are now all the sorer and sorrier for it. Those who bought cheap, in Melbourne, are nervous about the state of their already-frayed brogues.

I walk with little thought. Trouble only comes when I start remembering. Tomlins appears in my head and I'm back on the island, yet again, listening to his lordship spout his nonsense and hearing that cell door slam and lock behind me. I taste violent words eager on my tongue and thoughts roll through me, like great waves, 'til my head is punch-drunk, and my heart is all thunder.

235

The past is always at me. Even here. Even now. I wish I was a man who could forget. They seem to be the lucky ones. Nothing ever sticks to them. They float along the rivers of their lives, free from too much thinking and melancholy, and nothing weighs them down. They get on well enough and the world applauds them, and rewards them, for nothing of any great account. It's that injustice that I can't abide. It sours my having any great thought of God.

I drag myself out of the clutches of all that thinking and ask Adam about the likelihood of bushrangers.

"There's some around. How can there not be with all you mob pouring in from the island?"

He laughs. I pull a prison-yard sneer and point my fingers like they are a pistol at the ready.

"Well, now you say it, Adam, you best hand over your precious items."

We laugh together as we keep walking.

"Thing is, old mate, a lot of stories are told so someone can make a profit."

I give him a quizzical look. It seems to make him happy. He's not one who minds the chance to tell a story.

"If you have a shop in Melbourne selling guns, say, or if you want old Charlie La Trobe to beef up the constabulary up this way, then stories of lawlessness are your friend. You see? So the newspapers, who get their money advertising for the shopkeepers, make a fuss about terrible atrocities in places like the Black Forest up ahead. People love to read the worst, so more papers sell, and the shopkeepers can wave the printed stories under buyers' noses as evidence the worst that can be imagined is sure to happen."

"So a few more digger-bound men buy the guns."

"You've got it. Everyone is looking for their advancement. But I doubt we'll see any trouble on the road, save for what comes from those sorry bastards who can't manage their drink, and you'll find them in every hotel in this colony and every other, as you well know."

We are walking toward hill country. There's mention of a hotel called the Bush Inn, in a place called Gisborne, somewhere ahead. I pick up pace at mention of it. Sweet Jesus, one hot lick of the good stuff and I'll be right. We walk uphill and through a gap between two hilltops and then it's steep going down again.

There's a bullocky ahead, trying to steer his team so they don't get out of hand on the heavy downhill run. He's cracking the whip like there's no tomorrow but he's already lost control. The whole team have a bulbous mad panic in their eyes. The air is ripped through with their unholy hollering and thick with dust and the smell of the torrential splatter from their fear-struck bowels.

The bullocky's voice is turning from fury to pleading, then back again, as hooves slide on the gravel and tangle, and necks twist unnaturally in their yokes. The heads of beasts yank back and buck against the wood and strapping, desperate for their own deliverance, but all their consternation is hopeless. The whole of them is now a fierce knot getting tighter as every creature pushes away from the others. Their back-and-forth sets the top-heavy dray rocking ever more wildly. It topples and starts sliding down hill. Beasts are dragged down beneath it and behind it. Some are on their knees while others hammer their heels, wherever they can, to stay upright. It's carnage with bloody, broken beasts that need be shot, the air thick with dust, the bullocky on his haunches with his face buried in his hands, and all manner of goods scattered across the road.

Men about me are quickly split according to their instincts. The men of virtue look to help. The men of vice look to profit. I stand between the two, not sure which way to go. Adam goes over to the bullocky as the thieving mob scramble across the

237

carnage collecting bags of tobacco, flour, utensils, and whatever else they can lay their hands on.

"At least offer the man some money for what you take," Adam barks but it's a hopeless cause. The thieves are quick to race off down the road.

We sit, for a time, with the bullocky as others shoot the wounded beasts. Beasts that were still in fit condition bolted for the bush as soon as they were released from their entanglement.

The old man seems more weary than sad. His face is as worn as the country: a sunburnt leather that's furrowed and knotted from a life's worth of calamities.

"Australia Felix," he says, then laughs bitterly.

He says he will wait for a Melbourne-bound carter with an empty dray.

"Those bastards will be more than happy to load up and swing back for a short haul to the diggings for a sizeable cut of the profits."

We leave the man in his dark state and keep walking to the Bush Inn. It's a full house and the publican's yelling out greetings, racking up the glasses, and bouncing around the place with delight. We buy our drinks and weave through the crowd until we find seats in a corner. The faces around are all familiar from the road.

The room is full to bursting with dusty walkers, puffing at their pipes and knocking back their drinks, and all with something to say. Some are urgent with their plans about arriving at the diggings. Others are talking about the bullocky's ill-fate and how Breakneck Hill has claimed another victim.

I feel an itch to quiet the noisy bastards who are treating the man's misfortune as a joke. The itch gets stronger with every fiery mouthful I swallow. It settles in a heavy frown, the thick-browed ruminating building up inside me, my bodhrán heart fierce at play. And I'm giving a dagger look one way and then the other, sizing up each and every obnoxious blowhard in the room, and edging myself towards the sweet lip of bloody misadventure.

Adam notices. He pats me on the back, then shakes his head at me with a certain glee in his eyes. He tells me to drink my fill, as quick I can, so we can be back on the road and at the gold before this sorry lot can move their lazy arses. And, strange as it is, I do as he says without a hesitation. The heat of the moment has no sooner come than gone.

On the road, our eyes are set on a great mound ahead called Mount Macedon. We stop and make camp on the southern edge of the notorious Black Forest. I reckon I've been in more formidable wilderness in Van Diemen's Land, plenty populated by men worse than any likely here. And, besides, this forest, from base to the top of the mount, is black by nature as well as by name. The whole is scarred and bare from the early year's fire. Now it's a forest of charcoal, forking at the sky, with just a hint of new green buds bound round some trunks. There's light spread through it in daytime and no great opportunity for criminal surprise.

Apart from that, I reckon there's plenty of easier and more profitable pickings than the likes of me and Adam. We're too rough around the edges to cop the attention of the bad boys. Their eyes are bound to wander to those top-hatted travellers with the fancy silk cravats, and best riding boots, riding atop the finest mounts in the colony. They are a mark if ever there was one. There's plenty of already-rich men, bound for the diggings, and looking to steal the poor man's share as they always do. I wish the bushrangers good luck stripping those rich bastards of everything they've got.

Adam has been talking, through the afternoon, about getting decent meat for dinner. All I can think about is finest lamb, tender to the bone, with that good tail of fat hanging off it. How I love the oily good of that fat when teeth break through the crisp outside of it and all the juice spreads on the tongue with just that hint of salt that makes it grander.

Once we made camp, Adam took his gun and wandered off. Now he's back, half an hour later, with a possum slung over his shoulder. He's busy with his knife, skinning and gutting, as I build the fire and work on the damper.

"You eaten possum?"

I look over at him and think of saying I'd rather he got us a sheep. Best not offend a man with a knife like that though. I tell him I haven't had possum, but I've had my share of wallaby. This seems to make him happy.

"This is better than mutton."

He skewers the carcass and props it over the flames. Fat starts bubbling in thick globules and drops, causing a fiery surge of popping and sparking below. The flesh soon takes on a golden-red tinge as Adam turns it, so it's well-cooked on both sides. The smell of the meat and baking damper is as good as a banquet to me. I share a drink with Adam as we wait.

Beyond the fire is a land of shadows and murmurings. Mount Macedon, and the hills around, are silhouettes pressed against the sky. The firelight has turned the nearest bush into a bowl of light that flickers around us. We sit at the centre of it all and I feel the wonder of last night come back to me. It's there until my belly calls me back to order. I tear meat off the bone with my teeth and mop the drippings with the damper. I eat quick and my belly is soon full. A quiet ease takes hold of me. It has me stretch out and stare up at the stars. I look up there and I'm as content as I have ever been, held between the solid earth and all that endless sky.

Adam interrupts my reverie and says it's another day and night and then we will be at the diggings. I don't reply. It's as though I suddenly don't care. I just keep staring up to meet the stars, feeling strangely close to all that I thought lost and forgotten. I stay that way until I fall asleep.

CHAPTER 33

I have seen all manner of worlds in my twenty-six years: the joy and fury of Belfast; the savage prisons built for English law; the endless ocean with its beauty and dark, dread moods; the cruel system made to make men beasts to serve the island colony. All those sordid worlds dance to the same old tune: the rich get ever richer; the poor stay poor. And all the rest of high-colonial living, all its civilised ways and manners and law-making, are made to keep the order just as it is, so my kind have little to no chance for advancement.

But this promised land before me now, standing at the edge of Forest Creek, is of some other order. It's as though a great army of sweating, shirtless men are digging to make a different world. There's no coercion in it. There's no overseer. There's no push to slavishly perform for some meagre wage. There's no working to another man's measure and no laws that bind a servant to their masters. There's just men digging to find their own fortune, working out their best way as they do it, singing independence through the swing and strike of picks and shovels.

I look up and down the valley, as we make our way into the thick of it, and it's the same bustle as far as I can see. Some men are in holes, up to their waists, while others are no more than half-buried voices calling up to mates. They haul buckets of gravel out of narrow holes as a parade of staggering boys cart in the water. Others rock their cradles on the dried veins of creek beds and pause just long enough so their puffed red eyes can strain to spy some promise in the silt.

I want to hear a eureka cry. I want to see the promise made real. Nothing greets me save for the creak of cradles and

242

wheelbarrows, the ring of picks striking rocks, the holler of curses, the constant buzz of flies, and the eruption of dogs fighting over mounds of offal beside the butcher tents.

Most of the town is spread along a ridge line above the diggings. Gaudy shop signs add colour to the rows of canvas and bark tents and the many fires of campsites. The shops promise a cornucopia of all that's practical and luxurious. One offers the finest lemonade made in all the world. Many advertise they are ready to buy gold for the best price found on the fields. There are tents selling spades and picks. Some offer a meal of stew and fine bread. There are medicinal tents ready to deal with all manner of ailments, places to buy the latest newspapers, pick up mail, and secure a seat on coaches to the major towns down south.

Adam is walking beside me and taking in everything with cool eyes. I know there's judgement going on in there. The slight knot of his eyebrows hints it's not all for the best. It's no sure thing that he will share what he thinks with me. Everything he says and does is to a measure, and the views he does come out with are sometimes hard to fathom.

There is a lad with us called Jeremiah. Adam offered him a place in our team yesterday. We had no discussion of it beforehand. It made little sense to me that we should give shares to a skerrick of a boy with no meat on his bones. Besides, we had barely got to know him. I said as much to Adam and all I got was a bark that the decision was made, the boy was trustworthy, and there's no one thing more valuable than that. I said his quick appraisal of the child's moral standing was nothing short of naïve. Sure, there's thieves in every town who are nothing but skin and bones but with the face of angels. Adam gave up talking about the matter after that. We walked a number of miles, with no word said between us, with the boy following in our wake.

Today Jeremiah is full of more wonder than me. I can't help but warm to him on account of it.

"Have you ever seen such a thing, Con?"

His eyes are darting from one end of the valley to the other. His mouth is hanging open, in astonishment, despite the flies.

"Can't say I have."

"We'll be rich by this time next year."

"Sure."

"Are you ready to get rich, Adam?"

Adam's face tightens in dark disgruntlement, and I feel even warmer for the boy.

"I'm ready to find a place, stake a claim, and get to work lad. I expect as much from all of us. Wealth can look after itself."

The boy pulls a face at Adam's gruff words, and passes a look at me as if to say, "What a cranky bastard". I laugh and slap the boy on the back. I think he's won me over. We keep walking until we find a place to make our camp.

There are some men nearby, who are clearly trying to take our measure and decide if we are trouble. My friendly greeting doesn't seem to resolve the matter. They give each other a glance then keep on staring. Their distrust jars like ill-struck fiddle strings. I can feel my meagre measure of friendliness quickly shrivel to a hard stone. The beady twitching look of them invites calls for retaliation. I feel the itch but, instead, decide we need more flour.

I take a billycan and make my way to a nearby tent that has "shop" tar-painted across its side. There's two men before me in the line. They seem risen straight from the dirty bowels of the earth. Their woolly heads and clothing are full of dust. Their faces are grime-streaked with dirt and sweat. The shopkeeper seems a bastion of cleanliness in comparison. He is a portly type with a full moustache atop a pair of thick lips. He takes us all in with his gaze. It's not unfriendly but hardly warm. He's here to make his fortune the same as everyone.

The front man asks for flour. The shopkeeper scoops from a bag, fills the man's can, payment is made, and off the customer goes.

The next man nods at the shopkeeper who's now broken into a smile, as though he and the man in front are two good mates united at long last.

"I'll have your better-quality flour," the customer says.

The shopkeeper nods as though this is the wisest choice that could be made. He scoops from the same bag as he did the last customer and gives the man the same-sized portion. The man then hands over additional payment without a hesitation.

I look on bewildered and wait for the argument that will surely come.

"Now best we celebrate your wise purchase," says the shopkeeper.

He then pulls up a bottle and two glasses from under his table. The glasses are no sooner poured than the liquor's tossed down the throats of the two men. Both bottle and glasses are then whipped back out of view. The shopkeeper gives the man a wink as he takes his tin of flour and departs.

I step up to be served next.

"I like the look of that man's flour."

He gives me the same grin and we then proceed with the exchange and a quick-fire celebration at its conclusion. I come away from the shop with my tin of flour and a general sense of warm ease about this new world. There will be gold and there will be drink, and what more could a man want?

It hasn't taken long to set up the camp. It's a generous enough arrangement under canvas, slung over supporting branches, and pegged to the ground. There's room for all of us to sleep, and keep our possessions as safe as we can, with nearby space for a cooking fire and a scattering of tree stumps that we can sit on. The name is Forest Creek but a great amount of wood has been felled for campfires.

It's hard to imagine what this country once was.

Jeremiah has come back from fetching water for the billy tea. He has a bucket in one hand and a pamphlet in the other.

"Have you seen this?"

He hands the pamphlet to Adam and says there's more planted on the trees all about. I take a seat and ask Adam if he could read it out. He holds the paper a fair way from his eyes and squints.

"Fellow Diggers! The intelligence has just arrived of the resolution of the Government to double the Licence Fee. Will you tamely submit to the imposition, or assert your rights as men? You are called upon to pay a tax originated and concocted by the most heartless selfishness, a tax imposed by Legislators for the purpose of detaining you in their workshops, in their stableyards, and by their flocks and herds.

They would increase this sevenfold, but they are afraid! Fie upon such pusillanimity! And shame upon the men, who, to save a few paltry pounds for their own pockets, would tax the poor man's hands! It will be in vain for one or two individuals to tell the Commissioner, or his emissaries, that they have been unsuccessful, and that they cannot pay the licence fee. But remember, that union is strength, that though a single twig may be bent or broken, a bundle tied together yields not nor breaks.

Ye are Britons! Will you submit to oppression or injustice? Meet – Agitate – Be unanimous – and if there is justice in the land, they will, they must abolish the imposition. We meet at the shepherd's hut at four. Fie upon pusillanimity!"

Jeremiah has his eyebrows raised hearing it.

"Sounds serious."

I put aside my annoyance at the stupidity of being called a Briton and ask Adam if he had paid a licence fee. He looks at me

246

and scowls and tells me I would have known about it if he did. I'm too tired to be bothered with an argument. Besides, he seems more annoyed by the news in the pamphlet than anything I've said. It's as though it's taken him by surprise. That's a worry. I thought he knew all there was that needed to be known. It's no small part of why I agreed to work with him.

"Well, what can you tell us about this business?"

He frowns before he says a thing.

"It's thirty shillings a month already, for each one of us, before we swing a pick to break the earth. Thirty shillings a month whether we strike gold or not. Now that pompous bag of wind, La Trobe, is looking to double it come next year. Three pounds a month! And meanwhile, those bastard squatters pay ten pound a year to own half the bloody country and have the right, on account of all that land they grabbed, to vote in those politicians who will have no concern but for doing their masters' bidding."

Men start moving, down the valley, now that four o'clock approaches. Gunshots are fired to signal the time is near. Our camp is organised well enough. We can leave it and come back later. Jeremiah has drawn the short straw so he's staying behind to guard the tent. We had chance to stake our claim, in the early afternoon, though we barely scratched the surface. We've vowed we will get serious tomorrow and keep at it until we strike something.

There's a torrent of woolly-faced diggers, all achatter, bristling with excitement about the meeting and news of who's struck lucky and who has pulled up stakes. Many have an appetite for political talk and have concern for a great deal more than the increased digger's tax of old Charlie Joe La Trobe. A number are animated about a better future where every man will have a vote, regardless of owning land or not. There's talk elections should be held by secret ballots so there might be no coercion. There's even talk of paying the elected so the poor might have a chance to gain seats in government and have an equal voice in making laws. The air is full of these Chartist notions and talk of Frenchmen who call themselves socialists and preach a society of complete equality.

My head is fit to bursting with the agitation of views that are flying through the air all around me. There's even a few bombastic Americans with plenty to say about gaining independence from the tyranny of a wretched old empire's unjust taxes. The way they talk, all full of noisy swagger, a man might think they fought alongside old George Washington.

The one word that ripples through all the talk, in every direction, is democracy. True democracy. Everyman's democracy. And there's a ripple of certitude in the air that we are on the road to make it true in this land.

I can hear a band approaching from some distance. The thump of drum and cacophony of horns sends a further current of excitement through the crowd. There's cheers go up for no clear reason and a few more gunshots fired into the air.

I peer through the thick of bodies as the general shuffle comes to a halt. I can see a hilltop where there's a dray positioned. It's bedecked with flags as though for a county fair. There's a man atop the dray. Someone behind me says his name is Potts. Everyone is quiet, once they find a place to stand, as the speaker throws back his shoulders, extends his hands as though to embrace us all, and lets his voice rip out across the crowd as he addresses us as brother diggers and fellow citizens.

"I see before me some ten thousand or twelve thousand men, which any country in the world might be proud to call her sons. The very cream of Victoria, and the sinews of her strength. Now, my friends, let it be seen this day whether you intend to be slaves or Britons, whether you will basely bow down your neck to the yoke, or whether, like true men, you will support your rights."

The mention of our having rights stirs up everyone. There's hoots and hollers, and too right brother, and we need take action now, and hey let's shake La Trobe and see how well the bastard rattles.

I'm calling out, along with all the rest. I'm restless in my skin; restless to get busy and agitate. I feel the heat of it, right through my frame, charged by the sound of voices all around me, all united like the thunder of mighty cannons, and my heart's thumping with urgency and the air that's charged with a fierce belonging and a powerful brotherhood and the feeling we're ready to do anything to gain this greater freedom.

Someone in the crowd yells out "tiocfaidh ár lá" and there's enough Irish here to join that chant because maybe this is the time when our day will finally come. Maybe this is it now: enough numbers to force a just reckoning. Bold and bloody true now. Our day. Our freedom. Our chance to plant a claim, that can't be stolen from us, and make a better life.

Everything, all around, is like a good night in Belfast, but with grander ideas that might have a chance of sticking. I'm ready to march back to Melbourne right now if need be and ready for revolution if it comes to that. Everyone around is charged the same, and it takes a mighty effort just to settle so we can hear the speaker.

"The Herald describes us as a set of cutthroats and scoundrels; from that journal little else could be expected."

There's a loud chorus of booing all around at the Melbourne paper's wretched judgement of us.

"I defy the world to produce the same honesty among the same number as at Forest Creek. Is there anyone who locks their door?"

Now the booing has turned to laughter and calls of no fear.

"When I retire to rest, the last enquiry I make of those in the tent is whether they have put the skewer in the blanket. Men go to work, leaving thousands of pounds in their boxes, without lock or guard, and nothing but a bit of calico between that and a robber, that is, if there is any. Do not fathers bring their daughters among us, husbands their wives and children, and where has there been a single case of one being insulted?"

A man besides me murmurs Potts is gilding the lily on this point as, only this morning he'd been robbed and it's hardly a rare occurrence.

"We are willing to pay a little, but skinned alive we will not be! The Home Government do not require, nor do they possess the power to enforce, unjust taxation. It was such taxation that lost Great Britain, America. I hope, brother diggers, as a Briton, such unjust taxation will not be the cause of separating these splendid Colonies from the Mother Country. But mind, if from any misgovernment, the feelings and affections we at present possess as Britons are torn asunder by Government misrule, and fifty thousand British hearts are estranged by misrule – then, and then only, must violence be talked of. There are few here who would advocate separation; few who do not love the Country of their adoption; few who do not feel themselves free! And none, I trust, who will be slaves!"

I lift on the great wave of cheering, regardless of the nonsense about being called Britons. To hell with Britain, but ever onwards with the voice and force of freedom. And bring on separation too, as far as I'm concerned. Bring on independence for every man and for all these colonies. I'm all aglow with the power of the sentiment, but I notice Adam is unmoved in the raucous crowd. He is standing there as though all the commotion doesn't touch him at all. His eyes are on a group of natives watching from a hill beyond.

I catch my feelings ebbing, so I turn away from Adam and back to the dray. There's a further speaker, after Potts, who is

250

rallying against the Melbourne paper, and how it described the diggers as the scum of Van Diemen's Land, and the crowd cheers the speaker on enthusiastically. A man beside me yells, "Let them call us scum – we'll soon be richer than all those sons of bitches put together." Then the general noise mounts up to a roar when an older man, named Captain John Harrison, is up to speak. Someone tells him to put on his hat but the Captain says he'll keep it off in honour of the patriots before him. He has an energy about him, despite his grey mangled beard and worn features, and seems well-accustomed to being in front of a crowd.

"There is now a surplus of thirteen thousand pounds, which has been screwed out of the sinews of the gold-diggers, and what is to be done with it? They say it's for the Queen. Has the Queen not enough, or does she want it to buy pinafores for the children? They will tell you her salary is small. I wish to God I had one twentieth for mine! I called a meeting at Bendigo Creek the other day, and all came except the tent-keepers, to a man, and it was unanimously carried that we would not present a humble petition to withdraw the tax, but, like free and independent men, we decided that we would publish to the world, by every means in our power, our determination not to pay the tax!"

There's another roar from the crowd and the old man is pleased with his reception. The meeting goes on with the finest speakers I have ever heard, all men of learning. Through their words I feel myself made citizen and patriot, a man deserving a vote, a man deserving equality and the just protection of the law and a fair hearing in all matters. All shame and derision about my past and the past of my brother diggers, all thoughts of the inescapable boot heel of the wealthy classes applied to our necks, all the vilest judgements of the enemy newspapers, is burnt to nothing in the fire of this moment and the well-reasoned passion of these men.

I make no apologies for my tears. They are the tears of a saved man, for this is as close a thing to salvation as I've ever known. And I am not alone in this sentiment. I see hard men, all about, deeply moved as I am. How could they not be? Here is the power and resolution that might truly change the world, and each of us can feel our part in it. The world will become our world, our claim as strong and true as any other, and we will make this land the workers' paradise.

CHAPTER 34

Days pass, but the coals of the monster meeting still glow hot in me. I feel the chorus of those voices. It's like a song I can't shake from my ears. I've never heard words strong enough to burn the wrong out of this world. I'd never imagined such things could be said by working men like me. This notion of a better world has gnawed me into a sweet ache, and I can't be rid of it. I couldn't sleep last night on account of how close it feels. A better world: imagine such a thing. The only thing I fear is that the heat will lessen among all the men, and the moment will pass, and this world will go on as it has always been. I can't bear the thought of that loss.

I rouse myself, before the sun is up, and come out to the fire. Jeremiah is busy. He grunts a greeting at me, then takes my metal dish and loads it up with carved-off mutton and a hunk of damper. It's hardly finest lamb, but it will do. The boy has boiled the billy. He fills my cup with tea. It's hot and burns my tongue. I set it beside me, on the ground, as I take a seat on a stump. I gnaw the gristly meat, sip the tea, and feel relief in the cool night breeze that's still around enough to lick my face. That consolation won't be around for long. Once the sun is up there will be nothing but sweat and burnt skin and backache.

I finish eating and join Adam. We pile what we need into a barrow that we bought, along with a cradle, for too much money at one of the larger shops. We set out down the hill to our claim while Jeremiah stays as tent-keeper: gathering provisions and safeguarding our camp. It's the same routine at campsites all around. There's the murmur of arrangements for the day ahead, the gathering of tools, a joke of wealth that's sure to come today, the dusty trudge to the claims that are spread right through the valley.

I raise my pick then strike the dry earth. Up and down it

253

swings. Around and down my body goes. Weight raised to meet the claim of gravity: the steady ring of blade to rock; the steady fall of clods about my feet. Once I start, I am nothing but a moving thing. No thought. No imagining. Nothing but the doing and the scoured-out freedom beyond the grip of thinking. This has been my life, and will always be my life, to do a thing repeatedly: flax pressed firm to mill blades; strike of axe to timber; push and pull of pit saw; dig and toss of shovel. My knowledge is the callouses of my hands. My memories are knots, hard as beads, strung along my muscles.

I see plenty, at the diggings, whose soft bodies tell a different story. Anywhere else they would be the better off, but here is a different order. We work on, while their first swagger turns to blisters and exasperation. We keep steady, dusty men attacking the dusty earth, while their restlessness sours to melancholy.

Adam was right. Their kind don't stay long. They soon retreat to their Melbourne offices, their straight-columned book-keeping jobs, their regular wages, their titled positions, and their comfortable enough lives. Their kind are poor for not being poor like us. They don't have the hunger in them. There's no greater force behind the swing than that old ravenous beast. A man who knows starving will walk one side of the earth to the other, with his arse sticking out his trousers and his brogues worn down to nothing, and he will break his back with every ounce of effort to gain himself a meal. But their kind have clean options. Their spirits are made weaker by it, and their lives are made duller for it.

Adam is hauling water from further up the valley. I shovel earth into the hopper at the top of our cradle. Adam returns and cups water into the contraption. Just enough to get a flow without flooding the good out the bottom. I start the rocking as Adam keeps a slow and steady pour. I stop long enough to look for colour in the slurry as it's agitated through the sieve and down the slopes inside the box. The great hope is to see a nugget in the coarsest rocks trapped in the punctured tin mesh at the top.

My imagination stirs and is soon full of great gold nuggets, and glorious seams that are just a strike away. But what works through the cradle is mostly sand and grit, the wiggled-down slurry trailing down the cradle boards, and heavy dull sediment left behind the trap bars.

After time the heavy stuff is rinsed into the wash-pan for the final act. The decision of who works the pan is no easy matter between us. Adam claims to have the hand for it, but there's too much anger in him to bring a subtle hand to the business, and it's a subtle hand that's needed for the smaller grains. The man's sloshing about like a mad thing, and all I can see is hours of work and back-break wasted.

"You're tossing the lot out without a thought."

He gives me a cold stare.

"Do you think you're better than me?"

Only an hour ago I heard two partners, at a nearby claim, at each other with knives out. I'm sure there would have been murder if one hadn't stormed off to get drunk. There will likely be more trouble between them tonight.

I don't want that with Adam, and not just because he's bigger than me. I like the moody bastard. He roughly knows what he's doing here in all things but the pan. I decide to play the diplomat, for now at least, and see what comes of it.

"I think you're a man of commendable vigour, and probably best made for vigorous work."

He keeps at his cold gaze, for a few beats longer, then breaks into a wry smile. It's a look that could still see a man turn one way or another. There could be a hearty backslap or a savage knock from it. That's an uncertainty I've known all my life. I hope for the best with Adam, but I'm always ready for the worst. Humour's the hand that makes a moment right.

"Let's see how delicate a Belfast boy can be then," he says as he grabs the pick, jumps into our hole, and starts swinging like there's no tomorrow.

I start the gentle swirl of water and sediment, tilted just right, so the lighter dirt washes over the side and leaves the heavy behind. There are a few golden glints in the sandy bottom. Nothing extraordinary. The sort of gold collected on the tip of a thumb, then rubbed into a matchbox. There's enough to stir a murmur of hope that something greater might come. It has to come. If this is as good as it will ever be, then it won't cover the cost of our provisions, let alone make us wealthy men.

***

It's quiet through the valley before the evening meal. The air is laced with the smell of cooking. Sometimes there's the piss-sharp smell of frying liver. Each tent has a bucket of water for washing. It's a splash across the face and through the hair, to get the worst of the dust off, then another splash under the arms and down below to wash away the sweat and filth from cock and arse and all the rest. The final act is trying to tame mad hair into something close to civilised.

They call it an Irish Wash, as though other nations' washing is any better. God knows I've never met an English boy I couldn't smell a mile off. It's a known fact the English shriek like terrified pigs at sight of a bathtub. I roll that one out to anyone who'll listen. Have you not noticed they get jittery at the merest mention of soap? Adam laughs, and that's enough to keep me going.

"I have a view, Adam, I'd gladly put money on, that's how they conquered the world. Saxon Stench. One whiff of those bastards and whole nations are knocked to the ground. And before you're back to your senses, you've been invaded and subjugated by force of little more than their potent odour."

Jeremiah, who's a good lad and well-enough smelling despite his native origins, has an interest in what happened at the claim while he was busy guarding our tent all day. I show him the contents of the matchbox. He twists his mouth in a slightly-bitter smirk and crooks his eyebrows at the meagre sight of a couple of small golden grains.

"Is that it?"

"It's a start, lad."

He shakes his head at me, then says it's time to eat. It's mutton and damper again. I pray to God the colony's sheep keep breeding, otherwise there will be a riot across the goldfields.

We each take our evening share and settle around the fire. There's nothing but teeth ripping into the flesh of once-woolly beasts. A youthful belch from Jeremiah sets the tone. Talk only comes when the worst of the hunger is sated. It's slow at first, murmurs and grunts, and then it picks up when the valley stirs with a broader socialising.

The Welsh, across the way, start singing once they've finished their meal. It laces a gentle note through this rough world and sets minds drifting to other places. The soft of it makes me think of Mamai. She could hold a tune. I drop my eyes, so no one sees the feeling that creeps over me. All these years, and the ache still catches at my heel.

Adam grunts at the sound as though it's a nuisance.

"Those bastards might sing like birds, but they tunnel like dirty rats. We need make sure we never take a claim beside them. I heard they will hook underneath you and steal the gold beneath your feet before you're deep enough to know it. Don't bother me with your talk of diggers being a brotherhood with common cause. For all that grand brotherly ballyhoo, you need not dig too deep to know it's each to his own in this place."

257

He's having a go at me. I think I'm starting to like him less, but I won't be goaded by him. Not yet, at least.

"There will always be bad ones, no matter where you go or who you're with. It doesn't mean the overall good of others, put together, doesn't hold true."

"There's only one common cause here, Con, and it isn't about some new fairer world."

"Sounds like you didn't hear a word said yesterday."

"Sure I heard all them words. I would have thought you'd know, as well as me, that words don't amount to anything. The world don't change that easy. If it did, it'd be better already."

"Yesterday was different."

He grins at that, gets up, and walks off into the dark. I look across at Jeremiah.

"No point asking me, Con. I wasn't there, was I?"

I can't just sit here after that. I won't go after Adam. I know that would just end with a brawl and the end of our agreement. I decide it's better to go the other way. I pass a camp of boisterous Americans. I think most came from California but some from other places. They've grand opinions about most things, including the best techniques for the diggings.

They're a most peculiar tribe. It seems they rarely leave any thought unsaid. It's like they're still fighting their revolution and forever needing to spout their declarations.

They are not as serious as the Germans, though. Those heavy-browed boys are always mumbling about their work. They bark among themselves in a god-bothered, Prod manner that's squeezed of any joy. Unlike the Americans, though, the Germans seem to have solid knowledge of what they are talking about. Yet, for all their talk of mining, their greatest claim to expertise is making beer. I heard one claim, with a strangled kind of laugh, that the colony's beer was nothing but old dishwater and with a potency the same.

The Italians are the strangest of all. They are so fierce-full of energy I wonder how their skin hangs on. Mother of Jesus, how their words come flying out their mouths, and their hands go flying about in the most extravagant manner, and their faces turn red, with what seems a murderous rage, but next minute they're doubled-up with laughter. They are like jumpy wild beasts, and you can't help laughing along with them even though, most times, you don't have a clue what the joke is about. Chances are it's probably about yourself.

I talk to men who have come from back home whenever I can. Any scrap of news means something to me. Most stories are about the famine. It still has a bony grip on the throats of the poor. I've heard Belfast weathered the storm alright. Better than those in the country anyway. They've started shipping girls out here to lessen the crowds in the workhouses. People are leaving anyway they can. Most cross to America. The lucky ones get across alive.

The men get a look about them when they talk of what they've seen. They stare into the dark and see the dead mixed in with the living. They look down at their food as though it makes no sense: a full pannikin of betrayal in their hands. The skin-and-bone whisper of the dying is still in their ears. Some are so lost I'm sure they will soon be dead.

I talked to one man who broke down in tears. Back home he had gone out searching for any food. Not a bird in the sky. Not a beast in the fields. Even the rotten pratties had been eaten. There was nothing to be had but nettles and no taste in his mouth but the bitter shame of not providing for his family. By the time he got back home, himself no more than rags and bone, he found his wife and children clustered on the ground together, arms about each other, cold and gone forever.

He saw them piled atop others in the paupers' grave. He had no means to give them a decent burial. The man had so much

259

sorrow I'm surprised he could live. He said he would have gladly died back home. It was his brother who dragged him here. He said it as though it was more a curse than a blessing. There's one thing I have come to know from meeting men like him. Once a man has appetite to die there's little can be done.

I've noticed some of the broke men stir a bit once they've drunk enough and have been talking for a while. Some heat comes back when they turn to telling of the treachery of the landed rich. How their vile agents ride in with the constabulary, all on well-fed horses, to cast starving families into the cold. Not one stone is left atop another to tell where the poor man's home was. There's nothing left. Nothing left at all. Cold lonely stones where a hearth was once warm for all and the air was full of laughter and the telling of stories.

CHAPTER 35

Melbourne is madder than before. There's clamour and excitement from Yarra to the Flemington toll. The bay is planted with a forest of masts. Ships have lost their crew and will not be shipping out soon. There are mounds of discarded possessions beside the river, tossed aside by those desperate to be rid of any encumbrances so they can take flight the sooner. Those things that once mattered, now tattered and trampled underfoot, make a desolate sight on the roadside.

South of the river is a crowded canvas town. It stretches as far as the eye can see. Whole families are cobbling their plans beside the campfires, craving news, and scratching at their expectations until they are bloody raw with the wanting. Everywhere is stretched taut between the dream and nightmare. Some are more tortured than others. There's little peace in the place when men stagger home, their dread of missing out curdled to drunken anger. There's no end to the shame and bruises in canvas town.

Those who come back from the goldfields with full pockets, whoop up a good time in the hotels. The more outrageous the celebration, the more the general fever grows. I was having a drink in a hotel after I arrived last night, when a man came through the door and rode right up to the bar.

"I'll have a beer!" called out the rider.

The publican took the whole thing in his stride and enquired what the horse would be drinking. There was such a cheer in the hotel, and spilling out onto the crowded street, that I thought there would be no end to the celebration.

The summer heat has broken long enough for rain to fall in a torrent. Elizabeth Street is a fair bog, down the river end, with carts sunk down to their axles. Local dogs limp about in soggy states of misery without the strength to even offer a whimper.

Tethered horses look like clay statues half-stirred into life. Weens relish becoming unrecognisable. They race about looking to pick pockets, run amok, and spatter anyone who gets in their way. Their cries and curses echo through the streets.

The general run of people take the mud in their stride with hops and jumps and splattered trouser legs. A misplaced step, off a board, can see a man shin-deep in the worst of it but if he's colony-true he will laugh it off and have a drink to celebrate. The well-to-do ladies are a different matter, though. They cluck and rustle about in their floating fortresses of petticoats. They look on this soggy, stinking world like distraught chickens threatened with an axe.

God help us all; the way they carry on, you'd think a bit of mud is the worst curse they have ever known. The maddening thing is that's probably the truth of it. The whores don't mind so much though. They yell out offers from dry doorways, anything you want and something more if you're inclined. Their finer establishments even offer a man a bath.

The air is thick with languages from places I couldn't even name. The grander shops display the latest imports from England, America, and the Continent. There's a constant clatter of beasts and carriages along the streets, and guns occasionally fire in celebration of one thing or another. This town needs no reason for conviviality. There's faces, white and black and shades between, and natives who find amusement at the pompous specimens who pass them. They mimic and mock the exaggerated manners of the whites. They walk behind them and stir the air with their pipes, in a most illustrative way, then doff their hats and curtsy to each other, then collapse in laughter at the uppity whites who inspired their performance.

I have come down to meet Jimmy. He wrote and said he would be crossing the strait with intent to arrive sometime last week. I wrote back and told him to meet at the post office at midday today, but there's no sign of him. Maybe he's caught up in some business or drunk in a ditch. There's all manner of ways a man can be lost in this town. I'm not sure what to think of him coming here. I've got my own measure of this colony. He will be looking to have an opinion, and fill the air with it, and put me in my place for good measure. I can almost sniff the grief and complication. He's bound to not like Adam. I'd put money on that. I can see them eyeballing each other, and the decent agreement that I have with Adam will be ripped asunder.

I see a girl coming through the crowd. She has a determined stride. She won't bide any nonsense. She has the mark of the famine: hollow cheeks and a bony frame; worn down to nearly nothing but all the sharper for it. She has the dress of a maid but the way she tilts her head says something more. She stops, not far from me, and looks about in puzzlement. She frowns, then speaks to a woman who is coming the other way. The woman gives a curt shake of her head as she passes. The maid gets a crooked grin at that, then her eyes wander about and brush over me without a pause. The moment causes such a lurch inside me, an ache so old and long buried I can barely put a name to it. All I want is that she might turn back to look at me again. Long enough and there might be chance of something. She doesn't look my way, though. She's quickly folded back into the crowd.

"Well, if it isn't yourself."

I'm startled by Jimmy's face looming at me. I can barely hide the annoyance of it, but I know better than to make a fuss. He'd start digging and there would be no end to it. But still, he sniffs and knows there's something wrong. He twists his mouth in a quizzical knot and squints at me.

"You look like you've seen a ghost, boy."

I shake my head at him and tell him it's just his ugly face that's knocked me. He punches me in the shoulder, then holds his palm out with his fingers wriggling.

"Well, where's my share?"

I pull at my pockets to show what I have, then ask him if he's got everything he needs.

"I do, but we're not going straight off. I've a thirst, brother."

No sooner said than we're back at it with little to say until the first round is done. He has the look of a man with news. He's savouring his moment, knowing something that I don't. I give him the pleasure. He will be out with it soon enough and, sure enough, he's launching into it before my glass is empty.

"I have news of our old friend Tomlins."

"I've been glad to have no news of that bastard."

"This is good news now. You see, no sooner were you gone than the authorities sent their boot right up his arse and sent him packing from the local magistracy. He got the full comeuppance. And I'll tell you something else. There's an almighty gratitude, down the Huon, towards us taking him to court. You know what they're saying down there? We can breathe free, at last, thanks to those Donnelly boys. I've not had to pay any rounds lately. I'll tell you that much. Almost worth more than gold and, judging by your empty pockets, I'm wondering if I should have stayed back down there."

"Maybe you should have."

He shakes his head at me.

"But it's not just that, mind. Seems the man had a habit of getting himself into debt. So you know where it landed him?"

"Come on then, get on with it."

"Insolvency court. The man's life has fallen into ruin. What do you think of that now?"

"I think it calls for another drink."

We drink well into the night in this mad town that's made for drunken revelry. Jimmy tells me there were all manner of things written in papers about our case and many of the reports were strongly in our favour. He asks me about the diggings, and I tell him what I know. He asks me what kind of man Adam is. I tell him he's a smart one but prone to strange moods sometimes.

"Can he be trusted, though?"

"I wouldn't have got in business with him if I didn't think I could trust him."

"And what's the general feeling about the place?"

"There was a monster meeting at Forest Creek, the day we got there. It was like nothing I've ever known. It made me see things differently."

"You off on one of your flights of fancy, brother?"

"Nothing of the sort. I don't know why I bother with you."

"Oh, go on now. I'm listening."

"Working men like us were talking about having political power – every one of us having a vote, but not just that. People like us being able to run to be elected and get in government and have a say about laws."

"I'll believe that when I see it."

"You don't understand. This place is different. It's not like down there. Any man can get ahead here with a lucky strike. And even if you didn't want to go to the goldfields, this town is desperate for ordinary workers."

"I'm not here for that."

"No. The point I'm saying is, there's enough real change here to change the way things happen."

He gives me the old sceptical look, and I figure any more words are wasted with him. It's always back to the same old drudgery with him – everything bright and hopeful snuffed out before there's chance to see it fly. I settle into quiet drinking while he mumbles on about God knows what. I can't be bothered listening. I think about that girl instead. She was a one that one. If Jimmy hadn't turned up, I might have followed her and found out where she lives. I might have had chance to talk to her. There's little chance of seeing her again with us off to Forest Creek tomorrow.

How soft it is to dream of birds in flight. Glory spun above again and the Lagan well below but without a stink to it. I lean back so far I swear I'm lying on the air itself, adrift over all the old world, and full to bursting with sweet wonder. I can feel a pair of fingers wove with mine. I know it's her. I turn to look. Her eyes meet mine, but it isn't me she sees. There's a restless hunger that burns so fierce in her, she's bound to turn the world to ashes with just a glance. I fear there's nothing in me that can answer it. I'm daunted and undone and lose my grip. There's nothing below but a crowded street and all hope lost in the bustle. And now it's the same old lonely fall, as though it's in my blood to always find a crack to plummet through. I'm going at a great speed and about to strike the earth and break apart when I jerk awake with my heart pounding and my head sore and nothing but the southern night above me.

Jimmy is sitting on the other side of the fire, staring at me.

"What's that about?"

"Just a bad dream."

"What about?"

"Nothing. Why aren't you asleep anyway? We've got a way to go tomorrow to get to Forest Creek."

He keeps up his staring, then squints like he's trying to see inside my head.

"There's something you're not telling me."

"Stop spouting nonsense and let me get back to sleep at least."

He doesn't say another word, but he keeps looking at me, so I turn my back on him. That girl, whoever the hell she is, has eaten so deep into me she's planted herself in my dreaming. More fool am I for it. I'll never lay eyes on her again.

266

"Why don't you tell me, brother?"

I turn back. He has the look of a wounded creature, like I've gone and cut him and left him out in the cold. Old forlorn Jimmy is the worst of all the Jimmys. God help me. I know I have to give him something. There'll be no sleep if I don't.

"It's just a girl I saw. That's all."

"Who is she then?"

"I don't know. I just saw her in the street. She was there, then gone."

"Was she one of us?"

"I don't know. Sure, I'd say so. Maybe. She had the look of the famine about her."

"But worth a second look?"

"Yeah."

"So what are we doing here then?"

"What do you mean? We're going to Forest Creek."

He's shaking his head at me as though I've come out with the most absurd idea.

"There's not much point of that is there? I mean, take a look at yourself. You'll be good for nothing until you sort this out. You'll be mooching about with your head up your arse and getting cranky by the minute as though me and everyone else is to blame for it."

"I just saw her a few seconds. That's all. There's no point even talking about it. She could be anywhere now."

"Would you know her if you saw her again?"

"I suppose I would."

"Is it suppose or you would?"

"I would, Jimmy. Alright? I would, but none of that matters."

"She's one of us, you say?"

"Most likely."

"And how many of our churches are there in Melbourne?"

"Just the one I know in Lonsdale Street."

"Well, there's your answer. That's where you'll find her on Sunday."

I look at him, this brother of mine. He's already broken into that gormless grin. How he loves claiming the wiser older brother victory over me. There's nothing I can do but smile back at him, though. He's right. Why didn't I see it?

"Seems the wiser head's prevailed yet again, little brother."

CHAPTER 36

Catholic Melbourne is pressed around St Francis Church. Some churchgoers have spilled into Lonsdale and Elizabeth Streets, with a mind to make some noise before the herded-in business of quiet kneeling and Latin praying begins. Their chatter is punctuated by the sound of teetotaller band members tuning their fiddles and warbling on their horns. It's all a bluster in search of some polished hint of glory. My head started aching when I was still a block away from it.

I look at Jimmy, but he's no help. He's adjusted himself to be the upright man, all prim and proper in his bearing, and tilting his hat just right to those he passes. I swear I could walk away right now, leave his pompous self to it and be done with it, but no sooner do I think it than my brother's hand is firm on my shoulder as though he's read my mind.

"Steady ahead, little brother. God knows it'll take a saint to make a half-decent man out of you."

We make our way into the church. It's the first I've been in one since probation days. It's not like those old station chapels though. They were little more than rough cobbled barns and good for nothing but the grace of catching a breath from the general slavery of the system.

This church stretches long, in patches of light and dark, and smells of a sweet holy fog that's hanging in the air. It claws my lungs and tickles my throat and sends me into a spasm of coughing. I'm loud enough that people turn. They shoot me with pious frowns and tut-tutting.

I stare back at them: God's holy prunes, all lined up in a row, emanating their everlasting outrage at the sundry world. I'd rather hell's good company than be thrown into a heaven that's thick with the likes of them. I've a mind to turn tail, and be gone, but Jimmy sees me eyeing off the door and he's quick to shove me into a pew.

"Do you see her then?"

I shake my head. I'm pleased she's not one of them. Better to land a kind-hearted Prod girl than one of those snarling sanctimonious creatures. A year with one of them, rubbed raw by their hard praying and scouring goodness, and there'd barely be a soul left inside me to save. I tell Jimmy that I think we've made a mistake but, as I look towards the door, I see her come in and bless herself. I watch her walk towards the front then genuflect halfway down the aisle. Straightaway she's down on her knees. There's nothing in her that's looking to be seen, though. She's tucked inside herself so deep that I feel myself lean forward to see what I can of her before she's all but disappeared.

"It's her, then, is it?"

I manage a nod. Jimmy grins, elbows me in the ribs, and shakes his head.

"Well, I'll leave you to it, boy. I'm off to see a man about a horse now."

The religion starts with standing and singing, then churns along with the priest up there, lost behind the screen, making holy out of ordinary as the people stand and kneel and murmur.

She's well-practised in the business but in a quiet way. I don't know how it is that light and heavy manage to have a home in her. The wind could near gather up her famine-skinny self and set her flying but there's a weight to that way she's praying, and it keeps her anchored firm to the ground. It's both things at once in her, and it wakes such an awful ache in me. It's fierce enough, I feel that it could end me. My heart is tenacious, here inside my chest, and my tie feels awful tight about my neck. I'm fevered at the sight of her. That's it. I'm fevered and my mind is lost to it.

What am I doing in a church setting my eyes on a girl like this one? What am I thinking, to suppose I'd have a chance with her? There's nothing of me that isn't dirt and brokenness. That's a fact as clear to me as the sight of that quiet girl down there on her knees.

All my sorry life is heavy in me now. It pushes me down to kneel despite myself. Why would I do such a mad thing, though? God doesn't speak a word to the likes of me. I've never said a prayer that found an answer. I've never seen a wrong made right by God. But, for all that, my knees are planted hard against the earth. My head is cradled like a rock between my hands. How I hate the sweet stinking nothing of a place like this: all shiny with promise and short on any true deliverance. I close my eyes to be rid of the sight of it and find my head's soon full of too much trouble.

I think the priest is all packed up and gone. I can hear people moving out of the church and that's fine with me. I'll stay where I am for now, even though my knees are throbbing something shocking. Let the pious horde all be gone so I can disappear back to what I know. I'll find Jimmy, and we'll have a drink wherever we can find one on a Sunday. There's sure to be sly grog relief in the shadows of some alley in this town. We will get ourselves well soaked, and then we'll be back on the road to the diggings. We'll strike our fortune and live it up enough to forget this heart-troubling business and all the complications of it. A man should settle for being who he is and nothing more. That's the truth of it. It's wanting more that makes it all undone. All I need do is wait my moment, bolt from this place, and put this nonsense behind me.

It's quiet now. I think everyone is gone. I open my eyes and look up. She is right there, staring straight at me, and all I feel is shame at being caught in such a foolish state on my knees like some mangy beggar.

"I haven't seen you here before."

It takes a moment to make sense of what she said. She has her eyes on me, with no judgement about it, and the worst words are out of my mouth before I can catch them.

"You wouldn't catch me dead in a church."

She smiles at that, then looks around at the surroundings.

"You could have fooled me."

She starts towards the door and I'm near tripping as I try catching up to her.

"But I've seen you before."

She turns around at that and looks me over quizzically.

"And where was that then?"

"Down near the post office the other day. Seemed like you were looking for something in the crowd. I wanted to see if I could help, but you disappeared."

She breaks into a grin, then stops herself, mindful of being in the church, scratches the back of her neck and gestures me to come outside.

I follow her out and she turns and faces me.

"You wouldn't believe the thing that I was looking for."

There's a sudden life in her, dancing about her face, and she seems a different girl than the serious one who was all wrapped up in praying. The sun threads through her hair, as though it's some fine treasure now uncovered, and I forget to breathe. She is light and good itself to me, and I've a fear my words will stumble off my tongue and ruin everything.

"Well, what was it you were after then?"

She grins again and shakes her head.

"You won't believe it."

"Try me."

She leans into me as though it's a serious secret.

"You'll think me mad."

I almost say I'm starting to think it already, but I know I'd better play it safe or else I'll spook the horses.

"Well, mad or not, I really need to know."

"I heard it read from the newspapers that somewhere, in near proximity to the post office, there's an elephant, a bear and a monkey for sale. Can you imagine it? An elephant, a bear, and a monkey. And sure, I wanted to see it. Who wouldn't want to see a thing like that?"

She looks at me as though she's taking measure of my interest. The fact I'm smiling at the idea seems good enough to her.

"But I'll tell you, the looks on people's faces when I asked them if they knew about it. More than one of them said I need be locked up. A couple said it was surely the Elephant And Castle on Little Burke that I was after. I told them it was nothing of the sort and that it was a genuine elephant I was after. The kind with a big, long snout and an awful bellow and that could trample all of them, given half a mind. Didn't they race off like I was a lunatic let loose on the streets? The sight of them with their tails between their legs. I've never known how easy it is to scare a man away. Now I know the trick, I'm sure to keep it handy."

"An elephant, a bear, and a monkey you say?"

"Sure. That's exactly it. The elephant from India, the monkey from Madagascar, and God only knows where the bear has ventured from. Where is it bears come from anyway? And the truly astounding thing is, the lot of them are right here, somewhere hereabouts in Melbourne, and for sale. Imagine a thing like that now. If you had the chance, would you not have an interest in seeing such a thing?"

"I suppose I would. So where are they kept then?"

"You tell me. I haven't a clue and nobody seems to know. It's an elephant, a bear, and a monkey for God's sake! You'd think the whole city would be buzzing about it, wouldn't you? I find it

273

strange when people don't take an interest in the peculiar in this world. With everything that's all about, the wonder of it, still people go plodding around staring at the ground and they have nothing to talk about apart from shiny rocks they're hoping to dig up from the dirt. I swear I could shake them something fierce just to get them to look up, for once in their sorry lives, and see the golden world that's already all about them."

My heart near leaps out my chest at her words, as though some old promise has wakened in me. I take a breath and play it steady though. Too much sudden feeling wouldn't help my cause with her.

"Somewhere near the post office, you say?"

"Somewhere nearby. You'd think you could smell them, wouldn't you? I mean elephants are big aren't they, and a creature like that must make a lot of dung. What do you think an elephant would smell like?"

"It would smell like something big."

"Sure it would."

"Well, should we go looking for it then?"

"Not before a proper introduction. What kind of woman do you think I am? I don't go stepping out with boys without at least knowing their name."

"Con Donnelly."

"You're a northern boy?"

"Antrim."

As soon as I say it, I can't find another word to say to her. What foolishness is this that I should be so lost? She is staring back at me with amusement creased around her eyes. She's reading me like a book and there's nothing I can do but stare back at her, while I'm trying to catch hold of some convincing thing to say.

"Well, Con Donnelly, in case you're wondering, I'm Biddy Lyons from County Clare and now resident in this strangest of all towns."

I steady myself enough to get some words out.

"Well, now we know our names, should we go and find your creatures?"

"Not my creatures, but would you imagine having an elephant? Imagine the looks if you rode an elephant up Great Bourke Street. It would put the rowdiest diggers to shame for all their shabby stabs at trying for grand revelry. Wouldn't there be some looks about the place? And, atop an elephant, you'd be above the whole town like some lord or lady, grander than the lot of them."

I can't remember laughing as much as I am. In all the world, I swear I've never met a more peculiar girl than this one. But she's peculiar in some strange right way. All manner of bright old feelings are crowding the door to come back inside me, and my face is tight from grinning like a fool.

We start walking down Elizabeth Street towards the post office.

"How long have you been here then?"

"A little more than a year. What about yourself?"

"I came in '44."

"Before the famine, then. Aren't you a lucky one? How have your family faired with it?"

"Things haven't been too bad in Belfast from what I can tell."

"I imagine not. Clare was bad. Too many lost to count."

She blesses herself, and a shadow falls across her face. She stares down and frowns, then rights herself and turns her attention back to me.

"And have you been in Melbourne all the years you've been here?"

"Most years in Van Diemen's Land."

"I'm sorry to hear it. It's no surprise, though."

"What do you mean?"

"You've got a certain worn-about-the-edges look about you, that's all. No harm in it to me. The world dishes it up some, doesn't it?"

"I suppose it does. But anyway, that business is behind me now. It's the future that matters. The past can rot in a grave as far as I'm concerned. I'm done with it."

Her eyes are on me like she's back to reading my face and looking to know the splintery quiet stuck between my words.

"And now you're at the diggings, I suppose. Have you found yourself a nugget worth the effort?"

"We've found some. Nothing big but I've a plan to get the capital to set up business as a carter. The money is better and steadier."

"A man with a plan, then. Most men in this town can't think beyond the next drink. I've little time for that. I've seen men ruined and families torn asunder by it. It's nothing but the devil's curse."

There are those eyes giving me fierce attention, and I can feel the heat up in my cheeks. I nod, as best I can, to show I understand what she is saying. I hope to God the nod I offer might be enough. The way she looks at me, I think she knows the truth, though. There's such a desperate lurch inside my guts at the thought this might be the end of it.

"What kind of money does carting bring in?"

I'm no sooner damned than brought back to salvation with her question. I feel like all my fate is caught up in each next word she says.

"Three hundred pound for a decent three tonne load delivered to the diggings."

Her eyebrows go up at that.

"That's what I'm told anyway. And more if there's one or two travellers looking to get a ride."

"You'd be on your way to buying decent land."

"I suppose I would. I haven't seen a thing here I'd bother with, though. The big-name squatters grab all they can, then there's nothing but scraps left for working men. And I've no interest making a life in a town like this one. I know that for sure. I reckon Melbourne is on the road to being like Belfast, nothing but hovels and factories and workers falling back to poverty again. I've been there once. I won't have it again. The one good thing, in all that's happened to me, is getting away from it."

"So you've not a mind for Victoria. Is there anything you've seen down on that island that's promising?"

I look at her and feel the answer pressing from inside me. But I won't say it to her, even as I feel its rightness stirring pictures in my head: the green of valleys; the promise of good earth; the smell of decent forest and good tall timber waiting for the axe. That place cannot be the answer. There is too much poison riddled through the sweet. And she's clearly not one for a man who needs the consolation of a drink when dark memories come crowding in with vengeance.

"I haven't found the right place yet."

I say it, and she knows I'm lying. I can see a puzzled look brush across her face.

"One thing the famine's taught me. Owning land makes the mightiest difference when it comes to a family living or dying."

We keep walking down the street with no hope of finding her exotic creatures. I'm still desperate to find right words, but the quiet has gained a cool grip on the proceedings. No word seems enough to make things right. I look at her, and she seems lost to me, even as she keeps walking there beside me.

FOREST CREEK – VICTORIA
DECEMBER 1851

CHAPTER 37

All the promise of this place has dried to dust. There's barely water enough for men or horses, let alone for pan and cradle. Everywhere I go, the talk is about setting off to Loddon or even heading north to New South Wales. The next place could be better. It couldn't be much worse. I've seen some men tortured by uncertainty. They're set to leave, then turn to thinking maybe there's a nugget an inch away, right here beneath their feet. They get twitchy and distracted as their earlier promise unravels, and the little that is left is now honed to a lethal blade. They start hard drinking once they are well-cut, sink deep into the sullen dark, and soon enough its holy hell raging around the camps.

I've heard the New South Wales diggings are as bleak as here but in a different way. Hard to imagine their shafts are ruined by flooding. First comes too little then comes too much: the right swing to the jawbone then the left jab to the ribs. This land is braced to fight us with extremes. Adam smiles and shakes his head when I say such things. He points at the graveyard and says seems like we came to give the land a decent feed. He looks at the scarred land and says we gave it plenty cause for growing an appetite.

Jimmy worked hard to prove his worth as soon as I brought him here. He set to swinging the pick and shovel like a demon. No sooner did he find himself a vigorous rhythm than he was cut down with the dysentery. It's one of the common plagues in this air that stinks of fly-struck offal and shit. Never mind the netting over the face. It might keep the flies from crawling up your nose and in your mouth, but it can't stop the poisonous miasma that creeps in everywhere.

When Jimmy took the fever, he looked at me like I'd dragged him into hell itself.

"You always were a bastard, little brother! Mamai's favourite little bastard boy!"

That was his mild greeting on a good day. The bad days knew no end of all his nightmares: the cut of losing home and family; the shuddering remembrance of threats and beatings copped in all the stations. I'd see the fear rise in him, at thought of those worst overseers who were always looking for cause to have us locked inside the box. I watched him wither, on his sick bed, as though he was back before their sly scrutiny and all their wicked taunting. Then he started jabbering his yes and no sirs with all the panic of a bloody, mad rabbit trapped in steel jaws. There was nothing I could do but wet his forehead and tell him he was having nothing but bad dreams. Even in his fever, he knew the feeble nonsense of what I said.

On the worst night I heard Jimmy crying for Mamai as though he was a small boy. I couldn't bear the sound of that. Not from Jimmy. I could have slapped him one just to quiet him. Sure, he was in hell. I've no doubt of it. I'm well-acquainted with the place myself. I only have to close my eyes to see it. But it wasn't me who put him there. It was bastard life that put him there, this godless bastard life. And even here, with the golden promise in the ground, it's bastard life that taunts us. Dig a hole and I'll make you sick. Find a fleck and I'll give your nearest neighbour a mighty nugget. Step forward and I'll see you fall back on your arse. Buy a horse and I'll send someone to steal it. It is bastard life would have us stay as we have always been, nothing but poor, desperate men tortured with a thirst.

Once Jimmy's fever broke he looked at me, as clear-eyed as ever he had been.

"You promise me one thing, Connie. Will you do that much?"

I was so relieved to see him well, I nodded.

"You promise me you don't go and lose that mad girl your heart's gone and given itself to."

I frowned, and he grabbed my arm as though he'd squeeze the life right out of it.

"You hear me now. At least one of us needs have a chance, and there's not a moment that your head isn't thick and addled with thought of her. It's writ all over you, boy. But I know you too well, brother. That head of yours, with all its turgid thinking, will steal a good chance right out from under you. You close the door to that girl, you close the door to any hope you've got of making a decent life here. So, get on with it and do what needs be done. Best marry her quick 'cause there's plenty a man looking."

I am at a loss. My brother might be right, but what am I to do with it? Biddy's talk of wanting good land has left me thinking of that other place. The softest parts at least. All the burnt and dry of this mainland gives me a thirst for sight of the Huon and Kermandie. The thought of those good valleys steals inside me, but then it troubles me no end.

Surely leaving there was the best thing I had ever done? I shed the skin of the lowly man they would have had me be. And haven't I got on with life, away from it? Haven't I come to see I'm made for more than waiting for the scraps to fall my way?

All the dark that clawed at Jimmy's soul, when he was sick, is still down on that island. I'm sure of it. There's no getting bad memories, like that, out of bloody soil. And all the old unfairness is probably piled all the higher now. That place is well-ordered for keeping men like me and Jimmy down. The bastard Tomlins might be gone, but who's the man to take his place? Always trouble brewing. That's for sure. Always the uppity expecting heads like mine to bow. Best I'm away from it and for good. I've not got it in me to be held down anymore.

And yet that land would bring a smile to her eyes, wouldn't it? She would look at me as though I was sure the man for her. And isn't that enough? Isn't that better than anything this miserly dry wasteland could ever offer us? Here is good enough for gold but nothing else. But down there would be a lifetime's steady work, in the forests, and land to purchase and grow a decent thing. Truth is, those old midlands land-grabbers got nowhere near the best when it comes to growing. That's the one sweet secret in the place. It's the rich dirt, wild edges that are the place for it. It's only fools who call those parts the wastelands.

I don't know what to do, so I buy a bottle from a sly-selling mate I know and slide it in my pocket. There's a man ahead of me as I walk along a track. The worn old back of his head, with a fringe of raggedy grey, causes me to drag in a sharp breath. I'm sure it can't be him. Old Crooner would surely be dead and buried by now. He was ancient when we were still locked up in Dublin. But I can hear him singing in that half-mumbled way. *Óró 'Sé do bheatha 'bhaile, Óró 'Sé do bheatha 'bhaile*. It's him alright, the mad old crooner himself, stomping along the gravel of Forest Creek.

"Michael, is that you there?"

He turns around and squints at me. His face is ravaged to cracked leather by the years. It's him, sure enough though, in all his ignominious glory, with the red-coal glimmer playing in his eyes – still a man you'd half expect has a blade at the ready somewhere in his folds. He brightens at sight of me, and straightens up a bit.

"Young Donnelly, if it isn't yourself. Have you found any gold for an old man?"

"No, I haven't."

"Well, a drink at least."

I pull out the bottle and show him.

"Good man."

"Good man yourself, Michael. I'd never have thought I'd lay eyes on you again."

"I have a way of popping up, you know."

"You do at that."

We find a place to settle on a hillside looking over all the diggings. Old Crooner groans as he plants himself on top of a fallen log.

"I'm too old for this."

"Well, I guess it's you to say it."

"And what of you then, mo chara? What news have you got for me?"

I tell him about the trouble down at Franklin and the court case. He's amazed by it and says we were heroes to see a thing like that through to the end. He says justice might get truly done sometimes but never with a generous hand when it comes to treating poor men right. I raise the bottle on that point, then pass it over. I tell him about the diggings and the men I've worked alongside and the monster meeting, with the fierce good speeches, and the way the promise of something new and better seemed thick in the air afterwards, at least for some time.

"Old King Dan would have been at home at that one."

I smile at mention of O'Connell and tell him I'd thought as much myself.

"And have you got yourself a girl? I hear they're shipping them over by the boatloads."

"I met a girl. Would you believe we wandered around Melbourne looking for an elephant?"

"An elephant?"

"She was sure she'd heard there was one for sale somewhere, and she was determined to see it."

"And did you find it?"

282

"No."

"It would have been a sight. Will you be seeing her again?"

"A girl like that could do better."

He draws back and frowns at me.

"You're not that bad, boy. I've known plenty worse."

"I mean it. I watched her praying in a church. You know, some people, you just see the bright good in them. It fair leaps out their skin. And she's a one like that, not that she'd make a show of it. I reckon she wouldn't even see it in herself. That's the type she is. Genuine good. Lost in the mad thick of it. So anyway, I wouldn't want to be the one to ruin it."

The old man draws back again as though to get a better look at me.

"How could you?"

I lift the bottle.

"She doesn't like drinking for starters."

He chuckles and scratches his head.

"Well, there's plenty who don't. But I know one thing for sure. There'd be few marriages back home if stopping the drink was a condition to the act."

I nod. It's a fair enough point, I suppose.

"And she wants land. Have you noticed that way the ones out from the famine are?"

"Sure. They'd sooner be dead than dealing with a landlord, and who can blame them?"

"I wouldn't and I don't. The thing is, I know the kind of land she'd like the best."

He raises his eyebrows and spreads his hands out.

"So, there's your answer."

"Nothing of the sort, Michael. It would mean going back down there."

"To the island?"

I nod.

"Is that such a bad thing?"

"One time in hell's enough, isn't it?"

"Hell is it?"

He stops and weighs my words with a look of grave concern.

"Don't get me wrong, boy. I know there's places down there that I'd never go to again. I guess they are as close to hell as I've known. But bad places can be avoided, can't they? Sure, we've been doing that, back home, since ancient days. We know the places that would cause us trouble if we set foot in them, so we just don't go there. It's just respecting the wisdom of a place. That's all we ever need do, and I figure it's as true for here as home. The only difference between here and home is the evil places here are fresh-made. The blood's still wet in the soil.

"But saying the whole island is hell, well I don't know about it. Did you not have any good times there? Are there not friends still down there? We need make best with the meagre bit we have, you know. And besides, no matter where you go, there's always bound to be trouble. If it isn't the lingering trouble of the past, then it's the unknown variety waiting up ahead to clout you one. It's foolish thinking there's any getting away from trouble entirely. It's how you travel through it, that's the thing that matters, buachaill."

He looks me over with such a sad look and sighs.

"I feel sorry for you young ones. You're strangers to the culture in your veins. It's not your fault, of course."

"And what of culture then, Michael? What have you got for me from all that old business?"

The old man smiles then looks down at his brogues.

"Ta bróga orm."

He points at the smile on his face.

"Ta athas orm."

He bends his face to be downcast.

"Ta bron orm."

He raises his eyebrows at me, searches my eyes for understanding, then sighs again when he sees I haven't a clue.

"It's all putting on and taking off then putting on another thing: a pair of boots, happiness, sorrow, the shirt that's on your back. You put on the thing that needs be put on now. That's how old Tuan mac Cairill, the oldest man who ever lived, survived for generations. It was his gift of putting on and taking off that meant he could endure the lot of it. First, he put on being a stag, then the king of all the wild boars, then a high-flying hawk, then a salmon, then, once he was caught and ate, he came back as a man. That one endured more living and dying and living again than any other man."

"Ah Michael, it's a fine enough story, but I've no sign of sprouting feathers or scales. We're real men. We live and then we die at the end of it all, and that's all there is to say about it."

"So, you don't believe you've had any dying in all your years of living?"

"I can't see it."

"When we were piled in that wretched boat and they pulled up anchor, did you not die?"

"I don't know what you mean."

"Don't lie to me now. I know you know what I'm saying. We all of us died, didn't we? All the life we lived and might have gone on living, on our own land, was snuffed right out of us, just like that, when that anchor came up and we knew in our hearts we were leaving. Maybe you've forgotten how heavy the grief was. I remember you sobbing on your brother's shoulder, and there's no shame in it. It was our lives ending. It was heavy enough to crush the soul in every one of us, and it did. And you can be sure, back home, we're thought of more as lost among the dead than still happy in the company of the living."

I stare at him with tears rolling down my cheeks. Every word he's said is true, and every bit of it cuts me to the core.

"But here's the thing, boy, we put on the new of being on that boat. We got our sea legs, our lungs used to the salty air, and all the rest of it. And every bit of dying and living since – through the misery of the stations and thereafter – has seen us stripped of one thing and putting on something new. And here we are today, you the dusty digger with not enough gold to line your pockets, and me older and more worn than ever. You think the boy you were, back home, would know the man you are today? He wouldn't have a clue about it. There's been too much living and dying between one and the other.

"Point is we've all got a bit of old Tuan in us. So now, you take off being that sorry man beaten by the island. There's too much life waiting to be had now. You let that girl know the land that's calling to you. I'll tell you something, when land calls to a man, it's best he doesn't ignore it. You mark my words – the girl will understand and all the things that matter will be well enough, until they're not."

We drink until it's done then Old Crooner says he has a place to get to. I watch him wander off, and I sit for a while longer before going back to camp.

I feel strange in my head looking at the place. It's as though I'm standing somewhere and looking back at a memory. It's as though something has rightly broke inside me and, somehow, it has put me somewhere else. Jimmy is tending the fire. He looks up at me, then frowns. It's strange that I'm surprised he can see me at all.

"I can see you've been working hard, little brother."

I hear him say it to me, but I haven't a clue what he means at all. I'm surprised I still have my voice when I reply.

"You'd never guess who I ran into."

His frown disappears and now he looks amused.

"Tell me then."

"Old Crooner."

Jimmy gets his crooked grin as though he's caught me out being foolish.

"How much have you drunk, Connie? Old Crooner's been dead a good five years."

CHAPTER 38

I am on the road most days, carting goods to the diggings. I make more than I ever did with the pick and cradle, but carting is nothing but a hard slog for the money. This land is not a friend and never will be. The sun burns skin to a cinder. The rain falls and turns everything to mud. The team gets flighty at the sound of wild dogs, and mist rolls in so thick it's blinding. Then chaos comes to linger around the campfire. I steel myself against it. I think of her and that we are to marry. It's all a desperate dance with my precarity.

I readily play the hardened old lag and muster the beast in me when there's a sniff of trouble from those pimply boys who prowl the country looking for an easy score. They come along, with ruddy bluster, talking as though they have the measure of me. I show those rabbits my best blade, then strike with every dark word I can muster. It's those times I'm glad the devil's in me. Those boys no sooner sniff my sulphurous side than off they fly without another word.

Old bushrangers are a different matter, though. Those ones are true brothers to me. I curse the traps with a vehemence equal to them. I offer the brothers a drink to warm them up. I have one myself, and how I'm grateful she is in Melbourne then. It's not long before the stories come out of a once-dread flog or overseer, now worse for wear thanks to a night of it. Melbourne's a place well made for back-alley justice. As one man said to me with the reverence of a priest at the altar, "Where two or three are gathered in remembrance of the system, there you will find the makings for Vandemonian retribution."

There is a strange delight in dark things shared: the company of we who know, in this world that never will. We take a drink to push aside the veil: our stories writ in hidden scars and shadows. For a time, our dark truths are unbound. There is relief in it. We rage and weep and fight to feel those wild parts, not made for pleasant company. We sound the savage song of every ugly true thing that we've known, every brittle sharp thing that we've thought, every savage cut that's left us sore. It all comes out until we're bled-to-empty and finally free to lay down in the dirt.

I think of her when I get up from my ruin, and then I am ashamed. How I want to be the man that she needs me to be, but then, there's part of me that wants beyond it. Some part settled enough, for sure, but some part forever wild. There's no away from that fierce tangle that I carry in me. I told her the truth before I bought the ring. She at least deserved fair warning. She said there's nothing in the world that isn't broken. She looked at me with fierce, tender eyes and told me I would do, and then she kissed me. And I am sore with love for her. She is my treasure, finally found, and how I fear I might be fool enough to lose her.

I feel a sweet nostalgia when I hear the excitement of those fresh off the boats. They ask me what it's like at the diggings. I indulge them with stories of nuggets bigger than a fist, a morning's work that could gain a man a mansion, and celebrations that rage for weeks in Melbourne. They will know the grimmer truths soon enough and, besides, some are so elated by my stories they buy me a drink. I sit back then and watch the whole parade: dreamers and schemers and the light-fingers quick to profit when the drunk and wearies stop paying close attention.

Publicans sometimes gesture to me through the thick of fire and pipe smoke. I smile their way and know what they want long before they say it.

"And what is it in the dray today old son? Have you something good for me?"

They know they can offer me a good price, and still turn a profit themselves, when ill-equipped new chums stumble on their doorstep with little more than the clothes on their back.

Gold-fever is a stupefying business. It's getting worse as more clamber off the boats. Most new arrivals have more ready money in their pockets on the way up than they're ever likely to make at Forrest Creek or other diggings. Those gormless boys are ripe for the picking and, as far as publicans are concerned, if new chums are going to waste it, then it might as well be wasted in their premises!

I have six good beasts for the long haul. Tommy and Chancer are my lead pair in the yoke. They're all horns and muscle, black as night, and dim-witted to boot, but they don't cause me any bother. One crack and call-out and they brace to the task and it's steady along the way then.

"My team might be an ugly mob, sure enough," I say with a laugh to anyone who's looking for a carter in Melbourne, "but they've the best feel for the country in all this colony. I'll tell you now, they just keep on and on until we're where we're meant to be."

I have taught myself the patter of a businessman. I can read the likely concerns of people before they've even spoken. I bung on the charm where it's warranted and knit my brows in grave concern to match the manner of the serious.

"I have good record for hauling the most delicate goods across the roughest territory without a chip or crack to show for it," I say to a man but it's more said for the sake of the lady on his arm. "These good old ugly boys here have muscle, you see, and they're well-practised conquering the thickest mud that winter can dish up."

290

There's those whose eyes dart about trying to take in every option. They're always in a hurry to get somewhere but often have trouble settling on a deal. I've got my message well-polished for their scatty kind.

"Now, sure, those with horses might promise you a speedy delivery. I understand the temptation to go with what they promise – I'd be tempted myself. But I have to tell you" – I drop my voice to a secretive murmur – "I see plenty of dead horses along the way. There they are, the poor creatures, with their legs broken beside upended wagons, and with worldly goods broke beyond repair. I don't have to tell you, it's not a good start for a happy home at the diggings. But still, some take the gamble and there's nothing I can do about it. But, between you and me, it's bullocks get the job done, sure and steady in the heavy country. You mark my words. I'd put my money on certain delivery, at a slightly slower pace, rather than the jittery promise of horse-brained speed."

I have my regulars in Melbourne. I don't overcharge them. They're salt of the earth and ready to put in a good word about my business. Pompous arses are another matter, though. I see them coming towards me from a mile away with their noses in the air and the wrinkle of contempt around their eyes, but I'm well ready for their bounce.

I quote them high then watch them gasp and splutter with outrage. It's a pleasure just to see the shades of purple about their gills. What a hellish world it is that the likes of me are able to tell the likes of them what they have to pay for my service!

Some storm off without a further word, but others settle into a let's-be-reasonable tone. I know I'm in for fun then. They try to barter. I don't budge. They try to play at being an old mate. I smile and nod as though they've got me there. They cock their brow familiarly. Some go as far as giving me a wink. They have another run at bartering. I don't budge. They make appeals to my better nature. I sympathise with their hardships but then don't budge. The blood starts rising back up their necks and into their cheeks at that stage. Their tone goes hard. I don't budge. They bark the usual insults, then, about my being a thick-headed Irishman and a no-good Vandemonian and criminal filth that's a stain on all the colonies and the embodiment of all that's most despicable and wretched in the lower classes. I laugh in accompaniment to their raging performance and wish them all the best as they yell some more then storm off down the road.

CHAPTER 39

I wake listening to the bustle of the new world. There's the sound of carts and someone calling down the street. Melbourne is stirring from its slumber and slender threads of sunrise are streaming into the room. Ribbons of dust float about me, drifting and falling, with no hint of urgency. It feels like the whole world is bound to parade right past me and I am to watch it all as its benevolent judge.

I've been telling people that today will be my true Eureka day. I don't think Biddy's happy being called my golden nugget though. She'll have none of it. She gives me the stern look, whenever I say it, and says she'll not be called a lump of rock no matter how it shines. But then she smiles at me as though a thing's no sooner done than it is forgiven. There's the gold that matters. How it fires me up to see that smile and those eyes that fix me. Their tender grip tell me everything I need to know. How my heart trembles at the thought of those eyes opened to me for all the years to come. What days ahead we will have, and what fine children we will make. Let anyone dispute that fact and I'll be telling them a thing.

My girl has bought herself a dress, and pinned it with her little miracle medal, and organised a friend to put the child statue out to keep the weather off. I've paid for the finest garland of roses for her. They are threaded through with native ferns and I've given her a horseshoe for the luck. I have a fine new suit, a hat, a well-trimmed beard, and brogues well-polished to catch the sunlight as I'm walking down the street. I've never known a day when I've felt as fine as I do now. This is the lucky day where tomorrow really begins.

I walk through town to the church. It's quieter around the place than on the morning that I first saw her there. Everything looks right today: the gum tree and low scrub and the timber fence along the street line. I stop, straighten up my tie, and take off my hat then go inside. The noise of the city falls away as soon as the door closes behind me. It's calm inside and still has that musty holy smell that marks it as another world. It doesn't bother me today. I breathe it deep in hope it gives me blessing.

Our friends, the Newmans, are up near the altar rail, ready to do the witnessing. Jimmy is talking to Maurice Stack, the priest, who is here to do the business for us. I break into a smile at the sight of them all.

"There's the groom in all his splendour," says John Newman as he nods in my direction.

Jimmy grins and shakes his head at the sight of me.

"Time to make an honest man of you, brother."

He throws his arms around me and gives me a fierce hug. I can see his eyes are wet, with no hint of shame about it, as he stands back to size me up, then leans across and pushes my tie up tighter.

"I'm proud of you, Connie. You know that, don't you? And everyone back home would be proud of you, too. And Mamie and Da are looking down on you. I know it. I was right, wasn't I? If you wait, the good surely comes!"

All the feelings come, and I shudder to rein them in but, for all my effort, tears spill down my cheeks. The priest comes over and pats me on the arm and says some words to me in the old language. I haven't a clue what he says, but I smile and nod anyway.

Everyone's eyes turn down the aisle at the sound of the door opening. Elizabeth Newman races down the back to meet and accompany Biddy. There's some fussing over the dress to get things right before they start down the aisle. She is glowing, my beautiful bride, and with tears in her eyes already as she walks towards me. She has the flowers cradled in her arms and the horseshoe lying atop, as though to soak in all the good and blessing of the day so it is kept for all our years to come.

Have I ever seen a finer sight? I never have. I never will. She hands the flowers to Elizabeth as she takes her place beside me. She brushes her tears away, shakes her head, then smiles at me. We turn together to face the priest and so it begins: the prayers and the taking of vows and giving the ring. The whole of it unfolds like a dream and all I know is she is really there, beside me, and I am full to bursting with the joy of it.

We walk down the aisle afterwards, now married, and burst into the Melbourne light. Our friends give us a hearty cheer and I'm so elated I toss my hat so high it flies clear over the fence. I wrap my arms around her then, and kiss her and feel her hunger for it, and an urgent heat that we share. There are tears again, and not just hers, as we go down the path with our arms linked.

My brother exuberantly waves his arms about to get a cab. He is beaming as he does it. How long has it been since I've seen him aglow like that? Just goes to show there is life in the old boy yet. We all give him a round of applause when he finally manages to secure a cab. He laughs, gives a bow in return, then opens the door for all of us to tumble in. Then we are off, on a grand parade, circuiting the town. The whole party breaks into song, as the horses trot along Lonsdale then down Swanston. Jimmy has a flask that's passed around, to fire us up some more, and even Biddy smiles and takes a sip. Then she is leaning into me for another kiss as the others cheer us on. We nestle together, bound in warmth and joy, and we look at the town as though we own the lot of it.

Soon we are feasting and drinking and dancing in a hotel.

"God is making things right for us."

She whispers it in my ear as she presses my arm. There are

toasts to those we love, to the faraway and the departed, and to our old homeland. I feel the ache beneath the joy then and glimpse the shadows that dance alongside all that's bright. I see that Biddy feels the bruised whole of it too. Her eyes glisten with those other tears. She shakes away her thoughts of all the savage, hungry dead days, and then she's up for another dance and she's dragging me along. Our feet get a good stomp going, and the floorboards ring, as the fiddle plays a lightning-fast jig and Jimmy hollers an off-key song with all the breath that's in his lungs, and the Newmans watch us Irish with bemusement.

I feel the boisterous gambolling boy, on the boat, dancing alongside me; the child with his fingers woven with his mother's in that ever-ascending sweep to meet the sky. Up never down, up never down. All the best, bright past whispers through this moment – the whole of life crowding in to meet us – and then we swirl beyond the grip that aches for all that is gone and find our way into the joy that looks towards tomorrow. There is nothing but the heat betwixt us now. She leans towards my ear and whispers that it's time to go. The trace of her breath lingers on my neck, and I am stirred to hold her all the tighter.

"We need to go!"

Our party meets my announcement with a great laugh, then fond adieus, and Jimmy slaps me on the back and wishes Biddy all the best of luck because she will need it.

We are quick getting to the fine room I've hired for us. My fingers are clumsy trying to find my way through all the layers that wrap her. She laughs then does the work herself. I breathe in the soft of her as I clamber to get my britches down. The whole business between us is awkward and eager until we are both naked. She's soon on the bed and pulling me down on her. She wraps herself about me. Her fingers play through my hair. She looks at me as though I am some innocent thing that she is fierce in wanting. It is a look of tender judgement the likes of which I've never known. It curls around me, softening my heart, even as it stirs my body hard. I cover her with hungry kisses, graze her breasts with touches, and find my way inside her. We rock with such fierce urgency, the bed beneath us squeaks and groans. She laughs as though she fears the thing may well collapse beneath us. But then she surrenders back inside the fierce between us. Her thighs grip me all the tighter as she roars and shudders and I am all undone inside her.

We lay together in breathless relief. There's a tenderness that fills the room as all the world settles into quiet. The fierce soft knot of our marriage has now begun. I watch her, with wonder, as she falls asleep beside me. Everything inside me is awake: forever the wakeful boy in all the sleeping world.

I feel a strange tremor in me. The too-much of it all is moving through me, moving and breaking, dissolving the edges of my hard-wrought self. It presses me and I struggle against it. I don't want to wake her or have her see me in this spoiled state. There's no holding back the tears though. My face is soon all wet with them and, in my mouth, they taste of oceans. I am a man all undone right at the gates of heaven.

What is this sobbing song that's claiming me, that sounds of nothing but all that's broken in me? How is it that it's now I feel afraid, when everything's turned gentle in the world?

What is tomorrow in this world? What is tomorrow when everything is bound to fall, and everything is made to break, and more is likely lost than gained?

The girl who prays and has welcomed me into her is happily asleep. I gaze at her beside me. Her flesh, her breath, the quiver of her lips, are the holiest thing I am ever bound to see. Her truth is writ in scars across her skin, her hunger-weathered ribs, that tremor in her face that's part sorrow and part want. Her beauty is all the gathered pieces, the haunting and the hope, the fragile and the strong, unbroken beauty held in the broken

297

world. I lie beside her and there's no end to my tears.

CHAPTER 40

They gather on the deck as the Workington makes its way upriver to the township. Two brothers exchange glances. Their eyes are bruised with quiet familiarity. It is a strange thing being back, but they won't say it. Not here or now, at least.

The wife of the younger man is busy taking in the glistening river that's stretched between two distant shores. She sees, on the western side, a spread of farms on hills above the line of a sandy beach. The whole of it feels fresh and sweet-scented, a world that might be far enough to soften the haunting murmur of the famine.

She presses the feeling into a prayer, and whispers it, then squeezes her husband's arm the tighter as she sees a mountain looming up ahead. It stands there like an answer to all that has lost its way. Its hard-etched face looks out, through a cloudy veil, over an incidental world that is cradled below.

The woman sighs and leans her head against her husband's shoulder. The man she married: a man of shadows and broken pieces, loose-bound with tender threads. She looks up at him and knows the price he's paid. A tear rolls down her cheek. She watches as the sea breeze stirs white caps across the water. She hears the air rustling the canvas.

"Ta mé craiceáilte, do dhiaidh."

She whispers it, but he doesn't understand. He looks at her with his knotty puzzlement. It's not the first time, and it sure won't be the last. Marriage needs some measure of bewilderment.

I am cracked in your wake.

She thinks it, without saying it, as he looks up at birds in

299

flight. His eyes are bright and lost in boyish wonder as he watches them sweep and hover in the air. She feels the moment crack her all the more. Seems love might crack her until she is fine as sand.

It's now she hears the whisper of the sea breeze. It's full to the brim with soft persistent grace. Between the mountain and the sea, it comes to her: a whispered chorus born across the waters. She is far away. She is lost to all she knew. She is here now in this place. And one word mingles home with all to come. It is so close she can taste its sacrament. She leans into the breeze and feels the force of it: the days to come, the world to see, there ahead for both of them.

Amárach.

AFTERWORD

This book is born from a combination of protest and fascination. I believe the history of trauma, related to convict transportation, and the inter-generational reverberations of that trauma, is an important and under-explored subject. Transportation is a dark thread woven into the reality of invasion, land theft, massacre, child abduction, and cultural repression, that was perpetrated against the First Nations people of lutruwita (Tasmania). The violent social engineering of the nineteenth century has shaped much of the world we live in today.

I have used the convict records of my ancestor, Cornelius, and his brother James, in writing this book. The records are artefacts of a system that scrutinised bodies and relentlessly monitored and judged behaviours. They are records of control and punishment. I wrote this book in part so that an abiding memory of the brothers might be broken free from those scribbled lines that would have them forever labelled as convicts. The broader evidence of their lives tells stories of aspiration, adaptation, endurance, struggle, and hope.

The convict records, nevertheless, contain vital information about the brothers which I could not ignore. They were from Belfast. They were tried in Downpatrick for stealing "items of wearing apparel" and they had previously been convicted for stealing watches. They were sentenced to seven years' transportation for the theft of the clothes and were sent to the Smithfield Convict Depot, Dublin, where they were held for nine months. They were then shipped in the Emily II to Van Diemen's Land.

The two brothers were recorded as having the profession of "flax dressers." This was an unsurprising role in the linen-producing world of Belfast. Their father's name was George, and their siblings were Mary, George, and John. Their mother's name was not recorded. I have presumed, in the narrative, that she was deceased.

There were two James Donnellys on the Emily II. Cornelius's brother is recorded as James 2nd (a somewhat regal distinction!). Cornelius's physical description mentioned that one finger was missing and another one was crooked. I have attributed the injuries to the atrocious conditions of work in a linen factory in the mid-nineteenth century.

There was a period of rioting, in Belfast, in 1843. The newspapers of the day indicate there was significant tension, partly related to the rise of Dan O'Connell and the repeal movement, but it was also provoked by the British Government's suppression of the Protestant marching season. Newspaper accounts of the riots vary in assigning blame for the riots. The way events were reported was determined by each newspaper's sectarian allegiance. The Vindicator framed the troubles as "Orange Riots."

Cornelius and James are recorded as being Catholic. It is worthwhile noting that, at the time in Belfast, census information indicates there were Donnellys on both sides of the sectarian divide. The Vindicator's 19 July 1843 account of the riot that particularly informed this book's narrative, included a description of Protestants attacking a shoemaker named Cosgrove, and words exchanged between the attackers and Cosgrove's wife. There was further rioting following the shoemaker's funeral. I placed the Donnellys in that vigorous world of pitched street battles. It is hard to imagine they would have lived at a distance from that turmoil.

My account of the journey of the Emily II, from Dublin to Hobart, was informed by the journal of the ship's surgeon, John Munro. The pages of his journal provide rich details about the conditions on board, including the vigorous period of

302

seasickness in the early days of the journey, his particular concern for the old Irish speaking prisoners, the tendencies of certain convicts to feign sickness, the implementation of dancing and single sticks for exercise, and the particularly concerning behaviour of the convict Flannery. Flannery was punished by flogging, isolation, and heavy chains, as indicated in this book. He is the only prisoner recorded as having received significant punishment during the voyage.

I have placed a particular emphasis on the anti-transportation sentiment in Van Diemen's Land. I am mindful of historians who have framed the movement as a push towards independence and, therefore, a matter to be celebrated. My sense of the movement leans into a more complex take on the underlying motives of those involved. There are certainly instances where letters were written to newspaper editors protesting the inhumanity of transportation. But, in my reading, the thrust of anti-transportation protest was fuelled, more often, by self-serving interests rather than a humanitarian concern for prisoners.

I have, in fact, come to see the anti-transportation movement as a forerunner to the virulent anti-immigration sentiment that has troubled Australia up to our present day. The rhetoric of anti-transportation leaguers was often riddled with passionate concerns about the boatloads of prisoners who were coming and taking honest, free settlers' jobs; the inundation of prisoners causing devaluation of land values and economic collapse; boat arrivals as a real and present danger leaving settlers unsafe in their own homes and with a likelihood that crime will rise, progress will be undone, and that the moral standing of the colony will be forever degraded. The rhetoric is sadly familiar.

I included a rowdy theatre scene, where Joseph Allport addresses the crowd, as a concentrated instance of the anti-transportation passion of the day. The details of his speech are as recorded in the Hobart Town Advertiser, 21 February 1845.

I have taken an unashamed pleasure in portraying certain Vandemonian Lieutenant-Governors and senior colonial figures through the critical lens of convicts. I drew my inspiration from the writing of an American convict, William Gates, who was transported for his involvement in a Canadian uprising to overthrow British rule. Gates went on to write "Recollections of Life in Van Diemen's Land." He provided an exceedingly comical description of Lieutenant-Governor John Franklin. Gates described Franklin's breathing as coming "puffing from his brandy-bottled nose like steam from the escape pipe of an asthmatic boat." Gates went on further to say, "whether nature originally intended him (Franklin) to be a walking receiver of mutton, I am unable to say, but of all men I ever saw none ever gloried in such breadth of waistband." The writing of Gates provides a refreshing perspective on the convict experience from the inside.

Cornelius and James arrived in Tasmania at a time when New South Wales was no longer receiving convicts. A new form of convict management, known as the probation system, was implemented on the island just as the arrival numbers had started increasing. There was vigorous local opposition to the probation system. It's unsurprising that a sizeable part of the protest came from those settlers and major landowners who greatly benefited from the former assignment system.

I am particularly grateful for the insights that I found in Ian Brand's book "The Convict Probation System: Van Diemen's Land 1839-1854." It is excellent in its breadth of consideration of the system, its specific details of particular stations, and its inclusion of Charles La Trobe's 1847 report on the probation system.

I believe this period of convict history calls for a greater degree of examination and reflection than has occurred to date.

The probation stations, spread across Van Diemen's Land, were an industrial era design for efficiently carrying out the business of mass people processing. Thousands were circulated through the stations, moving through the probationary classes according to their length of sentence and behaviour, under the dubious banner of penal science. The extensive spread of this system, from furthest south to north, transformed Van Diemen's Land into a gulag island of the British Empire.

There is little evidence of the majority of probation stations in Tasmania today. Buildings were stripped down, bricks were repurposed, and the worst of the past was buried as much as possible. Some of the old buildings, in Jerusalem (now known as Colebrook), have been preserved as private residences. There are some crumbling remnants of the Jericho station still intact in a paddock. The Spiky Bridge still stands on the Tasmanian east coast. Darlington Probation Station, on Maria Island, is a well-preserved remnant of the system.

Tasmania's mass people processing past might not have been preserved in bricks and mortar, but it has lingered through the steady succession of political approaches, and dog-whistling campaigning, concerned with dealing with large groups of "problematic" people through offshore mass incarceration. Those of us descended from a far-from-welcomed mob of "offshore" detainees, people who were reviled and who continued to be monitored beyond the end of their sentences, surely have a legacy that calls for solidarity with those new arrivals who suffer as our people once did.

The letter from the character Toby Flynn to Charlie was largely inspired by a letter that the Norfolk Island convict, Denis Prendergast, wrote to his male lover in 1846. Prendergast was on his way to being executed for mutiny. I have come across few letters, of the era, that convey as much tenderness and love as that letter. It stands as a profound and beautiful counter to the vilifying homophobic rhetoric of that time and the long history of criminalising gay sex which lasted into recent years in Tasmania.

I have used an Irish expression in Chapter 22, "uaighneas an chladaigh." I encountered this expression, and its explanation, in the work of Manchan Magan. Manchan indicated to me that credit for this expression should be given to Pap Murphy. I have corresponded with Pap, who lives in County Mayo, and he was happy for me to go ahead and use the expression. Pap is dedicated to keeping language, local knowledge, and culture alive in his part of the world. The work of people like Pap in Ireland, and the Palawa communities of lutruwita, bring healing and restoration to a world scarred by colonisation. There is life and wealth in the recovery of what was stolen, suppressed, and lost.

Irish music has accompanied me during this creative journey. My listening has ranged from traditional songs to the contemporary sounds of Irish hip-hop. I've had many mornings, walking through the bush, with a diverse group extending from old Sean-nós master Joe Heaney to the Belfast rappers Kneecap singing in my ear. I am grateful to those fine artists, and boisterous confrontationists, who helped me hear the music in it all.

The paragraph, in the early section of chapter 24, where Denison writes "When we consider the elements of which society here is composed ..." is directly taken from a despatch that Denison wrote on 15 August 1848. The content of the despatch became known in Tasmania and was reported in the Launceston Examiner on 17 October 1849. The locals were far from impressed! I have been constantly surprised by the unfolding dramas waiting to be found in Tasmanian history.

The details of the court case, Donnelly v Tomlins, was given significant coverage in local newspapers in 1851. I used dialogue, in the court scene, based on the extensive account that was provided in the Hobarton Guardian 17 September 1851. This chapter of our family history was unknown until recent years. Awareness of the case, and the brothers' experience of false imprisonment, was made possible thanks to the National Library of Australia's wonderful resource, Trove. Trove is one of Australia's great resources.

I was tempted to finish the book with the story of Tomlins' ultimate demise. I decided a note of grace was a better choice as a conclusion. Nevertheless, for any readers interested, here is an account, taken from Launceston Examiner 8 June 1867, of Tomlins' final days:

"A letter by a recent mail from the Mauritius mentions the fact that Phillip Stanley Tomlins, once well known both in Launceston and Victoria, is dead. A letter from Port Louis, dated 4th April last, has the following passage:-" I was much shocked to hear yesterday that Tomlins was dead. He went on board a brig, called the Sea Nymph, in order to get something to eat, as he was nearly starving, and on coming on shore fell down on the wharf, and was picked up by some bystanders and conveyed to the hospital, where he died in about an hour and a half after admittance. Captain Fisher, owner of the brig, paid all the funeral expenses, although a perfect stranger to the old man, unless some-times meeting him in Fremantle constitutes an acquaintance. Tomlins was interred in the Western Cemetery, Port Louis, on April 3rd, the day following his death. The captain and I were the only persons who followed him to the grave." The writer added that, though they said at the hospital that the deceased died of fever, he believed that death was really caused by apoplexy, consequent upon intemperance. The deceased, who was possessed of considerable abilities, once occupied the position of police magistrate in Tasmania, from which office his habits compelled him to retire. He next went to Victoria, and Mr.

Michie, then Attorney-General, was on the point of giving him an appointment as police magistrate when a fit of intemperance disqualified him. Subsequently he was clerk of petty sessions at Echuca, and latterly came down in the world considerably. He sailed for Mauritius in the Hannah Nicolson some months since."

I drew inspiration, in the account of people making the crossing to goldrush Victoria, from the terrific book "Vandemonians: The Repressed History of Colonial Victoria" by Janet McCalman. I found this book provided rich insights into the origins of mainland perceptions, and the tired old tropes that have long been applied to Tasmanians. I would suggest, to Tasmanians with a passion for their family history, that they might find it worthwhile exploring the possibility that their ancestors may have had a chapter of their life spent on the Victorian goldfields. When my ancestor was interviewed, towards the end of his life, he was most forthcoming in talking of his days as a digger and carter. I suspect the goldrush provided a basis for giving shape to a new identity for many former convicts.

I framed the arrival of Cornelius, at the Forest Creek goldfields, to coincide with the monster meeting that was held there at the end of 1851. The text of the notice about the monster meeting, and details of the speeches given, have been drawn from an account given in The Argus, 18 December 1851. The monster meeting is little known beyond goldrush enthusiasts, but I understand it was an instance of political activism that proved to be effective. It caused La Trobe to back down from the increased tax on diggers that he was about to implement. It's interesting that this monster meeting is so little known while the failed rebellion of Eureka is known far and wide.

I found David Hill's book, "The Gold Rush" was a source of great information. Manning Clark's account of goldrush

Melbourne, in his series "A History of Australia" was an absolute delight to read. I must say, for all my reading, I found the best historical nuggets in the newspapers of the day, thanks to the access provided by Trove. This included my discovery of advertisements for the sale of an elephant, a bear, and a monkey in the pages of local newspapers. I couldn't resist including them in the story of my great great-grandparents.

The journey of writing this book has been made possible thanks to my wife Liz, who is a constant supporter of my creatve endeavours. Love and thanks, as always, to you Liz. I have received invaluable help from Richard Bradburn, an editor in Cork, whose beta feedback helped me open the door to a greater degree of fictional expansion than I had initally dared. I am partcularly grateful for the generous feedback and insights that were shared by my friend, David Dalton. Many thanks, Dave, for calling out my lackadaisical relatonship with hyphens and the many insights that can only come from a poet who has a great awareness of the power of our language.

The Cornelius of this book is a character composed of facts and speculation. I hope the man that my great-great-grandfather truly was might look kindly on my efforts in trying to bring to life something of his experience.

ABOUT THE AUTHOR

Rob Donnelly is a storyteller who draws inspiration from the physical beauty and tangled history of his island home, lutruwita Tasmania. He has a passion for the stories and wisdom of people who have been overlooked and silenced by mainstream society.

Rob's first book, Out of Order, is a memoir focused on the decade he spent as a member of a contemplative religious order and the drama involved in leaving that world. His second book, Con, is a vivid historical-fiction account of his ancestor's experience of transportation and life in Van Diemonian exile.

PREVIOUS BOOK BY THE AUTHOR

Out of Order

www.ingramcontent.com/pod-product-compliance
Lightning Source LLC
Chambersburg PA
CBHW070102120726
47909CB00002B/471